Howl
at the
Loon

Susan C. Daffron

An Alpine Grove Romantic Comedy

Book 6

Published by Magic Fur Press
An imprint of Logical Expressions, Inc.
P.O. Box 383
Ponderay, ID 83852

Howl at the Loon

ISBN: 978-1-61038-035-5 (paperback)
       978-1-61038-036-2 (EPUB)

Like all of my books, *Howl at the Loon* is dedicated to
my husband James Byrd,
my best friend and biggest supporter.
Thanks for everything!

Chapter 1

The North Fork

"How old is this photo? I think this kid is wearing bell-bottoms." Robin Sanders held out the brochure toward her boss, Darrell Lambert. "You don't see little kids wearing plaid pants like that anymore. It's 1996, not 1966."

"Yeah, yeah, I know. But see how happy that kid looks! The North Fork is a great place. It's right on the lake. When I was little, it was a resort like the one in *Dirty Dancing.* Remember that movie? With the woman who got the nose job?"

"Yes. And it had Patrick Swayze too." In the days when he was seriously hot. Darrell didn't need to know that Robin was an incurable romantic who had probably seen the movie three hundred times and knew half the dialogue by heart.

"Yes, yes!" Darrell slapped his hand on the desk. "The North Fork Lodge was just like that place in the movie. Then it was a summer camp for kids for a while. Then a bed and breakfast."

Robin held up a business card. "That would explain the dinner fork on the logo."

"Well, I suppose it *has* been a while since they redid the logo. Now they hold retreats and conferences there. It's practically a local historical landmark. If those walls could talk, they'd have stories to tell."

"I can imagine." Robin tried not to roll her eyes. Everyone at the company knew that when Darrell Lambert got an idea, he was like a dog with a bone, unwilling to let go. And because he was the CEO, his ideas tended to carry a lot of weight.

"The fact that they do retreats now is perfect for us because this merger has been a complete disaster. We need to get our team together and making sales as soon as possible. I'm tired of employees sniping at each other. Morale is in the toilet and it has gone on too long. All the attitude problems around here have got to stop. We need to be presenting a unified positive image to customers. I want you to go to Alpine Grove and get this retreat set up. My uncle Ernie is a great guy. He'll help you."

Robin stared at the brochure. Darrell was wrong. The swanky lodge in the movie had been made of stone. The North Fork was constructed of logs and was definitely more rustic. But the lodge did look pretty in a woodsy, mountain-cabin type of way. Or it had in the sixties anyway. Why on earth did he want her to do this? Shouldn't an event planner handle it? She gazed at Darrell, trying to muster a calm, competent demeanor. "I don't have any experience in setting up a complex event like a retreat. I'm an assistant buyer. Mostly I research merchandise, write purchase orders, and do some inventory planning."

"I know. But you are great at keeping things running smoothly and even after only a few months, everyone already loves you. You'll be working with Alec Montgomery. I've told him that he has to put aside his regular duties too, so he can handle the employee-training aspect. Almost no one knows more about the North Coast catalog and our customers than he does. Plus, I'm bringing in a team-building expert, Brett

Barker. All you need to do is work out details about the venue with my uncle. The main thing is to make sure there's lots of food, so people don't get cranky. You don't want them to turn on you."

Turn on her? Was he kidding? Momma always said nice girls didn't swear, but sweet blue blazes, this was totally insane. Robin didn't want to be responsible for a corporate *retreat*. Sure, Darrell was a genius when it came to retail, but this was nuts. Why did he want to hold an event in Alpine Grove? She put the brochure down on the desk and patted it gently. "If you want to have a retreat, why not do it somewhere closer? Alpine Grove is not exactly nearby."

"The place has been in my family forever, so I'm getting a great deal. Uncle Ernie has been having some financial problems and I can help out. It's a win-win. Our catalogs are supposed to represent the soul of the West and elegant country living, so the natural beauty of the location will be inspirational. You'll see!"

Robin made a serious effort to behave like a professional, but she wasn't sure her acting skills were up to this task. "When would you like to hold the retreat?"

"We need it set up in a week because that's the only time I could get on Brett's schedule before this summer. I guess we're heading into his busy season. So you need to drive down to Alpine Grove as soon as possible. I set up a meeting with Alec so you can find out what stuff he needs you to bring."

"What kind of stuff?" She had only a week to pull this off?

"Alec is getting together training materials and probably a bunch of old catalogs for everyone to review. He's got a lot of work to do to get everyone up to speed on the order-taking scripts, handling customer complaints—*everything*."

Robin had never officially met Alec Montgomery, although she'd seen him wandering the hallways occasionally. It sounded like he had a huge and possibly unpleasant task ahead of him. "I'm going to have to make some arrangements. I have a dog, but I've never used any of the boarding kennels around here, since we just moved to Portland. I wish I could take her with me. Emma loves riding in the car."

"Ernie doesn't allow pets at the lodge, but why don't you board your dog in Alpine Grove? There's probably a place somewhere around there. Ask Ernie. He'll know." Darrell pointed at the business card. "His number is on the card."

Robin looked down at the tattered rectangle. "It's only four digits."

"Yeah, every phone number in Alpine Grove has the same prefix." Darrell took the card, wrote the rest of the phone number, and started to hand it to her. He stopped and waggled the card emphatically. "Remember, I'm trusting you to make this retreat outstanding. I want an experience every single employee will remember."

"Okay, Mr. Lambert. I'll do my best. Thank you for trusting me with this opportunity." Robin stood up to leave. Maybe it wouldn't be so bad. How hard could it be? Even though the last event she had set up was a bridal shower for her friend Joanne, Robin was smart and organized. When she was growing up, her friends had always teased her about her tendency to make lists for everything. It was important to keep reminding herself that she was efficient and up to new challenges like this one. Presumably, the people at the North

Fork Lodge held retreats all the time, so setting everything up shouldn't be a big deal.

Maybe it could be like a vacation. Alpine Grove was supposed to be a beautiful little town, and traveling with Emma was always fun. The dog adored road trips and if Robin planned it well, maybe she and Emma could go for a few hikes and explore the area a little. Robin smiled as she thought about the happy eager expression in Emma's eyes when she hopped around, excited about the going somewhere in the car.

Emma was a pretty reddish-brown dog with a white chest and blaze down her nose. She was a mixed breed and Robin always told her that she was one of a kind, like a perfect snowflake. When Robin adopted the dog, the shelter had listed her as a chow mix, but the veterinarian said that was unlikely. At the vet clinic, their best guess was that Emma might be a mix of some type of spaniel and maybe some retriever. The dog's copper-colored fur was silky soft and longer than a Labrador retriever's, but shorter than a chow's. After looking through some dog-breed books, Robin thought Emma looked a little like a Brittany spaniel, but there was really no way to know what her heritage was. It didn't matter anyway. All that mattered was that Emma was the coolest dog Robin had ever met and it was love at first sight.

Robin walked down the hall past the executive offices toward the administration building where her cubicle was located. This trip could end up being great. Emma loved the outdoors, and with acres upon acres of forest, Alpine Grove was undoubtedly the ultimate doggie playground. Emma would have a ball. Getting away from the day-to-day monotony of purchase orders and merchandise lists for a couple weeks wouldn't be so bad either.

~

After a somewhat confusing conversation with Ernie Lambert, the owner of the North Fork Lodge, Robin called a property appraiser named Rebecca Mackenzie, who Ernie said knew about the boarding kennel in Alpine Grove. Although Becca talked faster than almost any person Robin had ever met, during the short conversation the woman gave Robin a phone number for the kennel owner, Kat Stevens. Becca also raved about how much her dog had enjoyed staying there. It was encouraging, particularly since Becca seemed to love her dog Mona.

Kat seemed pleasant on the phone and Robin made arrangements for Emma to stay with her. The whole set-up sounded incredibly cushy. If Emma got along with the resident dogs, she could stay in the house as a personal guest, but Kat also had a back-up plan. If Emma and the other canines or felines had differences of opinion, other dog-friendly accommodations were located in an outbuilding and Emma could stay there. To Robin, the arrangement sounded homey and sweet. Even if things were still up in the air with the retreat, everything was working out for the trip, and she was actually starting to look forward to the journey. It had been so long since she'd been able to take a vacation, and hitting the road with Emma would be fun.

Robin looked over her schedule on the computer screen in front of her. Darrell had set up a meeting that afternoon to talk to her and Alec Montgomery about the retreat. Two meetings with the owner of the company in as many days was more than a little stressful. Because Robin had only been with Eagle River for a couple of months, she'd never met Alec. She had been hired when Darrell bought the High Country catalog and merged it with Eagle River's existing North Coast catalog. Although both catalogs sold women's clothes, they had dissimilar marketing appeals and approaches.

The companies also had different employee cultures, which weren't meshing well. That was the polite way of putting it, anyway. The employees who had been brought over from High Country were particularly unhappy and took every opportunity to express their displeasure. In fact, Robin had replaced a buyer who, as the story went, had left in a rather spectacular way. The litany of complaints had been long and the words 'disgruntled employee' didn't even begin to describe the countless bridges going up in flames as Robin's predecessor had exited the company. It was highly unlikely anyone was going to give that woman a good reference after the things she had reportedly said.

Robin worked in merchandising, whereas Alec Montgomery was the head of communications and advertising. Up until now, their paths hadn't crossed. However, several women in Robin's department who had worked with Alec had less than complimentary things to say. The word around the water cooler was that he was a difficult person to deal with because he was creative to the point of hyperactivity. But he had been with the company almost since the beginning, and as employee number three, he knew more about Eagle River than anyone except the founders, Darrell and his wife Sue.

Robin walked down the hallway toward the conference room. She shouldn't let idle gossip color her view of Alec. Maybe everything would be fine. They were both professionals, after all. She walked up to the glass-walled room, hugging a pile of catalogs to her chest. Darrell's back was to her and he was sitting across from a man with brown hair who was leaning back in his chair with his arms crossed. Given the scowl on his face, Alec Montgomery was not appreciating whatever Darrell was telling him.

Alec had to be more than six feet tall, and the way his dress shirt stretched over his chest implied he had a fairly imposing physique. His dark, greenish-blue eyes were extremely expressive, and the flash of irritation that crossed his face left no doubt that he was not happy. An angry Alec was a bit intimidating. Maybe the gossips weren't so wrong after all.

Everyone always called Robin a peacemaker. Even when she was screaming obscenities at rude people in her mind, she generally was able to keep her cool and defuse conflicts. This ability had helped her make friends easily from as far back as she could remember. The now-legendary Crayola Skirmish in kindergarten was the first of many mediations to come.

Robin considered her persuasive abilities her secret weapon. Although it was hard to say exactly why, people often seemed to want to make her happy, which made it easy to reconcile disputes and convince people to see things her way. She tried to remember these past accolades as she plastered her most accommodating smile on her face, knocked on the door, and steeled herself to face two of the three top executives in the company. Darrell waved her inside and the two men stood up when she entered the room.

Darrell introduced her to Alec, who nodded and offered a perfunctory "nice to meet you" before Robin put her stack of catalogs on the long mahogany table and they all sat down.

Alec turned his attention back to Darrell. He tapped a stack of catalogs repeatedly and said, "What am I supposed to do about all of this while I'm off in the woods training these call-center people? The next catalog drop is coming up and there are a number of ad placements promoting the new merchandise. I know I'm not part of the creative team, but the draft copy for the products from High Country is pathetic. I don't know how they ever sold anything. You need to talk to Sue about it. This is like some kind of bad April Fool's Day joke."

Darrell shook his head. "Sue is aware of the copy issues, and I'm definitely not joking. Your attitude is exactly what I'm talking about. You need to get off this 'us versus them' bandwagon. It's not helping. Get the ads approved and then go down to Alpine Grove. You've got to make this work. We need the call-center employees up to speed before the next catalog hits the street. Everyone needs to have a complete understanding of the exceptional value of Eagle River merchandise and our high customer-service standards. We have a unique brand identity and your job is to drill that into those customer-service folks, even if it kills you."

Something about Alec's rebellious expression reminded Robin of the teenage Tom Cruise. Okay, a much older and taller Tom Cruise, but the mental image of Alec dancing around playing air guitar in a dress shirt, Ray-Bans, and his tighty-whities cracked her up. She smiled. "I'm sure we can find a way to make this work for everyone."

Alec glared at her. "You think this is funny?"

"No, I just think it's an opportunity to bring people together. Our customers love Eagle River and I know High Country customers were loyal too."

Darrell pointed at Robin. "See? She's got the right idea. Get it together, Montgomery. I want you in Alpine Grove

ASAP. Get what you need and load it in your car. Robin can haul some stuff too. You need to get moving on this now."

Robin said, "Do we have a schedule for the team-building exercises yet?"

"Brett is faxing that to me. I'll give you a copy as soon as I have it," Darrell said.

Alec grabbed an Eagle River ballpoint pen off the table and clicked it a few times. "That's another thing. How am I supposed to work employee training around all that stuff? Have you read about this guy? He's a snake-oil salesman."

Darrel gave Alec a hard look. "I took one of his seminars and I liked what he had to say. Plus he gets results. That's what we need. Do you know what the failure rate is for mergers and acquisitions?"

Robin shook her head and stole a glance at Alec, who appeared to be equally uninformed.

Darrell continued. "Let's just say that it's enough to give me heartburn. I've been popping Tums like candy. We need to beat the odds here, folks. I'll get you Brett's schedule as soon as I receive it and you'll need to work around that. Are we clear?"

Alec slapped the pen back onto the table. "Clear."

Robin moved to collect the catalogs and smiled brightly at Alec. "It was nice to meet you, and I'm looking forward to working together. Alpine Grove is supposed to be beautiful. I've never been there and I'm hoping to see some of the area while we're there."

Alec mumbled some sort of assent that may have included the word "Pollyanna." He got up to leave and met her gaze. "I've got a bunch of stuff to do right now, but I'll send you an e-mail later today."

Robin thanked him and left the conference room. She knew adopting a relentlessly positive attitude could frustrate grumpy people, but she was looking forward to the trip. It would be a break from her regular job, which truth be told was generally kind of boring.

If Alec could get over himself, the retreat might end up being a success. In the meantime, she needed to get this workday over with so she could start packing. She had a lot to do and not much time to do it.

∼

After two interminable days of meetings, lists, and countless phone calls, Robin finally hit the open road with Emma. The dog was set up with her travel pillow in the backseat, and behind her, the back of Robin's Subaru station wagon was loaded down with Eagle River training materials. She and Emma had reservations at a pet-friendly hotel for the night, but it was going to be two long days of driving. After they arrived in Alpine Grove, Robin would have the weekend to get everything set up before everyone started arriving for the retreat on Sunday night. The big event was scheduled to begin Monday. At the office, she'd been like a squirrel scrambling to get everything organized and ready, and it was a relief to be away from there and on the highway far away from the rest of the company.

A little downtime on the road with Emma would be a nice break before she had to play hostess for a whole lot of irritable call-center managers. Alec Montgomery wasn't the only one who was annoyed about the idea of a week of training and team-building. Darrell had gathered the scheduled attendees together and tasked them with absorbing knowledge and sharing what they learned with all of their front-line call-center personnel after they returned to work. The response to his spirited speech had been less than enthusiastic. More like low-grade dissent with a dash of defiance.

The windshield wipers whapped back and forth in an endless, monotonous rhythm. Rain was in the forecast for the entire drive from Portland to Alpine Grove. Weather reports showed a radar image that looked like a gigantic cloud was covering the entire West Coast. Robin had known when she moved to Portland, Oregon, that it rained a lot, but the gray reality was stunning in its monochromatic tedium. Growing up in Spokane, Washington, she hadn't appreciated how much more sunny it was farther inland. Portland had received a little tease of sun in February and early March, then more rain. And more rain after that. Sure, it was the Pacific Northwest, but even long-term residents were getting cranky about the continual soggy weather.

The brochures said Alpine Grove had a "true four-season climate," so maybe Robin would have an opportunity to see something other than rain for a change. At this point, any season that included weather without some form of drizzle would be a welcome novelty. If it rained for the entire retreat, the attendees might need more than good food to pacify them.

Robin made an effort not to dwell on things she couldn't do anything about, but the knot in her stomach didn't seem to want to go away. Although the meetings had been cordial, in subsequent terse e-mails Darrell had implied in a not-so-subtle way that her career at Eagle River was riding on this retreat. It wasn't fair either, since she hadn't been hired to do event planning. She gripped the steering wheel more tightly, reliving all the things she wished she could have said to him, but hadn't. Repressing emotions was supposed to be bad for you. If she actually made it through this experience, she'd probably end up with an ulcer. Or fired. Or both.

After two days of driving, even Emma was starting to get tired of the car. As Robin slowed the car to enter the town of Alpine Grove, the sun suddenly came out from behind a cloud, casting a brilliant glow behind the quaint brick buildings that lined the main street. The town looked like something out of a movie—like the little town in *It's a Wonderful Life*, except in color.

Robin squinted at the unaccustomed illumination and smiled. Alpine Grove was totally adorable, and it was obvious why it was such a tourist attraction. She drove by a gift store with a glittery window display, a bookstore, and a few restaurants and bars. The rest of the signs indicated small businesses like real estate and professional offices. People were walking along the sidewalk looking happy, obviously enjoying the sunshine.

Robin glanced at the directions to the boarding kennel that she had written down when she talked to the owner. The place was north of Alpine Grove, so Robin needed to drop off Emma, then go back through town to get back to the turn-off to the North Fork Lodge, which was located on the lake.

In town, the rain appeared to have washed most of the snow away. But as she drove farther north, small patches of snow still lingered in the shady areas alongside the road where it had obviously been pushed during a long winter of plowing activity. A few breaks in the dense forest provided stunning views of the surrounding white-capped mountains. All the natural beauty was a relief after so many hours on the interstate.

Glancing down at the directions again, Robin turned off the road into a driveway, or what passed for one anyway. The entrance was more swamp than driveway, and the car splashed through an immense muddy puddle, the tires grinding and bogging down in the muck. Sodden dirt spewed up onto the sides of the car and the windows. Emma sat up in the backseat and Robin looked in the rearview mirror at her. The dog looked excited about all the great splattery noises and eager to see what might happen next.

Robin was less thrilled with the off-road adventure. The long driveway wound through the forest and she attempted to slowly navigate the car around the sloppiest of the mud-filled craters. By the time she finally found this place, her car was going to be completely coated in filth. Was this even the right driveway? It seemed to go on forever.

At last a break in the trees revealed a rough-hewn log house with an old and extraordinarily dirty truck parked beneath a tree out front. Underneath the layer of filth, the truck might have been green, but it was hard to tell. Robin pulled in next to the pickup and got out of the car. She looked up at the enormous trees and took a deep breath. The air was clean and the verdant dampness was energizing, as if everything was trying to grow as quickly as possible. The door to the house opened and a petite woman with long dark hair came down the steps. She was wearing a grubby, tired-looking winter coat and clunky hiking shoes. All of the clothes looked far too large for her. Would it be rude to give her one of the Eagle River catalogs? This woman obviously had some issues when it came to fashion.

Robin waved. "Hi. You must be Kat."

"Yes, it's nice to meet you. I guess you made good time."

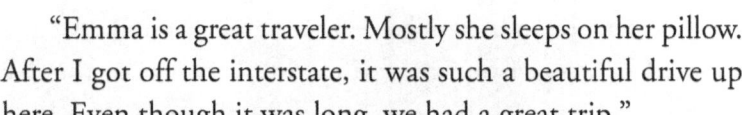

"Emma is a great traveler. Mostly she sleeps on her pillow. After I got off the interstate, it was such a beautiful drive up here. Even though it was long, we had a great trip."

Kat took her hands out of the pockets of the ugly coat and pointed at the happy canine face peering out of the car. "She's adorable. Do you want to let her out?"

Robin turned back toward the car and stepped in a puddle, splashing murky water up on her slacks. She leaped away and looked down at her shoe, which now was the same grayish-brown color as the driveway. "Oh, *shitake mushrooms!* I hope I remembered to pack more than one pair of shoes."

Kat said, "Did you say mushrooms?"

"Yes. I try hard not to curse, but it's a challenge sometimes."

"Well speaking of challenges, you're pretty brave to wear such nice clothes around here. I never wear black because of the level of dirt and dog hair."

Robin opened the door and clipped the leash onto Emma's collar. "They're from the Eagle River catalog. I get a 40-percent employee discount. Right after I started there, they had a sale and I went a little nuts."

"They look great on you. What kind of fabric is that?" Kat pointed to the puddle. "I'm sorry about the mud. The driveway has turned into a soupy mess. If it would stop raining, we might be able to do something about it."

"The slacks are linen, which means they have to be dry cleaned. They may not have been the best choice, I guess." She turned back to Emma and encouraged her out of the car. The dog daintily leaped down from the car and landed in another puddle, splashing Robin again. "Oh Emma, nice shot."

Kat said, "I'm not a big fan of dry cleaning. After I adopted this coat from the thrift store, I took it to the dry cleaner in town and they gave me the evil eye. After a long winter, I need to get it cleaned again, but I'm kind of afraid of what they'll say."

Robin laughed. "You *adopted* the coat?"

"It was cheap. I needed a warm coat and it needed a home. It was like an ugly junkyard dog and when I was at the thrift store, I felt sorry for it. The coat was almost brand-new, but it smelled sort of weird and was this revolting bubblegum-pink color. I thought if I got it cleaned and dyed it, the coat would be okay. Did I mention it was cheap? Unfortunately, the process only sort of worked. Let's just say the Rit dye folks wouldn't be impressed with my crafting abilities. I was going for blue, but I didn't think about how it would mix with the pink."

"It is an, well, an *unusual* color. But spring is coming!" The coat was a somewhat sickening grayish-purple color, and Kat had obviously not considered the fact that the zippers wouldn't take the dye, so they remained bright pink.

"I sure hope you're right. I'm ready to put this hideous coat in the closet and not look at it for a long, long time. Or maybe just burn it as a celebration of the season changing to something other than winter."

Robin paused. "Would you like an Eagle River catalog? I have lots here in the back of the car. We just merged with High Country, so there are some great new items too. You should check it out!"

"Their stuff is too nice for my hairy lifestyle. I'm more an REI or L.L. Bean kind of gal. I need new hiking boots." Kat looked down at her feet. "Obviously. These are falling apart."

"Well, we don't sell that type of merchandise." Robin turned, reached into the car, and grabbed a catalog. "But here's one just in case. You never know."

"Thanks." Kat rolled the catalog up and jammed it into her coat pocket. She crouched down next to Emma and stroked her shoulder. "Are you ready to meet a whole lot of other dogs?" Emma wagged happily and splashed a paw into the puddle for emphasis.

Robin handed her the leash. "I know I'll only be a few miles away, but I'm going to miss her so much. You said it's okay if I come and visit and maybe take her for a few hikes, right? I'm hoping to have a little free time after everything is set up for the retreat."

"Sure. Just give me a call. We'll be here."

Chapter 2

Batman & Julia

As Robin's car sloshed its way back up the soggy driveway toward the road, Kat walked Emma down the hill around the house to the back door, so she could introduce the dog to the five resident canines. She opened the door, peered inside, and waved the crowd of dogs away. "Hey, Emma has arrived. Could you help me do the doggie introduction thing?"

Joel poked his head out from his office. "Let me get my coat."

Kat stood outside with Emma and gazed up at the trees. Among the boughs, birds were singing and trilling to one another, obviously enjoying the break in the weather. It had been an incredibly rainy spring so far, and it seemed like forever since the sun had made an appearance.

One by one, Joel brought out the dogs. First to greet Emma was Linus, the huge furry brown dog who was attached on a harness to Tessa, the hyperactive golden retriever. Next was Lori the border collie, then Lady, the collie mix, and finally Joel joined the parade with Chelsey, the shy Australian shepherd mix who trotted alongside him on a leash.

Kat grinned at him. "This is great. Emma is a total sweetheart, and we have pack harmony. Want to join the expedition and go absorb some Vitamin D with me before the sun disappears again?"

"Sure." Joel took her hand and looked up. "Wow, what *is* that golden orb in the sky?"

"Isn't it amazing? Maybe Mr. Sun can do something about the driveway. The squish factor is getting extreme. If it gets any worse, the next time we try to drive your truck, it may get sucked down into the vortex of brownish-gray slime."

"I know. Jack is coming over later today to mark the trees that need to be cut down. I'm a little worried about his truck getting stuck."

"At least Robin's car is small. It seemed to float on top of the yuck. You guys with your big heavy trucks are doomed."

"You just hate my truck."

"It's well documented that your truck and I have issues with one another. At least you took the plow blade off. That must mean it's not going to snow and it truly is spring, right?"

"The torrential rain was another clue. April showers and all that."

"I'd better get some flowers out of all this crummy weather. At least I can see the garden fence again. That's progress. We also seem to have a river flowing next to the road at the end of the driveway."

"I think there may be a problem with the culvert, but the idea of getting down into the ditch and checking on it during a downpour hasn't been too appealing."

"I don't suppose you have scuba gear, do you?"

"No. But I do have hip waders."

Kat grinned. "Are you're kidding? Hip waders? I didn't think you liked fishing."

"I don't. They're for doing disgusting things like clearing out culverts."

"I'm warning you now that if you put on hip waders, there *will* be photographs."

"And now I have yet another reason to put off that task."

Kat gestured toward the forest. "I wish we didn't have to cut down trees for the new kennel. It makes me feel a little sick. I mean Abigail loved those trees, and here I am about to chop them down."

Joel squeezed her hand. "You know why it's necessary. The logging needs to be done to clear the spot for the building. Jack is also going to mark some trees that aren't doing well. He says it will actually improve the overall health of the forest."

"I know. Intellectually, I get it. I really do. But the idea of cutting down trees still makes me want to cry. Some of those cedars are probably sixty or eighty years old. They survived Prohibition. Maybe even the Civil War. Who knows? All I know is that Aunt Abigail looked out at those trees from the kitchen window and so have I. And we went to all that effort to keep the trees from being logged by her creepy ex-husband."

"That was different. He wanted to strip the property of *all* the trees, not just a few."

"Still. I feel bad. I'm going to miss them. I know Abigail would too."

"Abigail has been gone for more than a year. It's your house now." Joel stopped and looked down into her face. "You don't have to keep everything exactly the way it was when she was alive."

"Well, I did throw away the dining room rug. What that sheltie did to it was seriously gross."

"True." Joel stroked her cheek. "But I'm serious. I've sometimes wondered if you're trying to preserve Abigail's memory by not changing anything here. Starting the business is going to shake things up. If you're not okay with that, now would be a good time to change your mind about setting up the boarding kennel."

"I know. I think I'm having another entrepreneurial panic attack." Kat wrapped her arms around Joel's waist and hugged him. "I know things change. But sometimes I just want to stop time. It's a beautiful day and I'm starting to believe that spring may actually arrive. You're being incredibly patient with my arboreal meltdown, and Emma is a sweet dog. Everything is really good right now and I'm afraid to screw that up." She leaned back to look up at his face. "I'm sorry I keep freaking out. I need to stop being such a worrywart about everything."

"Would you feel better if some of the trees were turned into lumber? Then they'd still be here."

"Maybe."

"I had some of the trees on my property turned into boards when I was working on The Shack. There's a guy who has a portable sawmill that I can call. I'm not sure how much you actually save by turning them into boards, since if you sold the logs to a mill you'd get money for them. But as you know from the estimates we got, buying dimensional lumber at the building supply is expensive too."

"I noticed. Those numbers almost gave me a heart attack when I figured out what 'linear feet' meant. Once you start multiplying, all that math leads to disturbing dollar amounts."

"When you cut logs into boards, they have to dry for a long time, so we couldn't use the wood on the kennel building. But I'm sure something else will fall apart or need to be built."

"No doubt."

"I'll ask Jack about saving a few trees aside."

"Thanks. That's a good idea."

"Still, maybe you shouldn't be here when the loggers arrive and start cutting."

"I think you're right."

~

Robin drove south through Alpine Grove and turned onto a road that went along the lake. The North Fork Lodge was off Edgewater Road on ten acres of lakefront property. She'd seen the brochure, so she knew what it looked like. A weathered sign with a faded fork indicated the turnoff for the place and Robin navigated the car down a hill toward the lodge. She knew that the North Fork could accommodate around forty people. It had ten individual cabins and fifteen guest rooms in the lodge building itself.

As she got closer, two large structures came into view. They were surrounded by multiple smaller cabins that faced the lake. One of the large buildings looked like a meeting center or dining hall. The other looked to be the lodge where the guest rooms were located. Darrell's comparison to the resort in *Dirty Dancing* was even farther off than she had believed earlier. But even though the buildings looked nothing like the opulent stone edifices in the movie, their location on the lake was jaw-dropping. What a view!

Robin parked the car at the lodge building in front of a crooked sign that said "Lobby." The roof of the wooden structure had an odd tilt, and the steps up to the front door were a little worrisome as well, given that the aged wooden stairs had a definite sag in the middle. Gathering her purse from the passenger seat, she got out and walked up to the steps. She gingerly placed her foot on the bottom step, which seemed to hold her weight. She continued up to the wraparound porch and the old boards creaked under her feet as she crossed the weathered decking to the front door. Perhaps maintenance wasn't Uncle Ernie's strong suit.

She opened the door and walked into a large open room. The check-in desk and a stairway up to the rooms were on the left. To the right, a massive stone fireplace dominated the space. A number of small figures were displayed on the mantle and a grouping of antique bent-willow chairs and a sofa clustered around it. In front of the sofa, a vintage wooden coffee table sat on a threadbare floral rug. Huge wooden beams ran across the ceiling to the walls, which were made of log, so the room had the atmosphere of an old hunting lodge. On a positive note, there weren't any dead animals hanging on the walls, so apparently any hunters who had stayed here had taken their prizes away with them.

Someone with a scratchy male voice was belting out an extremely off-key rendition of "Love Will Keep Us Together" so tunelessly that even the Captain and Tennille might not recognize it. Robin rang the bell on the front desk and the singing stopped abruptly.

A tall, skinny man with grizzled grayish razor stubble and wild curly silvery hair opened a door behind the desk and thumped his cane on the floor. He raised his bushy white eyebrows at Robin. "Who are you?"

"I'm Robin Sanders. Are you Mr. Lambert?"

"Yeah. What's it to you?"

"I talked to you the other day. I'm Robin. I work for your nephew Darrell. We're doing a retreat here for Eagle River."

"What?"

"Eagle River. The catalog company? The one Darrell owns?"

"Oh yeah. Right. Who are you?"

Robin gripped the handle of her purse more tightly. The expression on the elderly man's face was utterly uncomprehending. It was like he'd never heard of her. But she knew she'd talked to him just the other day. She said more slowly, "I'm Robin Sanders. I'm here to get everything set up for the retreat. Remember? The attendees arrive in two days." Ernie seemed even more confused about the upcoming event than he had on the phone. This was not good.

"Right. I talked to Myrtle about that."

"Who is Myrtle?"

"My wife."

Robin breathed a sigh of relief. Maybe Myrtle was the one who actually ran this place. "Maybe I can talk to her too. But first I need to talk to your chef about the food. You said his name is Chuck?"

"Chuck?"

"Yes. You said he's the cook, right? Is he here?"

"Oh yeah. No. He isn't here. I need to give him a call."

"You haven't talked to him?"

"Nope."

Robin's stomach clenched and she made a dogged effort to keep her expression neutral. "May I please have his number?" What was going on here? She had talked to Ernie more than once. Why didn't he remember anything about their conversations? Was there something wrong with this guy? She needed to call Darrell. *Now.* Clearly, her boss did not have all the facts about his uncle or the North Fork Lodge.

Ernie disappeared into the back room and Robin waited as he crashed around, presumably looking for Chuck's phone number. With any luck, Ernie would remember what he was doing long enough to find it for her. If they didn't have food at the retreat, there could be a nasty riot. Robin was only a mediocre cook, and she certainly didn't have experience cooking for 25 people. She wouldn't even know where to begin.

She turned around and leaned her back on the desk. Taking a deep breath, she gazed across the large room, trying not to panic about the situation. A large black vinyl garbage can sat across the room from the desk and a blue tarp stretched from the ceiling to the garbage can. What was that for? Assuming Robin was able to resolve the food situation, she'd have to remember to investigate that bizarre set-up. Having a large trash receptacle in the room didn't exactly enhance the decor. Rustic was one thing. Proper refuse disposal was another.

The door to the back room opened again and Ernie came out waving a piece of paper. "I asked Myrtle about it, and I did talk to Chuck! I forgot. Here's his number."

Robin turned to face him and took the piece of paper he proffered. "Thank you. You told me that I would be staying in the Pine Cone cabin. I'd like to check in now, if that's okay. I need to make some urgent calls."

Ernie pointed to the phone on the desk. "This building's the only one wired for telephone. You'll have to use this one here. The phone in the back is my private line. You can't use that though. It's just for me and Myrtle."

No phone in the rooms? The attendees were going to love that. Robin sucked in another long breath, pausing to fill her lungs before responding. "All right. Could you give me the key to my cabin? I'll drop off my things and then come back here and call Chuck. I need to confer with him about the menu as soon as possible."

Ernie bent down and rummaged around behind the desk. "Here ya go. It's the first cabin down there on the left. It's a duplex and you're in the left one." He handed her the rusty skeleton key. "The door doesn't work that great. You gotta slam it hard to get it to close all the way. Otherwise, you'll have a pretty drafty night."

"Thank you." Robin took the key and left the building, glancing at the garbage can as she left. Was it there because the roof leaked? That was a depressing notion, particularly given the size of the garbage can. Was it full of water?

The whole place seemed to be dusty and decomposing. It was like the wood was opting to return to the land rather than holding up the various structures on the property. Robin needed a moment alone to gather her thoughts. Then she needed to call Darrell and tell him what was going on. Maybe she could stop this whole thing before it went any further. There had to be another place they could hold the retreat. Both Ernie and this lodge seemed to have some serious issues.

~

Robin drove her car over to Pine Cone 1 and parked. She got out and turned to look out at the lake, which was a stunning deep blue. The sun was streaming through the clouds, hitting the water and causing it to sparkle as if tiny diamonds were scattered on the surface. The lake was so beautiful and pristine, it almost didn't look real. Maybe some of those brochure photos weren't retouched after all. Sitting and staring out at that lovely water would be so much more relaxing than dealing with the ugly details of this disastrous retreat. Oh well. Maybe later.

Turning back to the car, Robin grabbed her suitcase and carried it to the door. The key didn't want to go into the lock, but after wrestling with it, she finally got the door open, tripping over her suitcase and falling into the darkened room.

A whoosh of dust hit her nose and Robin sneezed loudly, breaking the stillness of the cabin. When was the last time someone had walked into this room? And on a related note, when was the last time someone had stayed at the North Fork at all? The entire property seemed to have been utterly abandoned. The operation was definitely not a going concern. Robin opened the curtains and sunlight streamed through the dust motes into the room.

At one time, the cabin had probably been cute and charming. That time was evidently long ago. Now the bed sported a faded plaid bedspread that sank down into a large crater in the middle. The mattress had undoubtedly seen better days. Maybe back when the brochure photograph was taken.

Robin bent to take a closer look at the bed before placing her suitcase on it. If something was living inside that mattress,

Robin was absolutely going to scream like a little baby. She pulled down the covers, but nothing leaped out. Well, that was something, but the idea of actually sleeping on the bed was revolting. When was the last time those sheets had been washed? 1989?

Robin stood up again and straightened her shoulders. This was absurd. She was going to march back to the lodge, call Darrell, and tell him they had a big problem. No retreat of any kind was going to happen here if she had anything to say about it.

After fighting with the door and locking the cabin again, she walked back up to the lodge building. Ernie was nowhere to be found, which was a relief in some ways. She walked behind the desk and sat in the creaky wooden rolling chair. The harvest-gold phone had a rotary dial. Wow. When was the last time she'd seen one of those? She picked up the receiver and held it to her ear. At least it had a dial tone. Score one for telecommunications. Twirling the dial, she slowly called the number for Eagle River and asked for Darrell. After a long delay, he finally came on the line.

"Sorry, I was in a meeting. How's Alpine Grove?"

Robin cleared her throat. He wasn't going to like what she had to say. "Well, I'm sorry to say, we have a little issue with the lodge. Have you been here lately?"

"Nope. I heard through the grapevine that Ernie has been having some financial problems. That's why I wanted to do the retreat there. Ernie needs the cash."

"Well, I don't think anyone has stayed here in quite a while. I'm afraid the North Fork is in terrible shape. We can't do the retreat here. I know it's late to be deciding this, but it's not going to work."

Darrell paused and Robin could imagine the irritated look on his face. He finally said, "You'll make it work."

"I don't see how." Robin leaned back and covered her mouth to suppress a gasp as the wood creaked and the chair wobbled precipitously. Oops.

"You'll figure it out. I just heard from Brett and he's on his way down there. And we've rented a couple of vans to drive all the customer-service folks from the airport. It's happening. You're going to *make* it happen."

"Mr. Lambert, I don't think you understand. I don't know what to do. I don't think there have been any guests here in an extremely long time. Years maybe. The buildings… everything…it's a mess. Have you spoken to Ernie recently? I think he may have, well, some memory problems. Should I talk to Myrtle instead? I got the impression from him that she might know more about the operations of the lodge."

"Not anymore. Aunt Myrtle has been dead for five years."

"What?" Robin sat up in the chair, pitching it forward. "Ernie said he talked to her."

"Yeah, well, he does that. As long as Myrtle doesn't say anything back, it's okay."

"Mr. Lambert, I'm sorry, but that is *not* funny." The tightness in her chest increased. *Son of a nutcracker!* Ernie was crazy as a loon. What was she supposed to do now?

"Robin, I've got to go into a meeting now. I'm trusting you. Make it work. Alec should be there in a few hours, and I'm sure he'll help. Be sure to keep Brett happy too. He's doing me a favor here."

Robin said goodbye and carefully placed the receiver back in the cradle. It would be a miracle if she didn't get fired after this retreat. At the very least, every person in the

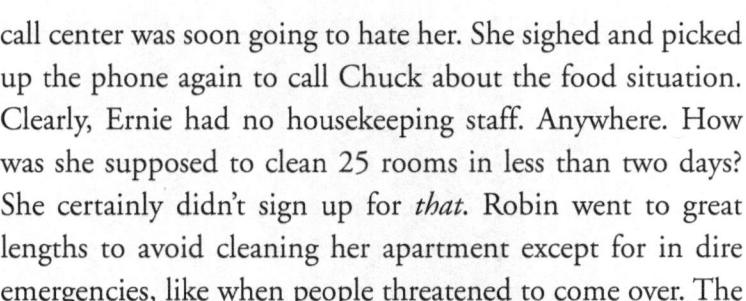

call center was soon going to hate her. She sighed and picked up the phone again to call Chuck about the food situation. Clearly, Ernie had no housekeeping staff. Anywhere. How was she supposed to clean 25 rooms in less than two days? She certainly didn't sign up for *that*. Robin went to great lengths to avoid cleaning her apartment except for in dire emergencies, like when people threatened to come over. The idea of cleaning an entire lodge was exhausting. On the other hand, she was definitely not going to sleep on those sheets in the Pine Cone cabin. No way. Even if she did nothing else, those sheets *had* to be washed before everyone got here.

A few hours later, Robin had talked to Chuck and found the laundry facilities, so she could begin the tedious task of stripping the beds and washing the sheets in all the rooms, starting with the ones in her cabin. She had practically collapsed with relief when Chuck told her that he actually did know about the upcoming retreat and that he would be bringing food over in preparation for it.

Ernie still was MIA, so Robin had gone behind the desk to get the keys to the various cabins so she could round up all the dusty sheets. Even though there wasn't much she would want to steal, it was strange that he'd completely vanished, leaving her here alone. Although she didn't think she looked like a hardened criminal, it was still odd.

At least the weather was nice. The only thing worse than having to do a zillion loads of laundry would be having to drag stacks of sheets through the rain. She was like Snow White with all the little birds in the forest chirping merrily as she dealt with her menial tasks.

It was actually peaceful out here by herself. After Alec and Brett, the team-building guy, showed up, all this tranquility would undoubtedly come to an abrupt end, so Robin wanted to enjoy it while she could.

~

Later that afternoon Robin was resting in the old wooden chair at the front desk. She had just finished putting newly laundered sheets back on some of the beds in the rooms upstairs. Making beds was one of her least-favorite tasks on the long list of housekeeping tasks she loathed. She didn't even make her own bed at home. What was the point? As soon as you go to bed, you're just going to mess it up again.

A large, burly man with a graying crew cut walked in and strode toward Robin. He smiled at her, revealing a gap where a lower incisor should have been. The missing tooth made his grin seem somewhat sinister, even though it obviously wasn't intentional.

Robin stood up and smiled politely. "Are you Chuck?"

"Yup. You must be Robin. Where'd Ernie get off to?"

"I'm not sure." It would be nice if he came back someday.

Chuck gestured toward the door. "He probably went out in his little boat. The sun is out, so he might be fishing."

"Isn't it a bit early in the year for that?"

"He doesn't actually catch anything, as far as I know. I asked him about fish for dinner once and he said he does catch and release. His description made it sound like he doesn't have to do much releasing, though. Mostly he sits out there and floats around, talking to himself. Since Myrtle died, he spends a lot of time out there on the water."

"Oh." Robin wasn't sure what to say. "I was sorry to hear about his wife."

"She was a nice lady. This place hasn't been the same since she died. People say the curse got her in the end."

"Curse?"

Chuck nodded. "Yeah. Didn't anyone tell you? A woman died here in the twenties and there's been stories forever that this place is haunted. Myrtle loved the legend and really played it up for a while. It was a great gimmick, and they had the best haunted house here for years. Hay rides and pumpkin carving. All kinds of Halloween stuff, and kids would come for miles around to get candy and get scared. My kids used to love it."

Robin glanced at the room beyond. It was all too easy to imagine it decked out for Halloween. They wouldn't have to put up those fake cobwebs, since there were plenty of the real thing available. "I'm from Portland, Oregon, so I don't know much about local history."

"Well, it's one of those stories that's probably been exaggerated over the years, but everyone who grew up in Alpine Grove knows about Julia, the ghost of the North Fork Lodge."

"There's a ghost named Julia here?"

"Well, that's what they say. Apparently, the Lambert family bought this land back in the twenties and there was nothing but a hunting cabin here. Back then, Aaron Lambert made a ton of money in mining and built a big house on the lake for his wife Julia. They had big parties here and did the whole Roaring-Twenties thing. They had a bunch of kids, but I guess one of the boys drowned in the lake. After losing her little boy, Julia went crazy with grief and her hair turned snow white. Then a fire burned down part of the house where the ballroom was and she died in the fire. Some people say she went completely mad and started the fire herself, but no one knows for sure."

"That is quite a story." Given Robin's recent interactions with Ernie, perhaps insanity ran in the family.

"Anyway, the place sat abandoned for a few years during the Depression, then one of Julia's kids tore down the rest of the house and built the lodge. It's been in the family ever since, and some people who stayed here claim to have met the ghost of Julia Lambert. They say she loved her home so much that she never left. Her spirit has a habit of interfering with hotel employees and guests. Ernie would probably be the first to tell you this place has always had trouble keeping staff.

"I haven't seen anyone else since I arrived." Certainly no housekeeping staff, that was for sure.

"Yeah, I think Ernie has given up on the place now. His heart's not in it anymore, I don't think. But I do know a few folks who've worked here over the years. The mom of one of my buddies did housekeeping for a little while. It was probably back in 1979 or so when she told us the story. It scared the crap outta me and Brian when she told us."

"Do you think she was just teasing you?"

"Maybe. But I doubt it. She wasn't that kind of lady. One night, she had to work late cleaning because a big group was coming here. She looked up and there's this translucent woman with flowing white hair wearing a white dress standing near that fireplace."

"Right there? In this room?" Robin stole a glance at the fireplace. No ghostly apparition. Phew. "This is all somewhat disturbing. I wish Darrell had told me."

"Yeah, lots of people around here have stories. My cousin Fred owns a bar in town and he said a tourist came in wanting a drink because he was out here and saw the woman. The guy was so freaked out he took off running and hitchhiked into town for a beer. But in all the stories, Julia vanishes right after she appears."

"You've catered events here for a while, right? Have you seen her?"

"Not really. But I did the food for a party a few years ago and one of the bartenders said glasses suddenly began to fly off of the shelves, one by one, smashing on the floor. And a waitress kept dropping trays. She said it felt like someone had pushed them up from underneath."

Robin tried to suppress a shudder. The sun had gone behind a cloud and suddenly she was cold. Nightfall was going to arrive all too soon. And she was completely creeped out. "You're still willing to do the food, so it can't be that bad."

"It's no big deal. Probably every small town has a place that's supposed to be haunted. It gives people something to talk about."

"I suppose."

Chuck gestured toward the door. "So, hey, sorry to talk your ear off. I should get moving here. I'm gonna bring in some food and put it in the refrigerator."

Robin nodded. "I should get more sheets out of the dryer. Thank you for bringing everything by. I don't know what I would have done if you weren't available to handle the food."

Chuck grinned, revealing his misaligned teeth again. "Maybe you could have gotten Julia to help you."

Robin laughed. "It doesn't sound like she's a particularly helpful or friendly ghost."

"Yeah, the fact she was totally nuts doesn't help. She ain't no Casper, that's for sure."

~

Robin was walking from her cabin back to the lodge as a car turned through the gate and started down the hill. When the vehicle got closer, she noticed that the pearl-gray sedan had some type of shiny hood ornament on it that was reflecting in the sunlight. Alec had mentioned he would be driving a Jeep Cherokee, so this must be Brett.

Robin had found Ernie's notes, which indicated Brett was staying in the North Star cabin. Unlike the other cabins, the North Star wasn't a duplex or triplex. It was a separate building set off away from the others. Honeymooners or hermits probably enjoyed the privacy and larger space.

The car door opened and a long leg stretched out. Brett extracted himself from the low-slung vehicle as Robin walked up. Dressed in a suit, he was strikingly handsome, with broad shoulders. His thick jet-black hair flowed back from his face and contrasted with his startling dark eyes. He had to be one of the tallest men Robin had ever met. Maybe six foot six? Six eight? Whatever the altitude, he was quite the towering presence. At five foot eight, she wasn't exactly tiny, but next to Brett, Robin felt like one of the seven dwarfs. Maybe Sneezy, after all the cleaning.

Brett turned to look at her and Robin smiled and extended her hand. "You must be Brett. I'm Robin. We exchanged a couple of emails, and it's a pleasure to meet you in person."

Brett stepped forward and ignored her outstretched hand, wrapping her in a bear hug and lifting her feet up off the ground. "Greetings and salutations, Robin!" He put her down and opened his arms wide toward the lake. "What an inspirational view. The energy from the natural beauty of this setting is going to help bring all of us into our personal power. Can you feel it?"

"It is pretty here." He might be less enthusiastic once he saw the inside of his cabin. Not to mention the lodge.

"Here in this glorious setting, I am going to help empower employees to make massive changes and give them tools to create dramatic growth in their chosen careers. We are all going to share in an entirely new mindset. Are you ready?"

"I guess so, although I'm not attending the retreat. I'm here in more of a managerial or administrative capacity." She clasped her palms together. "Darrell probably didn't tell you, so I should, well, let you know that this place doesn't seem to be in the greatest condition. I went into your cabin, and I'm afraid it may have suffered some rodent-related damage." Pink insulation had been everywhere. She'd tried to clean it up, but it was disgusting, and the scrabbly noises in the wall indicated that the current resident of the cabin wasn't planning on leaving any time soon.

Brett placed his palm on his chest and cast his gaze toward the lake. "I'm not worried. This will be another test that I can learn from in my own path to discovering my true identity as a leader. We're all here to learn new things." He glanced down at her. "But maybe you could find a mousetrap somewhere?"

"I'll keep looking." Robin pointed toward the largest cabin. "You're in the North Star cabin, which is down over there. The owner isn't around, but I can run into the lodge and get the key for you."

"Thank you." Brett leaned on the car, placed his hand on the hood, closed his eyes, and inhaled deeply. "There will be dynamic transformations here this week. I can tell."

"That's an interesting hood ornament. Isn't that the Batman logo?"

Brett opened his eyes. "Yes! How astute of you to notice. I identify with Bruce Wayne. Like him, I am a lone crusader trying to right wrongs. But in my case, the wrongs are in people's own perceptions. I try to help people see that we are *all* crusaders in our own lives. And we all have an identity that we hide from the world."

Robin tried not to roll her eyes. This guy needed a cape. "I see."

"And everyone needs a cohort. No one makes it through life completely alone. We all need a Robin." He grinned expansively. "Like you!"

If he called her the Girl Wonder, she was going to vomit. She was *so* not in the mood. Clenching her hands together, she smiled sweetly. "I'll run inside and get that key for you now. Be right back."

Robin turned and went inside the lodge. Ernie still wasn't around. Where was he? It had been hours now and she hadn't seen any boats out on the lake. She grabbed the key to the North Star cabin from its hook and went back outside. A Jeep was now parked next to the gray sedan and Alec Montgomery was getting out of it.

Robin was relieved that Alec had arrived. Although Brett was obviously trying to be cheerful and agreeable, the whole Batman thing was way over the top. He was a bit overwhelming to deal with alone, since he clearly needed a larger audience than she could provide.

She walked up to the two men. "Hi Alec. As you probably guessed, this is Brett."

The two men shook hands and Brett said, "Are you ready to learn some core leadership skills?"

Alec glanced at Robin quickly and withdrew his hand from Brett's. "Yeah, sure. That sounds great." He turned to Robin. "How was your trip?"

"It was fine. I dropped off my dog and have been… busy…here since I arrived. I need to talk to you about some logistics when you get a minute."

"Sure." Alec gazed out at the lake. "This is amazing. Look at how blue the water is."

Robin handed the North Star cabin key to Brett. "Here is your key. I put fresh sheets on the bed already." 'Fresh' was a more genteel way of saying the sheets had been washed within the last decade.

Brett took her hand and kissed her knuckles before taking the key. "Thank you. I'm sure we'll make a fantastic dynamic duo. I'll go acclimate myself to my new environment."

He walked around to the back of the car, opened the trunk, and pulled out a suitcase.

Robin said. "I'm in the Pine Cone cabin. Number 1 on the left." She glanced at Alec. Alec will be staying in the other side of the duplex, in the cabin on the right."

Brett waved behind him and said, "I'll see you later for dinner."

Robin looked at Alec, who was fiddling with his keys as he stared out at the lake. The guy certainly had a lot of nervous energy, considering that it was a long drive and he had to be exhausted. His blue-green eyes were bloodshot and he really needed a shave. Alec probably didn't have a cool dog like Emma for company on the road.

Dinner was going to be a problem, and it would probably be better to share the bad news with Alec sooner rather than later. Robin attempted to sound upbeat. "So, ah, I talked to Chuck, the chef, and his cooking duties aren't set to start until tomorrow when the attendees arrive. I don't suppose you like to cook, do you?"

He scrubbed his face with his hands and turned to look at her. "Not at the moment I don't."

"I was afraid of that." She gestured toward the lodge. "I need to get you your key and then I can show you what we're dealing with."

"What do you mean *dealing* with?"

"You'll see."

"Where's the owner of this place?"

"I wish I knew."

~

Robin went behind the desk and handed the key across the counter to Alec. "Here's the key to your cabin. I changed the sheets."

He raised his eyebrows. "How come you're doing that? Don't they have housekeeping staff here?"

"Look around. Do you *think* they have housekeeping staff?"

Alec twirled the key on his finger as he gazed at the open area. "That's a great fireplace. But why is that garbage can sitting over there with the tarp?"

"I think there's a roof leak. When it rains, it's probably like having a waterfall in the lobby. Perhaps we can pass it off as a water feature."

"This retreat is going to be even more of a nightmare than I thought." Alec fussed at the key in his hand. "What is wrong with Darrell? His family owns this place. He had to know it's a mess."

"After I got here, I called and talked to him about moving the retreat. He said, 'make it work or else.'"

"He really said that to you?"

"Well, maybe he didn't say 'or else' exactly, but it was implied." Robin carefully sat down in the wobbly chair behind the counter. "My situation is different than yours. I haven't worked at Eagle River for years like you have. I'm afraid I'm going to get fired if this retreat doesn't work out. I mean, look at this place. It's filthy and not in good repair. And the owner, Ernie, vanished right after I got here. Chuck said he might have gone fishing. But how long does fishing take? Ernie has been gone for hours."

Alec rested his elbows on the counter and leaned his forehead on his palms. "This is just like Darrell to do this." He raised his head to look at her, laid his forearms on the desk, and rhythmically tapped his fingertips on the wood. "You wouldn't know it, since it was a long time ago, but he used to pull this kind of stuff all the time when he first started the company. I can't tell you how many times I heard, 'you'll figure it out' in the early years."

"That does seem to be a popular phrase with him. But I guess you did figure things out, given how successful the company is now."

"Yeah. Most of the time. I had some pretty spectacular screw–ups, though."

Robin smiled. "That makes me feel a little better, I guess. You obviously didn't get fired."

Alec stood back up and jammed the key into his pocket. "No. But it's a big company now. When it was only the three of us working out of Darrell's living room, we all did everything. None of us knew what we were doing. In a lot of ways, it was a lot more fun back then. Every day was different. Now, I'm just a cog in a machine taking orders from the boss."

"So in a roundabout way, what you're *not* saying is that I could get fired."

"No, I didn't mean that." A corner of his mouth turned up. "Okay, maybe a little."

Robin's shoulders slumped. "I'm doomed. I know you've only been here ten minutes, but this place is a disaster. Even if I were a demon housekeeper, which I'm definitely not, I could never get this place sparkly in time. And even if it were clean, various parts of the buildings seem to be disintegrating."

A loud crash came from outside and they both looked toward the door. Alec said, "What was that?"

"I have no idea. Maybe something large fell apart...or off."

They walked to the door and Alec opened it. Other than a few birds singing, it was silent. No one appeared to be around. Lights were on in Brett's cabin, so it seemed he was still busy acclimating down there.

Robin leaned against the doorjamb and watched as Alec walked around the front of the building. He raised his palms to the sky and shrugged. "I don't see anything."

"Maybe it's another mouse. There's a rodent living in Brett's cabin. Maybe the little guy is looking for a new home."

"Whatever made that noise was a lot bigger than a mouse."

"Oh *fluffernuts*, don't say that! I have enough problems. I don't want to even consider the possibility of gigantic rodents." She shook her head, trying to banish the thought.

"Fluffer-what?"

Pressing her palms together, she gave Alec her most endearing smile. "Wait. I have an idea. How much do you think Darrell would pay for cleaning?"

"I don't know. He's a cheapskate and it's not his lodge."

"Yes, but it *is* his retreat. I'm going to look around for a phone book. Maybe I can get a power-cleaning crew in here tomorrow before everyone arrives. There's got to be someone around here that would be interested if we pay them enough."

Alec looked unconvinced and turned toward his Jeep. "Good luck. I should go unload my stuff and take a shower."

Robin glanced toward the Pine Cone cabin. Did the shower work? She hadn't checked. Guess he'd find out soon enough. "I'm going to make some calls."

True to her word, Robin spent the next few hours calling most of the businesses in Alpine Grove in her quest to find someone to clean the North Fork the next day. Not surprisingly, the idea of a last-minute cleaning job on a Sunday was met with limited enthusiasm, so she broadened her scope. First she asked Chuck, who had her call his cousin Fred who owned the bar. Fred suggested talking to the woman who owned a gift store because "she knows everyone." As it turned out, Bea Sullivan did seem to have the inside scoop on the Alpine Grove community. She suggested calling a woman named Eleanor. She and some friends in her church group were trying to raise money for roof repairs. It sounded like the roof of the nondenominational church wasn't keeping out rain much better than the roof on the North Fork Lodge. After a brief conversation, Eleanor and company were scheduled to come out right after church and set to work. Robin hoped it would be a collection of extremely hard-working, industrious people.

Robin looked up from her scribbled notes as the front door of the lodge opened. Alec walked in, looking much cleaner and less haggard. He'd even shaved. That was certainly an improvement. He was carrying a three-ring binder, which he placed on the desk in front of her.

Robin put down her pencil. "What's that?"

"This is the training manual for customer-service reps. It's the stuff I have to teach them starting Monday."

"All that to answer the phone and take orders?"

"Yes. I need to read it through again, but I was hoping to find something to eat first. I'm starving."

Robin had been so busy dealing with everything else, she hadn't thought about food in hours. Her stomach growled loudly. How embarrassing. She grinned sheepishly. "I guess I am too. Chuck has everything all organized, so I'm not sure what we're allowed to eat back in the kitchen."

"What if we order a pizza? I could use some nice greasy food."

"I doubt they deliver way out here. Plus, I have a problem. I found someone to clean, but it's not an official company. It's a bunch of women from a church and I don't think they take credit cards."

"So give them cash."

"I only have $40. Boarding my dog is going to cost money. And there's gas. My reimbursement check for this trip can't arrive soon enough."

Alec rocked back and forth on his heels. "So what you're saying is that you have no money to pay for the cleaning crew you just set up?"

"I moved to Portland a few months ago and I'm kind of broke. Could you cover it? Besides, as we've discussed, Darrell likes you way better than he likes me." Broke didn't begin to describe it. Her bank account had ten dollars and thirty-two cents in it.

"It's definitely dusty and dirty here. I guess I could stop by an ATM."

"You'll need the max amount you can withdraw."

Alec stopped tugging at the button on the cuff of his shirt and looked up. "Are you kidding me? For cleaning?"

"It's for a good cause. The church out on the highway needs a new roof. The ladies are raising money for it."

"I feel so much better now."

"Maybe you could pick up the pizza too? I'll check with Brett and see what he likes and then call it in."

Alec picked up his binder. "Fine. At this point, I'll do anything to get some food. You sure are one determined woman. I'll be back in a little while."

Robin plastered her sweetest smile on her face. She couldn't believe it—she'd actually talked him into paying. "Thank you, Alec. I really appreciate this."

Chapter 3

Greetings

Later, Robin walked down to Brett's cabin to let him know the pizza had arrived. She knocked on the door. He opened it wide and exclaimed "Robin! I assume that your presence here at my humble abode means that dinner has arrived."

"Yes. Alec is back with the pizza."

He closed the door behind him and took her hand. "Then let's go dine. Isn't this view with the sun reflecting off the lake breathtaking? You look absolutely lovely in the twilight. The reddish glow in the sky brings out the golden highlights in your hair."

"Thank you. That's very flattering."

"I'm sure I'm not the first to tell you that you're a beautiful woman."

Robin wasn't sure what to say. After a day of stress and cleaning, she had to look pretty rumpled by now. Was he coming on to her? If so, she wasn't in the mood. It was probably best to assume he was just being friendly and respond in kind. "It has been a long day and I'm afraid I'm not feeling terribly pretty at the moment, so that's kind of you to say."

"I'm simply expressing what I see. It doesn't hurt that I'm a sucker for blue-eyed blondes."

"Thank you. Is your cabin okay?"

"There seems to be an issue with the water pressure."

"What do you mean the water pressure?"

"There isn't any. I took a quick shower, but it was more like a misting, I'm afraid."

"*Holy schnitzel*, that doesn't sound good." Robin sighed and looked up at him. He was so tall, it was like holding hands with her father when she was twelve years old. "I'm sorry. If the owner ever shows up again, I'll be sure to tell him. Alec took a shower and didn't say anything was wrong. Maybe the plumbing in the Pine Cone cabin works better and you could try that one tomorrow."

He swung her hand cheerfully between them as they walked. "That's a great idea. You are always looking for solutions. I like that about you."

They walked into the kitchen, where Alec was sitting at one of the metal tables with a pizza box in front of him. The aroma of Italian spices and tomato sauce wafted through the space. Officially ravenous now, Robin eagerly settled onto one of the metal stools.

Even though the rest of the lodge might be seriously unclean, Chuck had obviously spent some time in the kitchen scrubbing down the shiny metal tables and commercial appliances when he brought over the food.

The trio sat around the table silently chewing pizza. It was delicious and Robin was finally starting to feel human again. She raised her slice toward Alec, "Thank you *so* much for going to town and getting this for us. Pizza has never tasted so good."

Brett said, "I appreciate your willingness to go forth and gather sustenance for us as well. I think we've all had a long day of travel and activities. This is exactly the type of team-oriented cooperation that I'll be focusing on this week."

Alec paused in his enthusiastic chewing and Robin was afraid he might say something sarcastic or snotty, but he just nodded. Robin said to Brett, "I've been somewhat curious about your program, actually. I hope the weather holds. Doing a scavenger hunt in the rain could be unpleasant for the attendees."

Brett set down his slice of pizza and leaned toward her. "Shared adversity such as bad weather can enhance the level of cooperation among team members. But I'm starting with simple ice-breaker exercises, which we'll do inside. That way people will feel more comfortable with one another before we send them out into the forest."

A crashing noise came from outside the kitchen and the door opened. Ernie walked in and nodded at the group. Robin hurriedly swallowed what she was chewing and said, "Ernie! Where have you been?"

"I was out. Had to do some stuff."

She stood up and placed her palms on the table. Maybe *stuff* was his term for fishing. "While you were gone, I washed all the sheets and gave Brett and Alec their keys. Also, we're having some women come in to clean tomorrow. I hope that's okay. And the nineteen people attending the retreat are arriving tomorrow evening. You remember that, right?"

Ernie waved dismissively, walked to the table, and took a slice of pizza. "Yeah. I'll tell Myrtle." He turned and left the kitchen.

Alec raised his eyebrows at Robin. "He's certainly a man of few words, isn't he?"

Robin sat down in her chair again. "To be honest, I'm not sure he's quite all there. Myrtle is his wife. Or *was* his wife. According to Darrell, she's been dead for years."

Brett said, "Sometimes people talk to their spouses, even after they are gone. It makes them feel closer to the person they've lost."

Robin sighed. "I suppose that's sweet in a way. Very sad, but sweet. Darrell said it was fine, unless Ernie thinks Myrtle is participating in the conversation. Maybe he does. I can't tell."

Brett put his hand over hers. "You've done a tremendous job of handling everything, Robin. I'm sure it will be fine."

She looked up into Brett's eyes. They were an unusual dark-brown, almost black color that was compelling. It was easy to understand why he was such a successful trainer. "Thank you. You've been very understanding about all the problems here."

Alec cleared his throat. "So. About tomorrow? I guess we set up in that other building across the way?"

Robin turned to him and said, "Yes. It used to be a dinner theater years ago, as I understand it. There are supposed to be folding tables and chairs in a closet, but I didn't have time to check it out. I was dealing with sheets. There were a lot of them. But I'll make sure the church ladies clean up that area too. I hope the roof is okay."

"Guess we'll find out." Alec stood up. "I think I'll head off to my cabin now. I've got a ton of material to go over before Monday."

They both thanked him again for the pizza and he left. Robin grabbed another piece of pizza and smiled at Brett. "There's only one more piece. Go for it."

He returned her smile and took the slice from the box. "I believe I will."

They ate companionably in silence and Robin stole a few glances at him. Brett was absurdly handsome, confident, and charming. Although he'd come on a little strong at first, it was difficult not to like him after he'd been so friendly and encouraging. Maybe it was just the fatigue talking, but she couldn't help thinking about him. What would those lips feel like? How would he respond? Moving and starting over in a new city had been complicated and she'd been lacking in any type of male companionship for a long time. All of her friends were still in Spokane, and her pathetic lack of social life was starting to feel hopeless.

A loud clattering racket from outside startled Robin from her reverie. "Flaming heck! What now?"

Brett stood up. "I don't know. Considering the remote location, it certainly is noisy here."

"Maybe it's the ghost."

He looked down at her. "Are you saying Ernie's wife is a ghost?"

"I don't know about her. But according to Chuck, the cook, there's supposedly a ghost from a long time ago. A woman who died in a fire here in the twenties, I think. Alpine Grove legend has it that she never left the North Fork."

Brett held out his hand to her. "It looks like you're done with dinner. Let me escort you back to your cabin. Just in case."

She took his hand and gave it a friendly squeeze. "Okay. Just in case."

~

The next morning Robin opened her eyes and squinted at the sunlight streaming through the window. The predicted bad weather obviously hadn't arrived yet, which was good news for the North Fork cleaning program. She sat up in bed, pulled her knees to her chest and wrapped her arms around them.

Even though the little brown Pine Cone cabin would hardly be considered opulent by anyone's estimation, it was still cute in a beat-up yet well-loved dollhouse kind of way. It had a tiny living area with an old sofa and wooden chest in front of it that acted as a coffee table. At the moment, the chest was covered with Robin's printouts of checklists and timelines, proving its ability to do double-duty as a micro-workspace.

The mattress on the old four-poster bed was a little broken-down in the middle, but Robin hadn't noticed when she crawled under the covers the night before. After the driving, laundry, and stress, she'd been exhausted and would have fallen asleep almost immediately were it not for the ghost—or oversized rodent—that had made a few more crashing noises before finally settling in for the evening.

Aside from the possible haunting issues, it was incredibly peaceful out here on the lake, which was quite a change from her apartment in downtown Portland. With a little TLC, the cabin could even be downright adorable. The tongue-and-groove paneling on the walls could stand to be refinished and the furniture desperately needed to be reupholstered and restored, but with those repairs, new bedding, and a few cute decorations, the little space would make an idyllic romantic getaway. Well, that and fixing the door. Getting in and out of Pine Cone 1 *was* a bit of a struggle. Shoving on the door wasn't sexy at all. It would completely ruin the whole traditional carrying-the-bride-over-the-threshold experience.

Robin looked over toward the bathroom with more than a little trepidation. It was time to brave the shower. There hadn't been any sounds of water running next door. Maybe she could get to the hot water before Alec did, since presumably the duplex shared plumbing. After yesterday's festival of dust, it would be fantastic to be clean again.

She turned on the water and held her hand under the spray while the water warmed up. After a prolonged wait, it became clear that the water was not *going* to warm up. Ever. She braced herself and finally leaped under the frigid stream with a shriek. *Fudge berries, kitty whiskers,* and *horse feathers*—it was *cold*!

Quickly leaping back out of the stream, she hurriedly shampooed her hair. This was going to be the fastest shower on record. So much for the relaxing morning. She was really, really awake now. Most of her nerve endings probably had icicles hanging from them.

As she shivered and toweled herself off, Robin made a mental note to ask Alec about hot water. Was he the only person in this place enjoying warm, revitalizing showers? Or was he just incredibly stoic? A crashing noise came from the other side of the wall, along with some shouting of expletives. Alec obviously had a preference for the type of four-letter words Robin's mother had forbidden her to utter. Maybe he wasn't so stoic, after all. After the initial outburst, Robin couldn't hear exactly what he said, but it seemed Alec had quite a range of lewd ways to express his displeasure over there in Pine Cone 2.

Robin hurriedly got dressed and tried not to think about the chill that had seeped deep down into her bones. Maybe in mid-summer a cold shower would be refreshing. In early spring, it just froze her entire body right down to her toenails. She grabbed a cardigan and went to the door. Grabbing the doorknob, she tugged and it came off in her hand. *Shostakovich!* Looking at the knob for a moment, she dropped it on the floor, peered into the hole in the door, and reached in with her fingertips. The door didn't want to move. How could she be trapped when half of the door lock was on the floor? And, more important, how was she supposed to get out? What was going on over there on the other side? Given all the stomping around, Alec was definitely alive. Even the thump of his feet didn't sound happy.

She pounded on the wall and yelled, "Are you okay?"

He thumped in response and said, "I'm fine. Good morning to you too."

"Could you help me? I'm stuck."

After an extended moment of silence, Alec finally shouted, "What do you mean *stuck*?"

"I can't get out of the cabin. The knob fell off the door."

After some more thumping noises and mumbling, the door on the other side of the cabin slammed. Robin's door wiggled a few times and Alec pounded on the wood. "Put the knob back on."

Robin bent down, picked up the doorknob, and held it up to the hole. "There's nothing to attach it to. It's gone."

"I know that. I've got it over here. Hold your side up."

Robin did as instructed. After some jiggling and rearranging, they worked together to reattach the knobs. With a bang, the door swung open and Alec practically fell on top of her. Having someone you didn't know land on you certainly was awkward. She mumbled a small "Thank you," as she stepped away from him.

Clutching a screwdriver in his hand, he backed onto the small porch landing. "Sure. No problem." Looking over his shoulder toward his side of the cabin, he said. "I've gotta go."

Robin peered out the door. "Is something wrong?"

"No. See you later." He ran around the building and the door to his cabin slammed again.

Robin shook her head. Alec was really kind of a strange guy. Maybe he drank too much coffee or something. He certainly was jumpy. She picked up her watch from the nightstand. The ladies would probably be getting out of church soon. Time to go dredge up some breakfast before they arrived at the lodge.

After a restorative bowl of cereal, Robin was sitting at the desk in the lobby looking over her lists when a short older woman wearing a colorful scarf on her head walked in the door. She marched up to the desk and put both hands on the counter with a slap. "You must be Robin."

Robin smiled politely. "Yes I am. You must be Eleanor."

"You can call me Ellie. Everybody does. Except my mother, but she's been dead for twenty years, so she doesn't get a vote anymore."

Robin stood up and walked around the desk. "I really appreciate you coming out here to help us on such short notice."

Ellie took off her silk scarf, revealing a mass of short tight gray curls that encircled her head like a badly crocheted hat. "All the rain we've had this spring sure hasn't been helping the roof at the church. Your call couldn't have come at a better time. I've already got that money spent. The boys are coming out tomorrow to get started before the whole thing caves in. The congregation will be a lot smaller if we all get squished during Bible study."

Robin pushed her hair behind her ear. Was Ellie kidding? It was hard to tell. She was a forceful little person and Robin decided she didn't want to get on her bad side. Opting for discretion, she said, "Let me show you around."

"Oh honey, I've been here a million times. My kids all went to the haunted house. Every single fall I had to bring them out here. Have you seen Julia yet?"

Robin shook her head. Apparently Chuck's ghost story was well known among the locals. "No, I haven't."

"But you've heard weird noises, right?"

"No. Or, yes, I suppose I did hear something. There was a squirrel or other animal outside yesterday that knocked something over. And one of the cabins seems to have a bit of, well, rodent damage."

"That wasn't rodents." Ellie waved her hand dismissively and walked over to the fireplace. Her flesh was so wrinkled with minute creases that it looked like crumpled waxed paper. Robin made a mental note to put on some sunscreen later.

Ellie reached up and ran her fingertip along the mantle. "That's some thick dust." She looked down. "The floors are nasty too. Okay. I can see what we need to do here. The girls are outside. Let's go round them up and plan our attack."

"I'm glad you're not too upset by the scope of work. I don't think this place has been cleaned in a while."

"Honey, a little dust doesn't scare me. I raised five children, three of them boys. When it comes to dirt, there's nothing I haven't seen."

Robin laughed and followed Ellie out the door. It seemed that things were well in hand. A Marine drill sergeant had nothing on this woman.

Even though the average age of the "girls" in the congregation had to be about seventy-five, they were a hard-working bunch and Robin had difficulty keeping up with them. She ran up and down the lodge stairs and throughout the North Fork property, making sure the women remained stocked with cleaning supplies. True to her word, Ellie was a cleaning machine, taking on some of the most unpleasant tasks, including the remaining rodent debris in the North Star cabin. Brett had wisely opted to get out of her way and had joined Alec in the former dinner theater to work on his program.

By late afternoon, the North Fork was as clean as it was going to get. Robin happily handed off the cash to Ellie, who reported that she was going back to the church to give the money to the pastor for safekeeping.

Satisfied with the day's major accomplishments, Robin slowly walked across the lawn toward the theater building. Like the lodge, the roof had a somewhat peculiar slant to it. Alpine Grove weather seemed to be hard on structures. She looked up at the eaves and the darkening clouds beyond. The rain was going to be arriving soon. All the roof had to do was last for one more week. After that, the entire North Fork facility could return to its leisurely process of decomposition, for all she cared.

She opened the door to the building and walked inside. The ladies had worked their cleaning magic here too. The tables had been set up in a large square with chairs surrounding the perimeter. The space was starting to look like an actual training facility, stage and piano notwithstanding. If things got tough, maybe they could do a sing-a-long.

Alec and Brett sat at opposite ends of the square of tables. Alec was surrounded by a disorganized mass of papers and Eagle River catalogs and Brett had a pile of notebooks neatly stacked next to him. They both looked up at her. Brett smiled and said, "Greetings, Robin. You have been one busy lady. Like a green dragonfly gracefully flitting from place to place."

Robin sat down in a chair on the side of the square closest to the door. "I'm exhausted. Tomorrow, I'm planning to take a nice, long, relaxing walk with my dog while everyone is doing their training and team-building stuff."

Alec said, "I think Darrell wants you to attend the training."

Robin glared at him. "Why do I have to do that? I don't work in the call center."

"*Everybody* answers the phones during the holidays." Alec twirled his pencil in his hand and pointed it at her. "They must have told you that when you were hired, right? The overflow calls get routed from the call center to the rest of the company. Everyone, from the lowliest clerk in the mail room to Darrell, has to take orders."

"I guess they did say that. But it sounded like it doesn't happen very often."

Alec put down the pencil and rested his elbows on the table, tapping his fingers sequentially as if he were doing scales on a piano. "It does if we're making sales. Believe me, you *want* those overflow calls happening a lot if you expect to ever get a bonus."

Robin crossed her arms in front of her. "I miss my dog and I told the lady at the kennel I'd take her out, but I haven't been able to so far."

Brett said, "Why don't you bring her here?"

Alec said, "They don't allow dogs."

Brett turned to look at him. "Well, if the dog is well-behaved, she could join in our outdoor team-building exercises. There shouldn't be any harm in that. The presence of animals often brings people together. A shared love of dogs, for example, can be a great way to break down barriers and initiate the bonding process."

Alec balanced his pencil in his palm, peering over the point at Robin. "What's your dog's name?"

"Emma. She is the best little dog. I got her at the animal shelter when I lived in Spokane. She might be a Brittany mix. I'm not sure what she's mixed with, but she's super smart. I took her to obedience classes and she did really well." Robin glanced out the window toward the lodge. "When I talked to him, Ernie was really emphatic about how dogs can't stay here. But would it be okay with you both if I brought her just for the day?"

The two men nodded and Alec added, "Sure. I like dogs."

Robin jumped out of the chair. "That's great. Thanks, you guys! I'm going to go call Kat now."

Talking to Kat had been reassuring. Apparently, Emma was being a fabulous house guest and everyone loved her.

And Kat had said that Robin could pick up Emma for a visit to the North Fork any time.

Ernie had pulled another disappearing act and hadn't been seen once during all the cleaning activities. Since he wasn't around to use the desk in the lobby, Robin took the opportunity to call Chuck again about the food and go through her list of attendees and their room assignments one last time. She looked at the clock. Everyone should be arriving soon. She went outside when two white vans filled with people pulled up in front of the lodge. Because Eagle River was a women's clothing retailer, almost all of the people who worked in the call center were female. The big employee discount was a major perk for women, but not so much for men.

Eighteen women and one man filed out of the two vans, talking nonstop as they stood in the parking area looking around. Robin moved toward the back of the vans as the driver started removing luggage. Brett would probably say that the van trip itself was good for bonding. Nothing like hours trapped in a vehicle to help people get to know one another. Maybe he wouldn't need those ice-breaker exercises after all.

People gathered around the vans, snatching suitcases as they were removed from the back. Robin waved her arms and said, "Hi everyone. I'm Robin and although I don't think I've met most of you before, I work for Eagle River. Welcome to the North Fork Lodge."

After a few mumbled greetings, Robin continued. "Darrell asked me to come here early and act as a coordinator for the retreat. If there's anything you need related to food or lodging, please ask me. I can act as a liaison to the owner of the lodge." If only she could ever find him.

Robin invited everyone inside and it became obvious that the employees had divided into two distinct cliques. The High Country and Eagle River call-center folks obviously did not mingle with one another. All the chatting was among their own "people." Darrell had a point. The undercurrent of animosity between the two groups was palpable. Robin didn't envy the task Brett and Alec had ahead of them.

Part of her was bothered by the fact that two men were going to be teaching almost all women. How patriarchal was this? And it was a women's clothing catalog, for heaven's sake. Couldn't Darrell have found a woman to talk about it? What did Alec know about the discomfort of twisted pantyhose, pinchy underwear, or tortuous pencil skirts? Well, she assumed Alec didn't know, anyway. It was probably best not to traverse that line of thought.

Realistically, Darrell's wife Sue was more qualified to do training on Eagle River merchandise and philosophy than Alec was. But she'd been swamped getting the latest catalog mailing out the door. Darrell probably didn't want her to be away from home or the business for long either.

The word around the company was that Sue was the real creative force at Eagle River. The catalog would never have gotten off the ground early on without her lyrical copywriting and design skills. Even though Robin had met Sue only a few times, she really liked the woman. She was certainly a lot nicer than Alec. It would have been interesting to get to know Sue better. Oh well. This was only one week out of Robin's career, for good or ill. She was *so* ready to get this retreat over with and return to her regular life again.

Robin stood behind the desk handing out keys and directing people to their rooms. Chuck had arrived and was working in the kitchen, and dinner was scheduled for later that evening.

Given the glares and significant pauses in conversation while Robin handed out room assignments, the social interaction among the employees would undoubtedly be tense. She was pretty sure high school cafeteria dynamics would come into play at dinner. Brett would probably have a field day analyzing the pecking order and the never-ending interplay among employees in their quest for dominance, control, and security. One thing was certain: it was going to be a long week.

Chapter 4

Stowaway

After dealing with getting everyone situated in their rooms, Robin went back to her cabin to lie down and decompress. She was too keyed-up to sleep, but lying on her back doing nothing, staring at the ceiling and enjoying the silence was a welcome relief. A howl came from somewhere outside her cabin. Apparently the local coyote population wasn't sleeping well either.

Normally, Robin spent a lot of her day doing calculations on her computer and filling out forms. Sometimes she attended a few meetings. It wasn't like she was some type of recluse or a closet introvert, but she wasn't used to spending this much time managing people, and it was taxing her ability to remain polite and friendly. Everybody had some little story they wanted to share with her. The van was too cold. The van was too hot. Someone was chewing gum the whole trip. Someone else snored. None of them wanted to be here, and all of them wanted to express their dismay.

Robin wanted to tell them to go talk to Darrell. This whole *freaking* retreat was his idea. None of this was her fault. How did anyone manage to be a psychiatrist and not want to kill someone or themselves by the end of the day? What a bunch of whiners.

A huge crash came from the other side of the duplex, and Robin bolted upright. What the *cuss* was that? She leaped off the bed, struggled with the door, and ran to the other side. She pounded on Alec's door. "Are you okay?"

A number of thumps and weird noises came from within and Alec said something unintelligible in an emphatic whisper. What the heck was he doing over there? She pounded again. "Alec! Are you hurt? Do you need me to get someone?"

"No. Go away."

"What happened?"

Footsteps stomped toward the door and Alec opened it a crack and glared at Robin. "Everything is fine. I'll see you at dinner."

"What are you doing over here? Did you break something? It sounded like something big fell on the floor. I could feel it on my side of the cabin."

"No. It's fine." Alec looked down as a large white canine nose pushed through the gap in the door.

Robin followed his gaze and laughed. "Oh, for the love of Benji, you're hiding a *dog* in here. *That's* what all this noise is?"

He opened the door, grabbed Robin's arm, and pulled her inside. "Yes. So now you know. Don't tell anyone. According to what Darrell said, Ernie is strict about the whole no-pets policy. He hates dogs because they chase deer. I guess it's a big deal with him and he'll shoot at dogs that go after deer. I don't know if Darrell was serious or just messing with me, but I don't want to risk it."

"Don't worry. Ernie will never know. Haven't you noticed? He's never around." Robin looked at the room, which was a mirror-image of her cabin. But while her side of the duplex was tidy, Alec's was a cluttered mess, filled with papers and clothes covering almost every available surface. No wonder

Alec had so vehemently declined any help from the church-lady cleaning crew and locked his door. The big dog stood in the middle of the debris, wagging his feathery tail. Although the dog was probably white, he was so dirty that it was hard to tell. The fuzzy beast walked over to Robin and encouraged her to pet him by pushing his head under her hand. She obliged and looked at Alec. "That is one filthy dog."

"I know. He doesn't smell good either. Underneath all that stink, dirt, and hair, there's not much dog. He's the skinniest thing I've ever seen."

Robin bent and rubbed her hands along the dog's sides, which he seemed to enjoy immensely. "Wow, no kidding. He's just ribs, skin, and fur." She stroked the dog's head and looked into the soulful brown eyes. "What happened to you, fella?"

Alec paced around the room, picking up items and throwing them onto the bed. "I guess he's a stray. I think he's been living off garbage for a while, since he seems to want to eat anything and everything."

"Why are you keeping him here?"

"He didn't want to leave. I kept trying to tell him to go home and that I have a lot of work to do, but he wasn't buying it. This dog is like my shadow now, following me everywhere. So I gave up and let him sleep in here." He smiled down at the dog. "That might have been a mistake. Now he's had a taste of the good life. Along with some of my notes for tomorrow. He's not exactly a picky eater."

Robin stroked the dog's head. "So I guess all those crashing noises weren't the ghost of Julia Lambert?"

"I doubt it. He's not the most graceful animal."

"No kidding. I was starting to think you were on drugs or something."

Alec paused in his pacing and looked at her. "What? No. Why would you think that?"

"You have to be the most jittery person I've ever met." Robin put her hand on her hip. "Don't you *ever* sit still?"

"I have a lot of stuff to do."

"Well as your neighbor, I know that you don't sleep much." Robin shook her head and scritched the fur behind the dog's ear. He was leaning on her and seemed to have no plans to move anytime soon. After a long day of dealing with humanity, the canine contact was comforting. She couldn't wait to see Emma tomorrow. "At least you didn't have to supervise the cleaning of an entire lodge."

"Starting tomorrow, I have to train nineteen people on everything having to do with Eagle River. I haven't dealt with half this stuff in years. And I...well...never mind."

"What?"

"Nothing. Don't you have something you should be doing now?"

"Well, dinner is in a little while, but I was resting until your illicit canine guest started making so much noise in here." Robin smiled at the dog. "Although I'm starting to see what you mean. He's really sweet. What kind of dog do you think he is?"

Alec dropped some notebooks onto the desk with a thump. "I'm guessing Great Pyrenees. Maybe mixed with some type of retriever?"

"You should find his owner. Someone is bound to be looking for him."

Alec scowled. "I doubt it, unless they starved him on purpose. In which case, I'd like to talk to them. No one should treat an animal like this."

"Maybe he just got lost." She reached around the dog's neck. No collar. "Someone might be really upset that their dog is missing and we just don't know it. Tomorrow, I'll make some calls. Is there an animal shelter here?"

"I have no idea."

"I'll look in the phone book. I'm picking up Emma at the boarding kennel in the morning. They might know who to call."

"Fine. Just don't let Ernie hear you mention the dog."

"Your secret is safe with me. Did you give him a name?"

"He's not my dog."

"You have to call him something."

Alec stopped wandering around the room and gazed at the dog. "Well, he does behave a little like my uncle."

"What do you mean?"

"He's kind of a goofball."

Robin giggled. "Your uncle is a goofball?"

"Uncle Leroy has always been a little weird."

Robin wanted to say, "You take after him, don't you?" but she refrained, since Alec hadn't seemed to appreciate it when she called him jittery. Didn't he know what he was like? Maybe he wasn't particularly introspective. Instead, she said evenly, "Weird in what way?"

"He always used to drop by and drink all my dad's beer. My mother couldn't really say anything, since Leroy is her brother."

"Having your uncle drop by doesn't seem particularly weird."

"Well, he always came in through my bedroom window. I think he thought he was being sneaky or something. It freaked me out at first, but after a while I kind of got used to it."

"Apparently, you have a long-standing problem with unannounced visitors." Robin ruffled the dog's ears, causing his tail to wag happily. "I think he looks like he could be a Leroy."

Alec shoved some catalogs aside and sat down on the end of the bed. Leroy walked over to him. "Yeah, he's really a nice dog. I've got to make an appearance at dinner." He looked up at Robin. "What do you think I should do with him? Last night I just let him follow me to the lodge. He stayed outside, but he made a lot of noise. I'm afraid Ernie is going to find out I've been harboring a fugitive."

"I noticed the noise." Robin sat down next to him. "I could sneak him some food from the kitchen."

"Oh, he's well aware of the kitchen. I've done that already. He likes pizza."

"See? Great minds." Robin smiled and got up to leave. "I'll see you later. You too Leroy." The dog wagged his tail, obviously pleased to have found a new friend.

～

Robin went back to her cabin and changed her clothes, since she was now covered with a lot of extremely dirty white dog hair. She made a point of wearing something from the Eagle River catalog. She'd gotten her outfit from a sample sale, which was another perk of working for the company. Manufacturers sent samples of items for consideration to be included in the catalog. Those items, along with returns, merchandise used in photo shoots, or items that were defective in some way, were sold to employees for absurdly low prices.

Robin smoothed the luscious fabric of her richly embroidered jacket. It retailed for $120 in the catalog, but she'd paid $3 for it at the sample sale. Success at a sample sale required power-shopping skills. All the employees had to get in line, and when the door was opened it was a free-for-all. Robin had learned that the key to scoring the best stuff was to grab first and ask questions later.

Robin walked down the pathway from her cabin to the lodge. She needed to talk to Chuck and see how things were going with dinner. At least that aspect of the retreat had gone well. Chuck was amazingly unflappable and told great stories. After catering events for so long, he seemed to know everyone in Alpine Grove.

As she walked through the large wooden door into the lodge, she mentally congratulated herself that the space seemed markedly less filthy. It still had the odd tarp-trash-can arrangement, but the lobby was substantially cleaner.

A tall blonde woman was sitting on the willow sofa in front of the fireplace. She was wearing a long flowing black jacket, which Robin knew was from the Eagle River big-and-tall collection. Of course, the catalog never used the word "plus size" or "full-figured," but some of the clothes were definitely optimized for certain body shapes. An Eagle River selling point was that whether you were four foot ten or six foot four, you could still find clothes that fit.

The woman had a concerned expression on her face. Robin walked over and stood in front of the coffee table. "You're Moira, right?"

"Yes." She stood up, towering over Robin. "There's no phone in my room and I came downstairs to see if I could get a signal on my cellular phone, but it's not working here, either."

"You have a cell phone?" Call-center employees made even less than she did and Robin certainly couldn't afford the exorbitant per-minute charges for both incoming and outgoing calls. Undoubtedly in a place like Alpine Grove, wherever you could actually get a signal, you'd be stuck with roaming charges too. Each call would cost a fortune. Maybe Moira had a rich husband. Must be nice.

"I *love* my phone!" Moira held the pink clamshell or "flip phone" in front of her. "Isn't it cute? I'm worried about my kids."

"Is something wrong? Are they okay? There is a phone here in the lobby if you have a family emergency."

Moira stuffed the tiny phone in her bag. "Oh, that would be wonderful. Mickey had a soccer game today and I need to find out how it went." She scuttled over to the desk and settled in for her call.

Robin shook her head and continued to the kitchen. Ernie hadn't said they *couldn't* use the phone. If he was going to pull this disappearing act all the time, it was his own blasted fault. Maybe after he got his phone bill, he'd realize it might be a good idea to pay a bit more attention to his facility.

She pushed the swinging door into the kitchen, where Chuck was standing over a huge stainless-steel vat on the stove. The aromas wafting through the kitchen were spicy and rich. Robin grinned at him and her stomach growled loudly. "That smells amazing. According to my list, it's minestrone, right?"

Chuck pointed a long wooden spoon at her. "You betcha. This is just the beginning. Today, we've got soup for the first course, along with salad and the main event. It's gonna be good."

Robin jumped at a crashing noise from outside. Although she knew it was undoubtedly Leroy hoping for a handout, she said, "Your ghost makes a lot of noise."

"Don't underestimate Julia. If she doesn't like you, you'll find out pretty quickly. I think everyone in Alpine Grove has met her at one time or another."

"You said that was a Halloween gimmick."

He waved the spoon toward the lake. "Well, yeah, the Lamberts played it up. But I told you about the things other people have seen. I know I've been here a bunch of times and there's been everything from hearing footsteps to hearing screams and whispers. Then there's the strange smells, like smoke from a fire. They say that's from the fire that killed Julia. And lights turning off and on. I mean, none of it is particularly sinister or scary. It's just strange. A faucet will be running, even though I know I didn't turn it on. Or a light is on that I know I turned off. So you gotta wonder."

Another loud noise came from outside and Robin wrapped her arms around herself. "You're doing it again, Chuck. Telling me ghost stories just to scare me. None of the ladies who came out to clean said anything. Are you making this up?"

"Nope." He mimed an X across his chest. "Cross my heart. Ask anyone."

"Well, if Ernie ever shows up again, I'll ask him. Have you talked to him about payment?"

"Yeah, I got paid before I started the job. It's best to get money up front in case he goes fishing."

"You're a wise man."

Chuck grinned. "I've been doing this a while. Even if I hadn't, it's a small town and word gets around."

After coordinating a few more details with Chuck, Robin went out to the dining room and noted that Chuck or one of his helpers had set all the tables. He referred to the kitchen staff that dealt with serving and clean-up as his "roadies." Whoever they were, Robin was glad he had a merry band of helpers and that dealing with all those dishes wasn't her responsibility.

She looked up as Brett moved through the lobby toward her to the dining room. He glanced at the garbage-can-tarp arrangement and went to the side of the room to take a look. With a shrug of his shoulders he turned, continued to the dining room, and sat down next to Robin. "Good evening. It appears the predicted rain has arrived."

Robin nodded. "The sound of the drips hitting the tarp and sliding into the garbage can is kind of soothing in a way. Like a slow waterfall."

"You have a wonderful way of looking at the bright side of things."

"I didn't have enough time to do anything about the roof. I just hope it doesn't cave in over the next week."

He put his hand on hers. "I'm sure everything will be fine. As long as you brought your raincoat."

Robin smiled. "I live in Portland, Oregon. I never go anywhere without it."

Alec came in from the kitchen and sat down at the table with Robin and Brett. He shook his head and droplets flew from his dark hair. "It's really coming down out there."

Robin smiled at Alec's wet-dog imitation. Where had he stashed Leroy this time? She hoped the dog wasn't sitting out there in the rain, but she couldn't say anything in front of Brett. She looked at her watch. Dinner was in fifteen minutes and the retreat attendees were starting to mill around and drift toward the dining room from the lobby, looking disoriented. Robin stood up and waved. "Welcome, everyone. Dinner will be over here."

A woman with jet-black chin-length straight hair strode purposefully across the room toward the table. Robin always envied women who could pull off the sleek glamorous look. No matter what Robin wore, with her dirty blonde hair and the splash of freckles that went across her cheeks, there was no way she could look anything beyond cute in a girl-next-door kind of way.

This woman oozed classy sophistication. She was dressed in a designer outfit that was clearly not from the Eagle River catalog. The gray suit was tailored to hug her slim form, and the painful-looking peep-toes with four-inch heels matched the suit perfectly. Her ruby-red lipstick emphasized the grim expression on her face. Stalking up next to Alec, she pointed across the table at Robin. "What is with all the noise here? We're in the middle of nowhere and there are all these creaking and crashing noises. Is there something in the attic?"

Robin raised her palms upward. "I'm not sure if there is an attic. What did you hear?"

"It's like being at Disneyland. Did you ever go to the dopey haunted house with all the wailing and creaking noises designed to scare six-year olds?"

"I'm sorry, but I've never been there."

"Well, it's incredibly infantile. Unless you believe in ghosts. Which I don't."

Alec said, "This building is old. Sometimes old wooden places like this make noise, particularly during storms." A piercing crack of thunder accompanied by a flash of lightning emphasized his point. The woman jumped backward and flailed at Alec, who reached out and grabbed her arm to keep her from falling. The lights flickered momentarily and Alec let go. He looked up as he released her. "Are you okay?"

"Yes, thank you. These shoes are a bit tippy. My name is Terri, by the way. You're Alec Montgomery, right?"

Picking up a fork off the table, he nodded. "Yes. It's nice to meet you." He pointed the fork at Brett. "This is Brett and I guess you already know Robin."

Terri flashed a radiant smile at Alec. "I know I'm new—since the merger—but I've noticed you around. You're hard to miss."

Robin wanted to roll her eyes, but managed to control herself. She stole a glance at Brett, who looked amused by the obvious over-the-top flirtatious moves. If he wanted to study interpersonal dynamics, here was his big opportunity.

Alec twirled the fork in his fingers. "I'll be doing the training. We have a lot of material to cover."

Terri tossed her head, her hair swishing against her cheek. "I'm looking forward to it. You have so much experience, I'm sure you'll be a wonderful instructor." Turning to look at

Robin, she said in a flat voice, "See if you can do something about the noise or I'll never get any sleep tonight."

Robin said, "I'll look into it." She gestured toward the chairs across the table. "Would you like to sit with us?"

Terri smiled at Alec and said, "I'd love to," as she settled down next to him, pulling the chair closer.

Brett said, "So you worked for the High Country catalog? How do you feel about the merger?"

Terri gave him a look of incredulity. "How do I *feel*? How do you think I feel? I've been treated like a second-class citizen. If I could find another job, I would!"

Brett looked somewhat taken aback by the vehemence, which was nothing new to Robin. He'd really put his foot into it, and now he'd get to enjoy the smell.

Alec said, "I'm hoping that once you learn more about the Eagle River process, things will get easier."

Terri put her hand on Alec's hands, stilling them and pressing the fork down to the table. "Perhaps that's true. But it won't fix the environment. I'm tired of people poking their heads into my cubicle like whac-a-moles when I'm trying to concentrate on a sale."

Brett said, "What can you do to change that reality?"

Terri turned to glare at him again. "Me? Why should it be me? I'm just doing my job. It's not like I can put up more partitions. People are so rude. I have no privacy!" Another woman wearing a pretty turquoise blouse walked into the dining room and Terri gestured toward her. "Then there's my cubicle mate. The lovely Loretta whose endless conversations with her gynecologist I get to overhear. Every. Single. Day. She keeps finding new maladies to whine about, and coughs constantly. Maybe she's got the plague. I don't know. What I do know is that I get to smell the horrible food she eats. But her various foodstuffs can't actually touch each other, so she has 350 plastic containers in the refrigerator."

Upon spotting Terri, Loretta turned away toward another table and sat down. Alec pulled his hands out from Terri's grasp and resumed his constant fiddling with dinner utensils. He was leaning as far away as possible from Terri, to the point that his ear was right next to Robin's face. She tilted her head slightly and whispered in his ear. "Do you need me to move over?" With a stony look, he sat up straighter, placed the fork back on the table, and put his hands in his lap.

Brett said, "If you could wave a magic wand, what would you want your work experience to be?"

Terri looked momentarily confused and finally said, "Well, I want better walls. *Solid* walls that are taller! And I don't want to share a cubicle. I don't think that's too much to ask, is it? And there should be rules about the microwave. No tuna. And no burning popcorn! Doesn't anyone ever read the instructions? How hard is it to pay attention to your popcorn so it doesn't stink up the whole building?"

Robin was relieved to see the roadies coming out with plates of food. At least there was no tuna on the menu, and the salads they were carrying looked tasty. Maybe eating would slow down Terri's litany of complaints. Or maybe not. It seemed like she was just getting started and really warming to the subject. Brett looked less enthusiastic, but he nodded at the right places, which encouraged Terri to persevere.

Alec quietly excused himself and headed for the kitchen. He was probably off to sneak some food to Leroy. Terri leaned across the table and gave Brett more information about the personal insults related to sharing a cubicle with Loretta.

Robin slowly chewed her lettuce, watching as Brett listened to the growing list of transgressions. Mostly he remained silent with a sympathetic look on his face. A few times, he asked Terri what changes she could make to improve matters, which she ignored. The questions only seemed to remind her of more things she didn't like. Apparently, she wasn't much of a solution-seeker. The continuing diatribe seemed to drive off the others, who congregated at the remaining tables in cliques that clearly delineated their association with Eagle River or the High Country catalog.

Alec returned to the dining room and crossed behind Terri to another table, where he sat down and began chatting with some other employees. Robin knew they were from Eagle River, not High Country. For all she knew, he might have known those women for years.

Darrell wasn't wrong about the resentments and jealousies running rampant through the company. As she finished her dinner, Robin tried not to dwell on what the next day might bring. At least picking up Emma and spending time with her would be great. Her dog wasn't hung up on injustices and allegiances. For the most part, Emma just loved everybody.

~

The next morning, Robin took another frigid shower and went to the lodge. Breakfast was a serve-yourself affair, and Chuck or one of his roadies had obviously stopped by early to set everything up. Robin practically pounced on a mug, eager for some coffee. A few early risers were scattered around the room, sitting at tables looking sleepy. Maybe they had hot water in their rooms. The cold showers in the Pine Cone cabin certainly helped wake a person up quickly in an unpleasant and jarring way.

Robin was eager to pick up Emma, so she grabbed a bagel and returned to her cabin. After listening to Terri the previous evening, she didn't want to hear more complaining about life at work. Terri hadn't been exaggerating about the conditions. They'd tried to cram far too many people into a small space and the situation was awful. The call center was a maze of cubicles with mismatched partitions and old office furniture. Robin didn't exactly love her cubicle either, but at least she didn't have to share it with someone else. No wonder Terri was angry. And Loretta probably wasn't loving the environment either.

Unlike Terri, who seemed to have no problem voicing her unhappiness, Robin was more cautious about sharing her concerns. She needed the job at Eagle River badly, and it was more than a little surprising that she been hired at all. After college, she'd worked at JK Manufacturing in Spokane, which was a family-owned contract garment manufacturer. By the time she left, the company was struggling because of competition from cheap foreign labor. As they lost more and more contracts to companies in China, Robin had started looking for a new job.

It had taken months before she'd finally landed the position at Eagle River. And she'd had to do some fast talking to convince them that buying fabric for a company that made ugly uniforms was similar to working in catalog retail. Robin still worried that her manager, Diane, wasn't completely convinced she was truly qualified. At work, Robin tried to be friendly with everyone, but also say as little as possible about her actual job. Coming up with a deposit and first- and last-month's rent for her apartment in Portland had cleaned out her savings. If she got fired, she'd have to crawl back home to Spokane and live with her parents. At her age, that would be utterly humiliating. And what about Emma? Momma was allergic to pet hair, so what would happen to Emma?

Shrugging her shoulders in an effort to shake off her spiraling thoughts, Robin opened the door to her cabin. It was useless to worry about things she couldn't control. If Darrell fired her because of this retreat, it wouldn't be like she hadn't tried her best. She had friends in Spokane who might take her in. Maybe Becky would let her crash on her sofa, even though her cat wasn't exactly thrilled with Emma.

The rain pounded on the metal roof of the cabin while Robin gathered her things for the trip out to Kat's. It was absolutely pouring and driving out to the sticks to get Emma was going to be a soggy adventure. The whole idea was probably stupid. Given the weather, it wasn't like she and Emma were going to enjoy a peaceful lakeside stroll. The lake looked gray and the wind was whipping up whitecaps on the water. But Robin missed her little dog. It would be nice to have a sympathetic friend, even one of the canine variety.

As Robin drove north out of Alpine Grove, water seemed to be everywhere. The ditches along the sides of the roads had turned into small creeks, which were starting to overflow their banks in some places. Because of the unusually wet spring, the ground was saturated and the water had nowhere to go. At the turn-off to Kat's place, the creek alongside the road was experiencing some type of fundamental drainage problem. Water was going over, not under, the end of the driveway. Robin stopped the car to evaluate how deep the water was and if her car had enough ground clearance to get through it without stalling out in the middle of the small stream.

It didn't seem *that* deep, so she inched the car through the rushing water. With a small cheer of victory, she successfully reached the other side and continued toward the house. That was a relief. Did Kat know that the driveway was under water?

She parked the car under the tree next to the filthy green truck again. The front yard had turned into a sea of muck and Robin was glad she had worn boots for the trip out here this time. She pulled the hood of her raincoat over her head and got out of the car. Running through the torrential downpour, she scampered up the steps to the landing in front of the door, shook the water off her sleeves, and knocked. The noise was answered with a cacophony of barking, and Robin smiled at the sound of Emma's high-pitched yips. Apparently, what Kat said was true—Emma was part of the pack now.

The sound of thumping footsteps came from inside, then Kat opened the door. Robin blushed slightly at Kat's rumpled appearance. She did not appear to have brushed her hair yet. Maybe it was a little early. Robin smiled weakly and said hello.

Kat said, "Come in for a minute and let me go get Emma. I'll be right back." She ran down the stairs and opened the gate at the bottom. With a great clattering of claws, Emma charged up the steps. Robin squealed at the sight of her dog, crouching down as Emma ran into her arms. She hugged the dog and ruffled her fur. "I've missed you!" Emma waggled and wiggled joyously, adding a few happy, chirpy woofs for emphasis.

Kat walked back into the entry area. "She sure is glad to see you. It's too bad the weather is so dismal for your day together."

Robin stood back up and gazed down at Emma. "We live in Portland. A little rain doesn't bother us, right Em?" The dog wagged in agreement and Robin looked back at Kat. "Did you know there's a bit of a river at the end of your driveway?"

Kat handed Robin her leash. "It's been getting worse, but thanks for letting me know. When are you bringing Emma back?"

"Probably after five. I hope that's okay. There's a break between the training and dinner, so I can run back out here."

"Okay. We'll check on the river along the road today. Hopefully my house won't be waterfront property by the time you return."

Robin clipped the leash on Emma. "We'll see you later!"

Chapter 5

Possessed

Kat closed the door and went into the kitchen. Where was the coffee? How pathetic was this? Actually misplacing the coffee indicated a critical need. She walked to the bedroom, where Joel was lying on the bed with his legs crossed at the ankles and sipping from a mug. He grinned at her, "Looking for something?"

"Did you steal my coffee?"

He reached over to the nightstand and handed her a mug. "No. I brought it in here, since I didn't think Robin needed to meet the pre-caffeinated, unwashed me."

Kat looked down at her wrinkled clothes. "I know. When she said she was stopping by, I didn't realize it would be quite this early. At least I was dressed." Barely.

"You might want to establish some pick-up and drop-off times."

"I know. Having people show up at our front door at all hours of the day and night is getting ridiculous."

Taking a sip of coffee, he peered over the rim of the mug and raised an eyebrow. "Well, at least the tousled look is kind of sexy."

"Tousled?" Kat glanced at her reflection in the mirrored closet door, uttered a tiny squeak, and put down her mug so she could yank her fingers through her long dark hair in an attempt to work out the tangles. "My hair looks like something is living in it. Or died in it." She put her face in her palms. "How embarrassing."

"Well, it's too late now. Maybe Robin didn't notice. Have some coffee. You'll feel better."

Kat crawled onto the bed next to him, picked up her mug, and took a sip. "I'm pretty sure she noticed my coiffure. Or lack of one. Robin is one of those women who always looks perfectly put together. She wears all these gorgeous clothes from Eagle River. When she dropped off Emma, she gave me a catalog. I don't think she was impressed with my dog-walking coat."

"It's utilitarian."

"I suppose, but it also makes me look like a bag lady. And after a long winter and record-breaking rains, it's become disgusting. Even I think it's horrible now."

"The dogs don't care. And I don't care because I know what's under the coat."

She poked him in the ribs. "Very funny."

He slowly ran a fingertip down the side of her neck and sparkly tingles skittered down her spine. Inclining his head to nuzzle her neck, he murmured, "I think we were analyzing the perfect proportions of the female form earlier."

"I think *you* were analyzing."

"The inquiry into cup size was particularly fascinating."

She put her mug back on the nightstand and turned to kiss him. "Yes, it was. You have been known to dwell on that topic."

"Just trying to be thorough."

Kat grinned. "Sometimes your focused analytical nature can be a good thing."

"It's important to capitalize on your strengths."

Later, Kat sat at her desk attempting to write an article. It was going nowhere. She stared out the window at the dripping trees. The deluge had subsided and now it was just cloudy and dreary outside. She got up and stepped over a few sleeping canines as she made her way across the hall to Joel's office.

Leaning in the doorway, she waited for him to look away from his computer screen at her. With a snort of disgust, he gestured toward the monitor. "I have no idea what the last programmer was thinking when he worked on this stuff. What a mess."

"Working on other people's code always makes you cranky."

"Only when the code is poorly written."

She smiled. "I think I've heard this song before. I noticed it finally stopped raining. Does that mean the guys with chain saws are showing up today?"

"I think so. Since they're only cutting down a few trees, they're working it in during their down time. All the logging equipment for their big jobs is stuck off somewhere in the boonies because of the load limits on the roads."

"I guess chain saws are light."

"It's expensive to get a gigantic skidder or feller-buncher machine stuck in the mud somewhere."

"I suppose. Given that I don't want to witness my trees falling to the ground, I'm going to head to town. My dog-caretaking responsibility is gone for the day, I can't do anything else on my article until they give me more information, and

Maria's new kitten is too adorable to be ignored. I need some tiny fuzzy feline time to take my mind off the forest carnage."

"It's only a few trees, and you know which ones they are."

"I know. Before I go I'll wander around and say goodbye to those unlucky conifers with the blue spray paint on them."

"They'll still be there. Just on the ground."

"Don't remind me."

Joel stood up, put his arms around her, and looked down into her eyes. "This is your last chance to stop this. Say the word and I'll send the loggers away."

"Nope, I'm in. We're doing this thing. But I'm still going to go out and apologize to the trees."

"Okay. I'll keep an eye on everything. Have fun with the kitten."

After a short foray around the forest to bid farewell to her trees, Kat got into the dirty green truck and went through her typical tirade of foul language to encourage it into motion. At the end of the driveway, the springtime seasonal river alongside the road was running high. It was a good thing the old Ford had good ground clearance. Robin's car might end up downstream on her return trip to drop off Emma. That was a disturbing notion.

After she got to Maria's place, Kat needed to remember to call Joel and ask him to look at the culvert again. Water seemed to be flowing everywhere *except* through the old rusty metal tube at the end of the driveway. The rushing stream was taking an increasing amount of the driveway rock away with it. The erosion was becoming extreme, and at this rate she'd soon be driving across the culvert itself, which was just asking for trouble. Having no way to get to the house wasn't exactly going to win new customers to her burgeoning dog-boarding business either.

~

Kat parked the truck at Maria's apartment building and walked down the main street to the old Frederickson's building, which was located a few blocks away. There was no way Kat would even consider parallel parking that evil hunk of truck in town. She valued her sanity too much to even try. Not to mention the fact that she'd probably hit five other cars in the process. Parallel parking was not one of her strengths.

Kat walked into the advertising agency office where Maria worked, and her friend looked up from the paperwork scattered across the large wooden desk. A computer and a big stack of books sat off to one side. Never one to dress down for any occasion, Maria was clad in a form-fitting purple dress that had strategically placed scrunches designed to emphasize her figure. She was already well-endowed, but the violet creases and crumples of the dress made her look like an Italian Dolly Parton. Even though the dress looked agonizingly uncomfortable, Maria assured Kat that the "miracle fabric" was fantastic.

After pressing a couple of keys on her computer keyboard with a final flourish, Maria said, "Hey girlfriend! You ready to head out?"

Kat pointed at the books. "Are you in the middle of something? I'm ditching all forms of work this afternoon, so I'm not in a rush."

"Nope. Michael found more psychology and advertising books. You gotta watch out for a guy who lives with a librarian. Jan keeps finding more of these things. To tell you the truth, I didn't think the Alpine Grove library was that large."

"You're certainly going to be well informed."

"And well rested." Maria tapped the top of the stack. "Some of these are serious sleep aids. Or they were until I got Scarlett. I thought cats were supposed to nap all the time. That kitten is bizarre. In fact, I'm pretty sure she's possessed."

"All kittens are like that."

"You mean they'll just be sitting there, then all of a sudden leap up and run around like they're being chased by an axe murderer?"

"Pretty much."

Maria bent to grab her purse from the desk drawer. "I think you gotta see this, girlfriend. I mean, Murphee wasn't like that when she was a kitten, was she? You never said anything."

"I was probably too tired. Murph was on the kitty night shift and it drove me nuts. I started making sure to play with her after I got home from work, so she'd stop waking me up in the middle of the night."

"Well, I'm still going with my demonic-possession theory. All the squalling noises that tiny animal makes are a little creepy. I need to get a microphone and record those sounds. They could use her scary kitty voice for special audio effects in horror movies. She could make me millions."

Kat opened the door for Maria and they walked out to the street. "I'm glad you're adjusting to the joys of pet ownership."

"Sort of. I still blame you for turning me into a cat lady. This is *so* not sexy. As if I didn't have enough problems finding a date around here."

"But Scarlett is so cute."

"I know. And she needed a home. But just you remember, her real name is *Katie* Scarlett like in *Gone with the Wind*. But it's also so I don't ever forget that my descent into cat-lady-hood is all your fault."

Kat gestured dismissively. "Yeah, yeah. You already love her and you know it."

A tall, lanky man wearing glasses was walking toward them on the sidewalk and Maria called out, "Hey Rob. How's your hard drive spinning?"

He grinned as he stopped in front of them. "Hi Maria. Hi Kat. I'm okay. What's up with you?"

Maria held out her hands and engaged in a complex handshake with Rob. Kat was impressed. She clapped her hands after the performance. "Wow, where did you guys learn to do that?"

Maria said, "It's a secret. Only those of us who work in the Frederickson's building know it."

Rob shook his head. "Actually, it's not much of a secret. Michael taught it to us. I have no idea where he came up with it."

"Hey, don't spoil the illusion," Maria said. "Where's your sense of adventure? We could have said that it's from an ancient Native American fertility ritual and she'd never know."

"Uh, I'm not sure I'm on board with the idea of a fertility ritual," Rob said.

"How's Tracy?" Kat asked. "Is she still mad at you?"

Rob shrugged and pushed his glasses back up to the bridge of his nose. "Probably. She went to another art class in

LA. She's probably spending the whole time telling her friend Shelby what a jerk I am."

"Women need their girlfriend time," Maria said. "Kat, for example, is here to tell me the latest stupid thing the engineer has done."

"I am *not!*" Kat said. "Joel is fine. They're cutting down trees at my place today and I don't want to watch."

Maria put her hand on her hip. "So you're not gonna say one word to me about the engineer? I find that hard to believe. Because, let's face it, men always do stupid things."

"No, I'm not. I am going to play with your kitten and share a few important cat-care tips with you."

Rob smiled. "Well, on that note, I have to go tend to my girlfriend's cranky dachshund now. It was good to see you both."

"I hate to break it to you, but I think Roxy is your dog too now," Kat said.

He waved off the comment and said, "See you later."

As he walked down the street toward the Frederickson's building, Maria said to Kat, "What's up with him? Behind those geeky spectacles, that man has the most gorgeous expressive eyes and they were telling me he's not a happy boy."

"I think he and Tracy are going through some adjustments."

"Adjustments? What's that supposed to mean?"

"They went on a great trip to Napa last fall and she wants to travel more because they've got more money now. He says he's got too many deadlines to go somewhere at the moment. Given that meeting all those deadlines is key to getting the money in the first place, they've reached an impasse. When I saw her at the vet clinic, she was definitely pissed off at him."

They stood at the crosswalk waiting for a car to go by. Maria said, "Life is short, so I see her point. On the other hand, I too have had to make some unfortunate life concessions due to dire financial considerations."

"I'm sure they'll work it out eventually. Getting out of town and seeing the sun in LA while she's at that class will probably help. She'll miss Rob and remember why they're together."

Maria grinned. "Wow, girlfriend, you sound so wise in the ways of the heart. What's happened to you?"

"Partly it's from living with someone normal, I guess, after so many years of serious dating disasters. Also, I've met a lot more people in relationships lately."

"No kidding, girlfriend. People board their weirdo dogs with you and fall in love. Wanna take care of Scarlett the scary kitten? Because, seriously, I *really* need a date."

"Very funny. And for the record, I don't plan to board cats."

"Not yet."

Kat nudged Maria playfully. "Don't even kid about that. You know all too well that I've got enough to do dealing with the weirdo dogs as it is."

~

Maria unlocked the door to her apartment and looked over her shoulder at Kat. "Watch out. She's small, but super fast."

"Don't worry. I'm bracing myself."

The two women scuttled into the apartment as a tiny orange tabby streaked across the room and into the hallway toward them. Scarlett had striking dark- and light-reddish-orange stripes that made a swirling pattern on her sides. She galloped down the hallway and crash-landed into one of Maria's pumps that had been sitting next to its mate near the door. The little cat jumped up, twisted sideways, and pirouetted into a frontal attack against the offending footwear. Maria bent to pick up the shoe and examined it. "C'mon, Scarlett! Those were *expensive*."

Undaunted, Scarlett resumed her attack on the other shoe, gripping the heel in her small paws and raking the toe leather with her back feet. Maria tried to extract the shoe and Scarlett reluctantly let go, jerking away with a squawk of irritation.

Swiveling away from Maria, the kitten made a loud screechy noise and shot out of the hallway toward the bedroom, her paws skittering across the tile, then thudding into something in the other room. Maria and Kat ran after her, turning their heads in an effort to spot the racing feline. Scarlett was near the window making *rrr-ing* noises as she batted at the draperies.

As she rushed toward the window, Maria yelped, "*No!* Not the curtains again."

The kitten's little tail was fluffed out and her back was arched against the enemy. With a mighty whap at the offending cloth, she somersaulted behind the curtains and started to scrabble upward. Maria whipped the fabric away from the wall and Scarlett rolled back down to the floor. She bolted back out of the bedroom toward the living room.

Maria held the curtain out in front of her and shook it at Kat. "We go through this every, single day."

Kat grinned. "I think you need more kitty toys."

A jingling ball rolled into the room, followed by Scarlett scampering around it, so she could bat it against the furniture like a pool ball. As the rolling toy came to a stop, she crouched down with a growl and began stalking it cautiously. Scarlett's tail whipped back and forth behind her as she sidled up alongside her spherical opponent. Apparently, the tip of the striped appendage entered her peripheral vision because the cat stopped suddenly and leaped at her tail, swirling around in a circle in an effort to catch the offending entity.

The cat missed her tail, fell down, and glared up at Maria. With a quick lick at a paw and a plaintive meow, Scarlett bolted back out of the room.

Kat giggled. "Kittenhood is so adorable. It's too bad they don't stay this way."

"Yeah, sure. Easy for you to say." Maria examined the curtains. "I think I'm gonna have to give up on window treatments for a while. You want something to eat?"

Kat followed Maria back into the living room, where Scarlett had settled into the sofa with one paw stretched out in front of her. Kat sat next to the kitten, who crawled into her lap. With her fingertip Kat traced the tabby M pattern above the kitten's striking golden eyes. "She's so pretty."

Maria busied herself in the kitchen, opening a can of soup. "Want a Twinkie? They make a fine appetizer."

"No thanks."

"You have no sense of culinary adventure."

Kat leaned back on the sofa and let Scarlett crawl up on her stomach for a power nap. The kitten curled up into a little fuzzy orange ball, and Kat slowly stroked the soft fur. "I got the invitation to Beth and Drew's wedding yesterday."

"That's the woman who dated the engineer, right? With the stinky dog?"

"Actually it was her mom's dog, but yes, Beth went out with Joel a long time ago."

Maria pressed buttons on the microwave and turned to face Kat. "So marriage, huh? That sounds so permanent."

"Drew is really nice. And he has the cutest puppy."

Maria gestured at the somnolent kitten. "You're just a sucker for tiny furry things."

"Maybe so. But when I saw them, he and Beth seemed so happy."

"You wanna eat over there on the coffee table?"

"Yes. I don't want to disturb Scarlett."

"It's always a fine idea to let the Tiny Tabby Terror sleep when sleep finally happens." Maria put the bowls of soup on the coffee table and sat down next to Kat. "So after all this time, you and the engineer must have talked about marriage. Is he for or against the institution?"

Kat sat up, readjusting Scarlett on her lap so she could reach her soup. "I'm not sure. The subject has never come up, I guess."

"He seems to be a permanent resident of your house. Don't you guys ever talk to each other?"

"Of course we do. In fact, today he was so sweet when I melted down about the loggers coming out to cut the trees."

"So if he asked you, what would you say?"

"You mean if he asked me to *marry* him?" Kat looked down at her hand on the kitten. "Give me a break. I don't think he's going to do that."

"Why not?" Maria looked at Kat and shook her head. "Okay, fine. Never mind. I don't want to pry, but as you know, I am a romantic. Given my lack of any action with members of the opposite sex lately, I have ample time to ponder your romantic life. I mean, you actually *have* one, which is more than I can say. But what if he does pop the question and you're not prepared? You need to be ready. I don't suppose you told him about your little adventure in Vegas, did you?"

"No. That was a long time ago. And I don't think it was legal, anyway."

"I know you've been putting it off since, well, I don't even know how long, but maybe it's time you checked. If you crazy kids filed a marriage license on that excursion, I'm guessing the State of Nevada thinks you're married, even if you don't."

"You know I don't remember what happened. Ned was such a loser, I can't believe he would have been organized enough to think about stopping by a courthouse. There's absolutely no way."

"You'll get no argument from me that he was a loser of the most extreme nature. My opinions on that particular subject have been detailed at length over many bottles of wine. But what if you did actually do the deed? If you end up getting married to the engineer, you'd be a bigamist and that's *sooo* illegal. Not to mention icky. You've got to get over yourself and check on this, girlfriend. We're talking one or two phone calls at the most and you'd know for sure."

Kat slumped down on the sofa. "I guess. It wasn't an issue for years, since as you know, I wasn't exactly Miss Popularity with the male of the species. And lately, I've had a lot of other things on my mind. All that mess with Ned was such a long time ago. I *know* I'm not married. I don't think anything happened. If it did, I would remember. Wouldn't I?"

"Maybe...maybe not. You're just too chicken to call the State of Nevada and find out."

"I am not!"

Maria put her hands under her armpits and flapped. "Chicken!"

"Okay, fine. What if I do call and I find out I really am married? What am I supposed to do then? I have no clue where Ned even is. And I never, *ever* want to see that creep again."

Maria took a sip of her soup and waved her spoon at Kat. "I just thought of another thing. When you inherited the house, did anyone ask if you were married?"

"No. And I'm *not*."

"But technically, if you *are* married, Ned might have a claim on your house. I don't suppose you ever mentioned Ned to Larry, did you?"

"Larry, the lawyer? No. I have made it a personal mission to try to think about Ned as little as possible."

Maria splashed her spoon down into the soup. "This is bad. Really bad. You need to talk to Larry, girlfriend. I know we broke up, but he's a decent guy."

"Yeah, he was great about everything that happened when I inherited the house."

Maria pointed her spoon at Kat. "You have to talk to the engineer too. That's not optional."

Kat closed her eyes and covered her face with her palm. "I know. But I *really* don't want to. I was so incredibly stupid. That's a story I'd rather leave in the past."

Maria put her hand on Kat's forearm. "Sorry girlfriend, I know you've spent a lot of time trying to forget about Ned, but I think it's about time you fessed up."

Chapter 6

Do You Feel Rosy?

Robin drove back down the driveway to the North Fork. The rain had stopped, although heavy gray clouds still glowered over the lake. She looked at Emma's eager face in the rearview mirror. "We're going to have a great walk today, Em. You'll love it!"

As she drove through the lodge complex to her cabin, Robin looked around for any evidence that Ernie had made an appearance. Everything seemed quiet and peaceful, so maybe she could run into her cabin for a minute to change her shoes without the elusive dog-hating proprietor discovering Emma sitting in the car.

Robin sat on the end of the bed and yanked her boots off her feet. Good thing she hadn't bothered dressing up. Kat certainly hadn't. It looked like the woman had just crawled out of bed. Maybe Robin shouldn't have stopped by so early. But at least she and Emma still had a little time to squeeze in a walk before Robin had to attend the retreat. The fact she had to attend the training was so irritating. She and Emma needed to make the most of any recreation time they could get.

Even though the lake was not perhaps at its most picturesque, Emma was able to engage in some frolicsome, fun off-leash time splashing along the water's edge. Robin looked at her watch and called Emma back. She clipped on the leash and they stopped by her cabin so Robin could switch footwear again, then they walked across to the theater building where Brett was scheduled to do a few ice-breaker exercises.

After the whine fest at dinner, Robin was somewhat concerned about breaking ice with her co-workers. It was entirely possible that in this case, honesty might not be the best policy. The call-center employees could easily transition from not being able to work together to more actively hating each other. But Brett didn't seem phased by Terri's litany last night, so maybe Robin's concerns were unfounded.

She opened the large wooden door and found that many of the women had gathered around the square of tables. Terri was sitting next to Brett and leaning so close she was almost touching him. Maybe overnight she had thought up some exciting new complaints to share with him.

Robin had grabbed a towel from her cabin and she laid it out on the floor in the corner for Emma. She explained to the dog that this was now her bed and she needed to stay on the towel. Emma wagged her tail, spun in a circle, laid down in her new spot, and began a complex cleaning operation on her paws. Robin stroked her head. "Good girl. I'll be right here."

Pulling out a chair, she sat down next to a woman with close-cropped gray hair who was wearing a lavender jumper and oversized glasses with purple frames. The woman was scowling and looked like she'd commit a murder if anyone even considered taking her coffee mug away from her. Robin turned to her and said, "My name is Robin. You're Claire, right?"

The woman frowned more emphatically and took a sip of coffee. "Yes. I remember you. You're the one I need to talk to about my room."

Robin tried not to roll her eyes. Everyone had problems they wanted to share and she couldn't do anything about most of them. Where on earth was Ernie? She needed to talk to the man. With her most conciliatory polite smile, she replied, "Perhaps we can discuss the situation after this session." She gestured toward the woman's necklace "I love your necklace. Is it from the catalog?"

"Yes."

Given the look on her face, it was clear Claire was done talking. Robin folded her hands in front of her and glanced across the table at Brett, who was still attempting to look interested in whatever Terri was telling him. Robin scratched her ear and wiggled her pinkie finger slightly to catch his attention. She quickly pointed to her wristwatch and raised her eyebrows. A corner of his mouth turned up and he put his hand on Terri's for a moment. She leaned back, away from him, and he stood up.

With a wave toward the table, Brett said in an authoritarian tone, "Let's get started, everyone. First, as you can see, there is a well-behaved dog here in the corner. Is anyone allergic or does anyone have any issue with this dog being here?"

Everyone in the room shook their heads in unison.

"Okay, that's good. Now then, I'd like to say that it has been a pleasure getting to know some of you at the mealtimes last night and this morning, but as of now, my focus needs to move from small talk to more serious topics. Darrell has given me a formidable task, which is to transform the anger and resentments that I have seen into a new reality."

He leaned forward and put his palms flat on the table. "I want all of you to close your eyes and place your hands in front of you with your palms on the table like I have. Then listen to your breath as you inhale and exhale."

There was some grumbling, and someone said, "What is this, a yoga class?" Robin opened one eye to peek. It looked like despite the grousing, everyone was following his instructions. Undoubtedly, it helped that he had such a compelling voice. She closed her eyes again. Brett said, "Now, I am going to walk around the room and when I touch your shoulder, I want you to give us your name and one word that describes you now or who you aspire to be in the future. That word must begin with the same letter as the first letter of your name. So for example, my name is Brett and my word is *bold.* If you want, you can even call me Bold Brett if it helps you remember my name and embrace the transformative experience we are trying to have here."

Robin frantically searched her mind for words beginning with R that wouldn't sound stupid. The other people were probably thinking of a few choice words to describe her right about now, but at least they couldn't call her *rude.* She'd made a supreme effort to be unfailingly nice and polite to everyone. Right now, she was dreading the touch on her shoulder and couldn't think of anything beyond, *Don't pick me first!* Finally, a word popped into her head: *rosy.* People always said she was an optimist. Close enough. It was all she could think of, so it would have to do.

Brett said, "I'll give you a few minutes to ponder your choice. The reason I've had you close your eyes is because I want you to listen and meet the people in this room with no judgments about what they look like, what clothes they are wearing, or what company they worked for in the past."

Robin had to admit that it wasn't a bad idea. Too bad Alec had ditched this session. He could use some perspective.

Brett continued in a soothing voice. "I want you to be creative about this. And please don't be shy. Once you have thought of a word, raise your hand and we'll begin."

Even though she had a word, Robin kept her hand down. She *so* didn't want to go first. *Please don't pick me.* She peeked and noticed that everyone else still had their hands flat on the table too. *Fudge*! If no one was going to say anything, she was going to have to put on her big-girl panties and be first. She slowly raised her hand toward the ceiling, and the sound of Brett's footsteps indicated he was coming toward her. His warm hand settled on her shoulder and he squeezed gently as an unspoken thank you.

Robin cleared her throat. "I'm Robin. And my word is *rosy*."

"Why did you select that word?" Brett asked.

"Well, my mother always said I wear rose-colored glasses."

Brett chuckled and said, "After spending time with you Robin, I think *rosy* is an ideal word to describe you. Thank you for being the first one to participate. Who's next?"

Robin let out a sigh of relief. Even though she wasn't exactly shy per se, she didn't like being singled out in front of people she didn't know. She would give anything to be sitting around chatting and laughing with her girlfriends in Spokane instead of doing this right now.

The woman with the desperate need to use the phone the other day was next. She said her name was Moira and her word was *motherly*. Robin nodded her head. That was a good word. Moira did seem to be extremely involved with her children's lives. When Terri the complainer said her word was *tough,* Robin had to admit that the exercise was surprisingly illuminating.

A few other people recited their words, some of which required more detailed explanations. Claire the cranky woman with the room problem said her word was *capable.* Robin had no idea if that was accurate or not. After a few more people had their turns, Robin was desperate to open her eyes because her curiosity about which voice went with which human was starting to get to her. A woman named Darlene had started with *drab* and Brett had gently suggested that she go with a more positive word. After agonizing about it, she opted for *decent* because her pastor had told her that "bragging is a sin." After a small hissy-fit about how difficult vowels were to deal with, a woman named Angela settled on *ambitious.*

A heavy object settled on her thigh, startling Robin so badly that she almost fell off her chair. She looked down and Emma's dark brown soulful eyes were gazing up at her. Robin stroked the smooth fur on Emma's head, tracing the outline of the white blaze on the dog's nose. She whispered, "Go lie down, Em."

Emma indicated her lack of interest in returning to her towel by thumping her muzzle down on Robin's thigh again more forcefully. Robin looked up at Brent and mimed, "Sorry." He just nodded and gestured toward the door.

∼

Robin got up as quietly as she could and clipped on Emma's leash. As she tiptoed out the door, the soggy spring air hit her face. The breeze was refreshing, even though it was cold and damp. Getting away from the intensity of the ice-breaker exercise and being outside again was a welcome relief. It was almost break time anyway, so she needed to check on the food. She walked with Emma over to the lodge and went around the side to the entrance to the kitchen. As she attached Emma's leash to a little tree near the door, she told her to stay. The dog looked pouty, but sat resolutely in her spot.

Robin peeked in the door where Chuck was busy setting up sandwich platters for the buffet lunch. "Hi Chuck. Everything okay here?"

"Yup, I'm good. Alec just stopped by and grabbed some food. Do you want something?"

"That would be great." She walked over and made up a sandwich. "My dog is here for the day and she's outside, so I have to run. It looks like you've got everything under control. I'll see you tonight."

"Yup. The roadies and I have it handled."

She exited the kitchen and untied Emma, who yanked on the leash. Robin turned to see what the dog was so excited about. Leroy the big white dog came bounding over to say hello. Alec was walking behind him and waved at Robin.

The two dogs circled one another, sniffing and wagging furiously, thrilled to have found another canine wandering the area. Emma stared up at Robin with an imploring wide-eyed look. Robin smiled. "You want to play, don't you?" Leroy wagged to show his support for the idea.

Alec grinned at her as he walked up. "That's a happy pair of dogs."

"Do you think it's okay if they play together?"

"Fine with me. I don't have to teach anything for another hour, so I can keep an eye on them if you want."

Robin unclipped Emma's leash and looked at him more closely as she stood up. Something was different about him.

He was just standing there with his hands in his pockets, but the drawn look on his face was gone and the lines around his eyes seemed less pronounced. He also was actually standing perfectly still. That was new. She gestured toward Emma. "Look at them go! That's going to be one tired dog by the time she returns to the kennel tonight."

"Yeah, it's a lot of fun to watch dogs play."

Robin wasn't sure what to make of him. That had to be the most cheerful thing she had ever heard Alec say, and a far cry from his typical surly attitude. "You seem, uh, more relaxed. I guess that means you're ready to talk about answering the phone?"

"I'm ready to roll."

"I guess something good happened between yesterday and today."

"Well, I finally got a decent night's sleep. And I gave Leroy a bath, so he doesn't stink."

"I thought he was a lighter color today."

"Yeah, check it out. He's a white dog, after all."

Robin stopped walking and jammed her sandwich into her pocket. "Oh *swizzle sticks*! I forgot to look up the number for an animal shelter. I'm sorry. I left so early this morning, I couldn't call around. And then by the time I got out to the kennel, I was thinking about picking up Emma and I didn't ask Kat either."

"It's okay. I kind of like having him around. Doing all that reading was pretty tedious, and he kept me company."

"I guess reading about selling women's clothes isn't the most interesting thing, is it?"

He pulled his keys out of his pocket, twirled them around his index finger idly a few times, and put them back. "Not

really. But I've always had this problem. When I am tired,
I have more trouble reading. It's like my eyes and brain are
jumping around all over the place, so it takes me forever to
get through stuff. Leroy was sympathetic."

Robin laughed as the two dogs chased each other in a
circle around them on the path down toward the lake. "Dogs
often are. Emma has been incredibly supportive since I
moved so far away from all my friends. I don't know what I
would have done without her. My long-distance phone bills
would be even worse than they are."

"When did you move?"

"About three months ago. I hate to admit it, but moving
has been more of an adjustment than I thought it would be. I
wanted to get out of Spokane forever, so I was thrilled to get a
job in Portland." She flopped her arms in a gesture of dismay.
"But be careful what you wish for, right?"

"I thought you liked your job. You're always so happy
and cheerful. Darrell is certainly impressed."

"Well, nobody likes a Gloomy Gus. I'm just trying to
fit in. And this job is better than what I was doing before.
But it's still just a paycheck. I don't know what else I would
do, either. In college, I couldn't even figure out a major.
My friend Sara majored in business so I did too, for lack of
anything better. It was fun being in the same classes together,
so we had a good time."

He smiled. "At least you got a degree."

"You didn't?"

"No. I dropped out before I graduated. Maybe if I'd had
a dog I would have made it through the reading. The only
good thing was that before I bailed, my roommate broke my

typewriter, so I had to learn how to use a computer to do my papers. My handwriting is so bad no one can read it."

Robin turned to look at him. "It can't be that bad. Well, unless you're a doctor."

"I'm definitely not a doctor, but I had to do essay tests on a typewriter or computer because my professors couldn't read what I wrote in blue books."

"Now I'm curious. You need to write something so I can see it."

"No you don't. You won't be able to read it, anyway. Sometimes I even write letters backwards." He chuckled. "My profs said it was like I was writing in code."

"Wait! I've heard of this before. Are you dyslexic?"

"Probably. Or just weird. When I was a kid, no one could figure me out. They tested me every which way and my reading comprehension scores were off the charts. I may read slowly, but I remember what I read. So no one knew what to do with me. I hated school, and most of the time I was bored out of my mind. I definitely don't miss that."

"Well, I can see why you weren't happy about reading that whole gigantic binder of tedious stuff then."

"Exactly. I hate being bored" He looked at his watch. "We should round these guys up because I have to get my stuff and get ready to teach now. It's been nice talking to you."

"You too."

Robin called Emma and the two dogs rushed over. After clipping the leash on her dog, Robin and Alec walked with the canines away from the beach and back up toward the lodge buildings. As they strolled slowly down the pathway,

Robin nibbled on her sandwich and pondered all the things Alec had told her.

You never knew about people. He had good reasons to be grumpy about doing the training. Maybe he wasn't such a bad guy after all. But she wasn't going to argue with him about the weird part. He was definitely an unusual character.

~

Alec paused at the turn toward the Pine Cone cabin. "Leroy has decided he likes the indoor life. Now that he's all tired out, I'm going to leave him here at the cabin."

Robin shook her head. "But you're not supposed to have dogs in there."

"Have you seen the owner anywhere? I'll clean it before I go. If Ernie is out hunting or fishing or whatever he does, I don't want him shooting at Leroy."

"I think you're becoming attached to this dog."

Alec stroked the dog's head. "Maybe. I just don't want him to get shot on my watch. Why don't you leave Emma in your cabin? She'd probably be a lot more comfortable."

"I can't do that! It's not allowed."

Alec shrugged. "Suit yourself."

Leroy cavorted around Alec as they strolled away toward the cabin and Robin smiled. It was obvious that Leroy was devoted to his new best buddy. And it was sweet that Alec was so protective of the dog. Ernie's absence was starting to go from odd to somewhat disturbing. What if something had happened to him while he was fishing? The water in the lake had to be frigid. If he had fallen overboard, he might be hurt. Or a corpse languishing on the lake bottom.

She glanced down at Emma, who was looking a little sad that her new canine playmate was going away. Robin crouched down and scratched the dog's ears. "Are you up for a little call-center training?" Emma wagged enthusiastically and Robin chuckled. "At least we're pretty sure the teacher likes dogs, right?"

After another short stroll along the lakeshore while she ate the rest of her sandwich, Robin walked back up to the building, went inside, and settled Emma back into her corner on her towel. Once the dog seemed composed again, Robin sat down at the table. She smiled at Alec as he walked in. He'd changed out of the old faded jeans he'd been wearing while walking Leroy into more instructor-appropriate dress pants. Brett had disappeared, which wasn't a surprise given that he undoubtedly had limited interest in learning how to take phone orders for women's clothes.

Alec put his huge binder on the table and handed a pile of comb-bound booklets to Terri for everyone to pass around. Terri took her booklet from the stack and plopped it on the table with a thud. She glared at Alec. "So where were you when we all had to come up with words? What's your word?"

At the confused expression on his face, Robin said, "It was an ice-breaker exercise. We all had to say our name and then one word to describe us that starts with the same letter as our first name. For example, my word was *rosy*."

Terri said, "Mine is *tough*."

Everyone looked at Alec and Terri said, "We all had to come up with one, so you do too. Come on, what's your word?"

Alec put his palms on the big binder and leaned forward. "Okay. I guess I'll go with *adaptable*."

"Oh brother." Terri rolled her eyes melodramatically. "That's the best you can do? What does that mean?"

He sat down and patted the binder, "I have adapted to more things than you might imagine, including teaching this class, which I've never done before."

Terri crossed her arms in front of her chest. "That's just great. So you're telling us you don't know anything."

"I didn't say that." Alec leaned forward with his elbows on the table. "Most of you know that I was Eagle River's third employee. So I probably know more about the company than even *I* think I know. I took orders before it was computerized and I helped Sue Lambert come up with the scripts you all use."

Terri scowled. "Well all that ancient history doesn't help us *now*."

"At first, I didn't think it would either, but it does." He stood up and began walking around the table. "I'm going to assume you all know the basics of taking orders. I know you all already have the call scripts memorized. Someone says, 'I'd like to place an order' and you say 'I'd be happy to help you with that' and so on."

At the collective nodding of heads, Alec continued. "You also all should know how to use the software, because you deal with it every day. So we're not going to talk about how the software works—or doesn't work. I am well aware everyone hates it because it's cryptic and completely unintuitive. All the idiotic function keys where you have to press F3 here and F4 there. It's horrible and I get that, because I've used it too. But frankly, there's nothing I can do about the fact that the software stinks. What I can do is help you understand more about the company, who our customers are, and what to do when things go wrong. I'm going to talk about what happens when a call goes off the rails. We've all been there. What we're going to be talking about is the service part of customer service. If you know what to do, it's a lot less stressful when you're talking to an angry senior citizen in Georgia who just got the wrong size jacket and wants to take out the fact that her diet isn't working on someone. Unfortunately, that someone is you."

There was more nodding in agreement, and Robin looked over at Emma. Even the dog seemed intrigued. Robin had never taken an Eagle River order herself, so she had no idea what talking to customers was like. Even Terri was smiling at what Alec was saying. He'd managed to win over a ridiculously tough crowd in seconds. Robin was impressed. Apparently, all that slow reading and preparation with Leroy paid off.

Alec proceeded to tell a story about a woman who had called so many times that he was able to recognize her voice. After the company grew, she continued to ask for Alec by name, even though his job no longer was supposed to involve taking phone orders anymore. He said, "Back in the early years, Gladys was Eagle River's number-one customer. It's possible she was just lonely and wanted someone to talk to, but I think she bought almost every product in the catalog. As you know, there is no time limit on calls. Although call time is one of the metrics we track, and shorter is better financially, because customer service trumps everything else, you can take as long as necessary to take an order. If that means you hear all about Gladys's grandchildren like I did, that's okay."

A woman with shoulder-length bleached blonde hair said, "That's ridiculous. If we listen to people blab all day, it will take forever to finish orders. That's certainly not how we did it at High Country. We were supposed to be businesslike and get through calls as quickly as possible. Get the order so you can move on to the next call."

Robin recognized the woman's voice, partly because she spoke extremely fast. It was ambitious Angela, and given her rapid-fire speech patterns, she probably could win order-taking-speed awards.

Alec didn't seem phased by the outburst and picked up a pencil, turning it in his fingers. "From the beginning, Eagle River has worked hard to be the Nordstrom's of the catalog world. Caller wait times are negligible, even though like I said, our reps can take as long as necessary to take an order. Whether someone is ordering an entire wardrobe or just one piddly scarf, it doesn't matter how long you're on the phone. That's why we have so many employees at the call center."

Angela said, "I guess that makes sense."

He looked down at the pencil in his hand. "I think after the merger, Eagle River didn't do a particularly good job of explaining what the core values of the company are. We showed you what to do—with the software and the scripts and all that—but we didn't tell you *why*. I'll get into that this week too. If we expect you to present our vision for customer service out there into the world, we should probably tell you what it is."

Angela looked more relaxed. "Yes. You should."

Alec sat down again and put his hands in his lap. "For the next few days, you'll have the opportunity to get all your questions answered. If you've ever had a horrible call that made you want to scream or cry, we can talk about it. I don't promise to have all the answers, but together we can come up with solutions, so I encourage you to share your experiences. We'll do a lot of exercises and then go over them. If you don't understand something I'm saying, ask and I'll try to figure out a different way to explain it."

Everyone nodded in agreement. Robin looked over at Emma, who was wagging the tip of her tail on the towel. She seemed pleased too. Who knew Alec would end up being such a good teacher? Maybe even after all the issues with the lodge, this retreat wouldn't be a disaster after all.

~

After the training ended, Robin gave Emma one last walk along the lake before they had to return to the kennel. It was starting to drizzle and the clouds were looking more serious about precipitation again. Robin needed to make sure she got out there and back before dinner.

She called Emma, interrupting the dog's beach-cavorting extravaganza. Emma was being so good, and it wasn't fair that Alec was keeping a dog in his cabin. But Robin knew better. It would be just her type of Murphy's Law to be the one who got caught breaking the rules.

After loading Emma into the car, she headed back north through town and out toward the kennel. The rain was steady with fat droplets hitting the windshield, and Robin flipped the wipers to high. The smell of wet dog pervaded the car. Maybe after she got home, she'd give Emma a bath. All this running around in the rain and mud wasn't improving her aroma.

An old grayish sawhorse sat at the turn to the driveway and a man was standing in the rushing water alongside the road. The old green truck was parked on the other side of the creek. Robin pulled over to the side of the road and parked. She looked over her shoulder at Emma. "I'll be right back, Em."

Opening the door, she popped open her umbrella and tucked herself underneath it. The rain was coming down in sheets. She walked over to the creek and pointed. "Hi. I need to go to the house."

The man was wearing hip waders, a raincoat, and a leather hat. Water poured off its brim as he looked up at her. "Sorry, but the driveway is closed."

As he blinked, droplets flew off his lashes. Robin had never met anyone with eyes that shade of deep green. She gestured toward the driveway. "But my dog has to stay here."

"Are you Robin?"

"Yes. I took my dog Emma out for the day. She's staying here. Who are you?"

He splashed toward the edge of the creek and clambered out into the sodden weeds alongside the road. "I'm Joel. I live here with Kat." He turned and pointed toward the creek. "The culvert got crushed completely when a truck went over it, so there's a crater where the driveway used to be. It's pretty deep. We're going to have to dig out the culvert and replace it, which is going to take a while."

Robin shook her umbrella. "What should I do? Emma isn't supposed to stay with me."

"I'll carry her across and take her back to the house."

"All right. Let me go get her." Robin turned and went back to the car. Maybe this wasn't such a good idea. Hiding Emma with her in the cabin was looking more appealing. But if she got caught, Robin could lose her job. And she was supposed to be available to everyone during meals, where she definitely could not take Emma. There were health regulations about that, weren't there? Ernie would have a fit, assuming he was still around somewhere and not dead at the bottom of the lake. She opened the car door and clipped the leash on Emma. "Sorry Em. I guess you have go with this guy."

Emma wagged her tail and jumped daintily down from the car. At the sight of Joel, she ran to the end of the leash, obviously eager to see the man again. Robin smiled. "I guess she knows you."

Joel said, "Emma is a great dog. We spent some time hanging out together."

Robin crouched down next to Emma and hugged her, even though her fur was getting soggy. "I'll see you in a few days, Em. Be good." She stood and handed the leash to Joel. "I'll call Kat and see how she's doing. If you get this fixed later in the week, maybe I can take her for the day again. We had a wonderful time."

"Okay." Joel walked down into the creek and once he was in, he pulled the dog closer to him and gathered her in his arms. "Let's go Emma." The dog squirmed a little during the ferrying and happily leaped down on the opposite shore. Joel clambered up and waved at Robin. "See you later."

Robin watched as they walked to the truck. He hoisted Emma into the cab, got in, and turned the truck around. Robin waved as they disappeared around a bend into the deeply forested property. Emma was muddy and the truck cab would be soaked by the time they made it all the way back to the log house. She shook the umbrella in annoyance. *Horse hockey!* She'd forgotten to ask about an animal shelter again. What was wrong with her? Well, if she couldn't find anything in the phone book, she'd ask Kat the next time they talked. Leroy's owners might be frantic by now, particularly because of the rain. They probably thought he was shivering out in the cold somewhere. Fortunately, in reality, the dog was enjoying the good life in Alec's messy but warm cabin.

Robin got back into the car and drove up to the next driveway where she could turn around and head back south toward town and the lake. As she drove down the misty country road, the rain began to let up. The weather here certainly was fickle. In Portland, she'd experienced a long winter of perpetual gray, usually accompanied by dreary, methodical rain. Right before she left to come to the retreat, the flowers of spring were starting to appear, which gave her hope that the dismal weather finally might be subsiding. Everyone said that Portland summers were glorious, but far too short.

In Alpine Grove, the weather was more capricious. Within a few hours it could go from pouring rain to glittery sunlight. No matter what the weather was doing though, it always was beautiful to Robin. Something about the lake, trees, mountains, and the long, winding rural roads gave her a sense of peace.

If she was going to have to manage a retreat with a bunch of contentious people at a dilapidated old lodge, at least she was getting to do it in a gorgeous place. Maybe after she'd earned enough vacation time, she could come back here with Emma. If she planned ahead, she might even be able to convince a few of her friends from Spokane to come too. She'd love to be able to really enjoy the area, relax, and have some fun.

∼

Kat sat on the sofa reading a novel. She started and uttered a small yelp as a cacophony of barking erupted from the downstairs hallway. They certainly never had to worry about burglars here. The outside door to the hallway opened and closed and Joel said something to the dogs before opening the gate and coming upstairs.

He stalked through the kitchen toward her with a grumpy look on his face. Presumably he'd been wearing a raincoat, but he looked like he'd been on the losing end of a carnival dunk tank. Kat put down the book. "How is the culvert?"

He stopped at the hallway that led to the bedroom. "It's dead. And I need towels. Lots of towels. Emma has returned and she is sopping wet."

"I guess it's still raining?" Given that he looked like a surly drowned rat, it wasn't much of a guess.

"Yes." He went into the bathroom and yelled back, "It finally started to let up right when we got to the house."

Kat got up off the sofa as he walked back out with a stack of towels. He was scrubbing at his hair with a threadbare old beach towel that sported a faded image of a beer bottle. He handed it to her. "Let's go dry off that small smelly canine."

They went downstairs and Kat bent over Emma and began rubbing the towel over the dog, who writhed with glee at all the fun. Kat handed the sodden towel to Joel, who handed her another. After Emma was somewhat less soggy, Kat paused and stood up. "So what do you mean the culvert is *dead?*"

"It no longer serves its primary purpose of transporting water under the driveway."

"Oh." Kat dropped the towel on the floor to mop up some of the water from dog-shaking activities. "That sounds like a problem."

Joel leaned against the door frame to his office. "When the logger called to let us know his truck might have damaged the culvert on the way out, he didn't go into detail about what that meant. In this case, *damaged* meant *killed*."

"So does that mean the driveway is completely flooded?"

"Flooded and gone. There's a big hole where the driveway used to be." Joel gestured toward the door. "I'm guessing the guy neglected to mention he got his truck stuck in there. Maybe he winched the rig out somehow. I don't know. I put an old sawhorse at the end of the driveway, so people won't try to cross."

"How did Robin get here?"

"She didn't. I carried Emma across the creek and she rode with me in the truck, which now smells like wet dog."

"Well, to be fair, it didn't smell that great before."

"The scent of used motor oil and a few decades of dirt was better than wet dog."

"I suppose I can't argue with that." Kat pushed a towel along the floor with her foot to sop up some of the dog-shaking spray. "It sounds like we can't go anywhere. How are we going to fix this if we can't get out? And who fixes culverts? I doubt there's an entry for culvert repair in the phone book."

"No, but I'll call the hardware store and find out what culverts cost. Maybe I can get Jack to pick it up. We're going to have to get a load of rock to go on top of the culvert, but no one will be able to come out here with it until they take load limits off the roads."

"So *you're* going to fix it?" Kat bent to pick up a dirty wet towel. "That sounds horrible. It's going to be expensive too, isn't it?"

"I'm afraid so. And no, digging out an old rusted culvert is not my idea of a good time."

"I'll help."

"That would be great. In the meantime, think sunny thoughts. All this rain isn't improving matters."

Kat gave him a thank-you hug and picked up the towels so she could throw them in the laundry. Emma had curled up into a small ball and was working on a nap. If they didn't get the road fixed, Kat might be stuck caring for this dog forever. Emma was nice, but the last thing Kat needed was another dog. After starting up the washer, she returned to her office to work on her article. It was time to get busy making some money.

Later, Joel stood in the doorway of her office and tapped lightly on the door. "Your dogs are becoming obnoxious."

She looked up from her monitor. "Why are they always *my* dogs when they're obnoxious?"

He gestured at the dogs milling around his legs. "You may have noticed that they would like their dinner."

Kat stood up and stretched in an effort to get rid of the crick in her neck. "I know. I've been beating my head against the wall trying to figure out this stupid software. Trying to write a how-to article about software I don't understand is an exercise in frustration. The help file is not helpful. In fact, it's actually *un*-helpful." She pointed at the monitor. "I want to commit bodily harm against the incompetent tech writer who wrote that worthless pile of drivel. I mean, who writes 'A view of the page is shown in the page view'?

Gee, how illuminating. Not to mention it takes advantage of some seriously awful passive tense. Really? Are they kidding me? And yet, there is no explanation of what you might actually do using the various screens. Nowhere. Nothing! As a recovering technical writer, I am offended. This is a disgrace to my former profession."

"Maybe you should take a break."

"I've *got* to get this done!"

He sat down on the bed. "You have a few days before the deadline, right?"

"I know. I'm having trouble concentrating because I'm so disgusted with the software. And now it turns out we're marooned here. I feel like Gilligan."

Joel chuckled. "I don't think it's that bad. Maria can come out and pick you up if you get a desperate urge to go to town."

"Eventually we will run out of food, you know. And if we run out of dog or cat food, then we're *really* in trouble."

"If things get tough I'm sure Maria will share one of her cases of Twinkies with you. And we'll get the culvert fixed before the canines figure out that we're cut off from all sources of dog food."

Kat sat down next to him on the bed in her office, leaned her head on his arm, and sighed. "I also have to talk to you about something that I don't want to talk about."

His arm stiffened and he gently pushed her away so he could stand up. "Okay. Maybe you could feed the dogs first." He pointed at the group of canine faces staring intently at them. "They're looking pretty anxious. I'll go figure out what we're having for dinner."

Linus came over and plopped his big muzzle on Kat's thigh to emphasize the fact that dinner was late. She stroked the soft brown fur on the dog's giant head as Joel left the room and went upstairs. "Yeah, Linus, I know. I'm dawdling. Give me a minute, okay? Joel isn't gonna like what I have to say, so you guys need to eat super-slowly tonight." Linus looked unconvinced, but wagged his tail in sympathy anyway.

~

After feeding the dogs, Kat let them upstairs, where they all settled into their favorite napping spots for some important after-dinner slumber. Joel was in the kitchen and Kat peered around him to see what was on the stove. "That looks good."

"It's rice. I haven't figured out the rest. Any ideas?"

Kat walked over to the refrigerator and gazed at the contents. "How much chopping do you want to do?"

"As little as possible."

She walked over the pantry, grabbed some cans, and held them up. "Here you go. Water chestnuts and bamboo shoots. No chopping required."

He turned and leaned back on the counter, crossing his arms across his chest. "I suppose it's a start."

"You look mad."

"I'm not mad. More like concerned. Usually, you want to talk about things *I* don't want to talk about. I'm a little worried that now there's something that *you* don't want to talk about."

She smiled. "Hey, I'm supposed to be the worrier, not you. You're invading my territory."

Joel uncrossed his arms and walked back to the refrigerator. "Not funny. Are you going to tell me whatever it is you don't want to tell me?"

"Do you promise not to get mad?"

"No."

"Maybe we should make dinner. You don't seem to be in a good mood."

"Fine."

Kat chopped some veggies and threw them into the saucepan while Joel stirred in stony silence. He was obviously now even more upset with her, but she couldn't think of a low-key way to say, "Gee, here's something I never mentioned before—I might be married." There wasn't any easy way to begin a conversation like that. Of course, the fact that he was now already irritated was not a good lead-in either. Sometimes she needed to just shut up instead of blurting things out.

After an uncomfortably quiet dinner, Kat went back to the sofa to curl up with her novel. Emma was snoring on the rug in front of the couch, and Joel silently disappeared into the bedroom. Kat tried to focus on her novel, but now that she'd made such a mess of things, even the trashy story in the book wasn't enough distraction. She sighed and led the dogs downstairs. "Time for bed, guys."

After giving the canines a final outing and settling them in for the evening, Kat went into the bedroom. Joel was lying on top of the covers with his arm over his eyes. She crawled onto the bed next to him and he lowered his arm and put it around her. She hugged him and tugged on his flannel shirt. "So okay, what I've got to tell you...I'm pretty sure you're going to get mad."

He sat up straighter on the bed. "You sure know how to open a conversation."

She looked into his eyes. "Remember when you told me about the car accident with your parents and your sister and you said sometimes you didn't come off as the greatest person?"

"Yeah, I remember."

"This is kind of like that. Well, except way worse, because you were young and did the best you could in a horrible situation. In this case, I was just stupid. Really, really stupid. I'm afraid you're not going to think about me in the same way anymore."

He shrugged his shoulders. "Everybody does stupid things sometimes."

"Not like this. It's pretty much the dumbest thing I've ever done."

"So what is it?"

"Well, um," she leaned her head on his chest and cleared her throat. "I ah, well, a long time ago I went to Las Vegas with this guy named Ned. And, um, I might have gotten married."

"What? Is this some kind of joke?" He moved away from her so he could look into her face. "You're *married*? And you're telling me this *now*? After all this time?"

"I know. This is the part where you get mad, and I'm sorry. But it's not like that. I don't think I actually am married. I mean I never did, but Maria thinks I might be. So I'm not sure."

Making an obvious effort to collect himself, Joel said in an overly controlled low voice, "How can you not be *sure*? You were there, right?"

"I was." Kat closed her eyes, not wanting to see his reaction. "But I don't remember. It's kind of a long story."

"I think I'd like to hear this story."

She opened her eyes. "Okay, but this is the not-good part where I don't come off very well."

"I'm listening."

Kat sighed. "A long time ago, I was sort of dating a guy named Ned."

"Sort of? How do you *sort of* date someone?"

"He was a jerk. You may have noticed that Maria sometimes makes comments about my pathetic dating history. He's one of the reasons why."

"Okay. So you *married* the jerk?"

"No. Well maybe. I don't know. Anyway, it was right when I started working at my old job. I was incredibly nervous and I didn't know anyone, so when they all invited me out to happy hour at a bar, I said yes. It was one of the first times I went out with Maria, actually. It was how we first started getting to know each other. An editor I worked with—I think it was Sharon—introduced me to the friend of a friend of a friend. Ned had been watching from some corner of the room. I'm not exactly sure how he was connected. But he bought me a drink and we talked for a while. Like I said, I was really nervous. I kept drinking and he kept talking."

Joel arched an eyebrow. "I think I know where this is going."

"No, it's not what you think. The bar was near my apartment and he walked me home. It was all kind of sweet, so I gave him my phone number."

"Okay. So you *did* go out with the jerk."

"We went out for a while—mostly we went to a lot of bars. He told me all about his job. He said he bought and sold merchandise, and it was all ridiculously complicated. So I tended to drink too much and pretend to be interested." She looked into Joel's eyes. "This is some of the stuff I'm not particularly proud of."

"It doesn't sound bad so far. You know about some of the people I went out with. I'd like to point out that I didn't marry them though." He leaned closer to her face. "And if I had, I would have *told* you by now."

"I know, and I'm glad to hear that. Anyway, like I said, a lot of the time I spent with Ned was in bars. I suppose when you meet a guy in a bar, it shouldn't be a big surprise that hanging out in bars is what he likes to do."

"Did you go out for a long time?"

"Too long. Maria was constantly after me to dump him because it seemed like he was lying about some things."

"Like what?"

"Like the fact that he didn't actually have a job. He stayed over at my place a few times, and in the morning he made it sound like he was going off to work. But he never gave me the number for the place. Finally, Maria called around trying to find it. But it turned out the company didn't exist. No business with that name was in any records anywhere in the vicinity."

Joel smiled faintly. "This is getting more interesting."

"It gets worse. Finally, I sucked up the courage to say something. I mean, it's not like I had huge experience with men and relationships, but I thought asking if he had a job was a pretty reasonable question."

"I guess it didn't go well?"

"No. We met at a bar…again…and when I asked him about the job, he started to make a scene. It was so embarrassing. He was shouting that if I really loved him, I wouldn't be asking that kind of thing."

"So did you dump him?"

"No."

"You're kidding. After all that? Why not?"

"He started to cry. Then he went on this whole long story that he was afraid to tell me about the job." Kat shook her head. "Anyway, now in retrospect, I think it was just more lies, but I bought it. This is another part where I was really stupid."

Joel nodded, but didn't say anything.

"We had this awful, strange, weepy conversation and I drank some more. I drank a lot. There was a lot of drinking and crying. Then Ned called some friend…I think his name was George. I'm sort of fuzzy on the details. He's the one who drove us to Vegas."

"You went to Las Vegas?"

"Yes. I was in the backseat and I fell asleep for a while, but Ned kept making proclamations about love and life and how this was going to change everything. George kept yelling 'road trip!' like John Belushi in *Animal House* and driving scary fast."

"So did this guy mean getting married was going to change everything? Didn't you see a problem with that?"

"They kept saying it was a road trip and reminiscing about a lot of places and people I didn't know anything about. By that point I felt sick, and mostly I was focusing on not hurling all over George's car. We got there late at night and I remember opening the door and throwing up outside in the gutter."

Joel scratched the short beard on his chin. "Wow, this isn't good."

"Ned proclaimed that if I really loved him, I'd do this."

"Do what? Get married?"

"Well, yeah, I know that *now*. At the time, I thought it was some melodramatic way to get my attention. I don't know if technically a man can be a drama queen, but if so, that's what Ned was like. Plus the place didn't look real. Everything was plastic and Elvis was there. It was like a sort of bizarre dream."

"I suppose Vegas is like that."

"So Elvis goes through the thing and I barely make it before running off to the ladies room to throw up again. I was lying on the tile for a while. I think I fell asleep."

"What happened?"

"A cleaning lady kicked my shoe, probably to see if I was dead. That woke me up. It was morning and even though I was alive, I wasn't sure I wanted to be. I threw up again and went back out to the room where Elvis had been. But Elvis, George, and Ned were gone."

"Gone? They just *left* you there? Where did they go?"

"I have no idea."

"That's horrible. What did you do?

"I took a bus back home and called in sick to work for a few days."

"Didn't you try to find Ned?"

"No. The whole thing was humiliating and I didn't want to wander around Vegas smelling like barf. I'm sure the people on the bus weren't too excited about sharing a ride with me."

"And you never tried to find him after you got home?"

"No. I never went to any of the bars we frequented ever again, just in case."

Joel ran his fingers through his hair. "I don't know what to say. Are you married?"

Kat sighed. "That's the thing. I always assumed the answer was no. But now I'm not sure. Maria says that Ned would have had to have gotten a marriage license for it to be legal."

"Like at a courthouse?"

"Yes. Apparently the Clark County clerk's office is open until midnight."

"Do you think he did? Did you sign anything?"

"No. Or I don't think so. I was so sure I didn't, but I was so drunk and so sick, who knows? What if I *did*?"

"Maybe you should find out. I can't believe you never checked."

"I wanted to forget about the whole thing. I figured if I never signed anything, it was just a stupid trip to Vegas." Kat threw up her hands in exasperation and let them drop on her thighs. "For a long time, being married was never an issue anyway, since no one was interested. After that disastrous relationship failure, I kind of swore off men completely for a while."

Joel looked at her and sighed. "It is an issue to me. I'd really rather not be sleeping with another man's wife, thanks."

Kat leaned over on his chest and started to cry quietly. "I'm so sorry. I should have told you about this a long time ago."

Joel wrapped his arms around her and kissed the top of her head. "Probably. But you can't change what's already happened. I'm glad you told me now."

Chapter 7

Lights Out

As she sat down to dinner, Robin was still thinking about her reaction to leaving Emma behind and watching the old truck disappear into the forest. It was like when she had to let the veterinarian take Emma into the back to do a procedure. A little piece of her heart went with the dog and she worried that Emma wouldn't ever come back. She couldn't imagine how mothers were able to watch their babies get vaccinated at the doctor's office. It was easy to understand why Moira worried about her children so much.

Brett walked up to the table and Robin smiled at him. "Would you like to join me?"

He settled into the chair beside her and said, "You looked to be deep in thought. And not particularly *rosy*. Is everything all right?"

"Yes. I was thinking about responsibilities and parenthood. Even being a dog parent is hard sometimes. Do you have pets?"

He shook his head. "I travel too much."

"That must be exciting. I'm a bit too much of a homebody for that, I think."

"Yes. As it turned out, my ex-wife wasn't too fond of my lifestyle either."

Robin took another sip of water and considered the kind of woman who would be bold enough to marry Brett. A man who came on as strong as Brett undoubtedly did not lack for female companionship. It wouldn't be a surprise if he'd had a woman in every city. Being involved with him would likely be complicated and ultimately disastrous. "I'm sorry. That must have been difficult."

He looked into her eyes. "Not everyone is quite as accommodating as you are."

A low screeching noise arose from outside and Robin jerked her gaze away from Brett. "What was that?" She twisted her napkin in her fingers. The room was freezing for some reason all of a sudden. "*Good gravy,* why is it so cold in here? Please excuse me. I need to go ask Chuck about the heat."

She got up and went through the doors into the kitchen. Chuck was standing in front of the stove methodically stirring a sauce. She cleared her throat to get his attention. "Excuse me, Chuck. Do you know where the thermostat is? It's cold in the dining room."

He turned and pointed his whisk toward the far wall. "Over there. Last time I looked, it was set to 68 I think. But with the stove, I can't tell."

A long mournful howl came from outside. It seemed to seep though the air like a long tendril of smoke as Robin walked across the kitchen. "What was that?"

"Maybe coyotes?"

"I've heard coyotes before and they don't sound like that. Unless maybe something is wrong. It sounds as if something is dying." She turned the thermostat up a degree and crossed the room to the outside door. Peering out into the misty darkness, she shuddered. At the sound of rustling leaves and snapping branches, she closed the door quickly. "I think there's something out there."

Chuck looked over his shoulder. "Well, you know about Leroy, right? Alec probably brought him by for a handout again."

"I've heard Leroy before and whatever made that awful wail was *not* a dog. Unless he's hurt. Oh, no! What if something happened to Leroy? Alec was worried he might get shot if he's caught wandering around. I should go see if he's okay."

"Well it could be the ghost." Chuck grinned at her. "Don't forget, you gotta watch out for Julia."

Robin clenched her fists and put them at her sides. "Cut that out." She stalked out of the kitchen and back into the dining room, which was filling with people.

At her table, she put her hand on Brett's shoulder. "Please excuse me. I'll be right back. I need to check on something."

Crossing the dining room to the lobby, she stopped when Alec walked in the door. She waved at him and pointed at the fireplace to indicate that she wanted to talk to him there. She scuttled up to him and whispered. "Where is Leroy?"

Alec grinned. "Fast asleep in Pine Cone 2. I gave him dinner, and between food and all the running around this afternoon with Emma, that dog is wiped out. I think it was the best day he's had in a long time."

"Are you sure?"

"Of course I'm sure. I just walked up from there five minutes ago."

"That's a relief. There was this horrible noise outside. I thought he might be hurt." The wailing started again and she locked her gaze with Alec's and whispered, "That's it! Isn't it awful?"

"I agree that it's creepy, but I know it's not Leroy. Do you suppose there's another stray dog here?"

Robin looked toward the windows. "Or maybe a cat? I don't know, but whatever it is sounds like it's in pain. It makes my heart hurt to hear it cry like that."

"I'll go take a look." He turned and went back out the door.

Robin returned to her table and found most of the room was abuzz with conversation. She wasn't the only one who had heard the anguished cries from outside.

A crack of gunfire echoed through the room, followed by a collective gasp of surprise from the attendees. Then silence as people seemed to hold their breath, waiting for another shot. Robin turned, speed-walked back to the lobby, and peered out the door. She jumped as three more shots were fired in quick succession. Where was Alec?

She walked outside onto the porch and wrapped her arms around her body in an effort to ward off the damp, chill air. From her perch near the steps, she gazed out across the lawn toward the lake. The wind was whistling through the trees, but other than that, everything was quiet. Where had Alec gone? Did someone shoot at *him*? Should she go look? What if something had happened? It was dark and he could have been shot by accident. Maybe he was bleeding to death right now. What if she had to do CPR? Did she even remember how?

At a touch on her shoulder, she screamed and whirled around. Alec grabbed her by the shoulders so she wouldn't fall down the steps. With an alarmed look on his face, he said, "What happened?"

She shook herself free of his grasp and pressed her hand to her chest to encourage the pounding of her heart to return to normal. "*Holy Mother Fussbucket!* You scared me. I almost had a heart attack. Why did you sneak up on me?"

"I didn't. I just walked up the steps, then caught you before you took a header *down* the steps."

"I thought someone might have shot you."

"I heard the gunfire too." He gestured toward the forest. "It sounded like it came from over there somewhere."

"Did you see anything?"

He opened the door to the lodge for her. "No. I walked around the whole building and didn't find anything. Whatever was making the noises must be gone. Sometimes animals go off into the woods to die, I think. Or maybe someone found the animal and shot it to end its suffering."

Robin stopped next to the front desk. "Oh, that's terrible. The poor creature."

Terri ran up to them. "I heard a scream from outside! It sounded like a woman. And there were gunshots. Is someone dead?"

Robin gestured toward the door. "I was outside. The scream was me."

Alec said, "I startled her when I came up the stairs."

"I apologize for disturbing everyone. Let's go sit down, relax, and have something to eat." Robin tried to muster up her most placating smile. "I was in the kitchen a few minutes ago and dinner smelled heavenly."

With a scowl of irritation, Terri turned and sauntered back toward the dining room. Robin and Alec followed. She looked up at him. "You probably think I'm nuts. But I do think something is out there."

"I didn't see anything, but if there is something, I sure hope it stays outside."

~

Robin returned to her seat at the table. Several women and the lone male attendee had joined Brett and were quietly eating their salads. The man was named Nigel and during the introductions, he had said he couldn't decide if his word was *naughty* or *nice* because it depended on the day. Everyone had laughed and ambitious Angela volunteered that *nasty* described the cologne Nigel's boyfriend had given him for Christmas. Nigel retorted that Angela was just cranky because she was the one who had eaten all the holiday candy from the dish on his desk and he hadn't restocked. Brett had then interceded and returned everyone's focus to the task at hand. Robin was again impressed with Brett's ability to deftly and efficiently redirect conflict.

Robin had met Nigel at work a few times. He had black straight hair and was extremely slender, with the type of sleek male-model good looks that served to emphasize his impeccable attire. Compared to him, Robin was downright frumpy, but he was an exceptionally friendly and helpful person, so the word *nice* was an apt choice. Whenever Robin couldn't decipher the description of an item from a manufacturer, he was always more than willing to answer questions about fabrics, styles, and terminology. The uniform manufacturer she had worked for in Spokane didn't exactly deal in upscale clothing, so a lot of the fashion lingo they used at Eagle River was new to her.

The salad was delicious and Robin dug in, gobbling it down with gusto. Having Alec scare the socks off her was the culmination of another long day. She couldn't wait to crawl under the covers in the bed in her little cabin and pass out. This retreat was certainly not turning out to be the relaxing vacation she'd hoped it would be.

A loud crack of thunder followed by a flash of lightning broke the silence of the meal as several women shrieked in involuntary surprise. The dining room lights flickered a few times as heavy rain started pounding on the roof. Robin looked up as if examining the ceiling would give her insights into the structural integrity of the building. The noise got louder and changed pitch. It sounded like thousands of BB pellets were hitting the roof. Was it actually hailing out there?

The wind howled outside and another massive thunderclap rang through the air. The lights flickered a few more times and finally went out. Robin stood up and said loudly, "Please stay where you are, everyone. I'll get some matches from the kitchen so we can light the candles on the tables."

Nigel said, "How romantic," and a woman at the table giggled. A glow of light came from around the swinging kitchen door and Robin walked toward it, stumbling a few times as her eyes adjusted. Chuck was standing in front of the flame from the stove. He smiled. "I had a feeling I'd see you in here."

"Do you have matches?"

"Yup. Now you know why those candles are on the tables. Those little votives aren't just for decoration."

She took the box of matches from him. "Thank you."

One of the roadies, who was sitting on a metal stool, said to Chuck, "Should we start taking out the main course?"

The young man was so dimly lit, Robin couldn't make out which roadie he was. Chuck said, "Why don't you help Robin light the candles?"

He lurched off the stool and took another box of matches from Chuck. "Cool. I'm on it." Robin followed him and they went around to the tables lighting the candles, so soon the room was bathed in the warm glow of candlelight. The hail had subsided, but the low drumming noise of the rain continued on the roof.

Roadies came out with food, which seemed to cheer everyone up. Finally, Robin sat down next to Brett again and eagerly returned to her dinner. Brett was patiently listening to a woman named Linda describe her recent golfing vacation. Linda's word was *logical* and Robin tried to tune out her long-winded analysis of the perfect golf swing. Robin wasn't sure how interested Brett was in golf, but overhearing the story made Robin glad she was sitting where she was. Golf was boring on TV, but Linda took the tedium to a new and more soporific place. Robin yawned and glanced across the room at the windows. A shadowy figure moved outside and she dropped her fork, which clattered on her plate.

Brett turned to look at her. "Are you okay?"

"Y...yes. I thought I saw something, but I think it was my imagination." Nothing was there anymore. Suddenly the door to the lodge opened with a whoosh, and someone came inside. Robin couldn't see the person, but she looked around the room. Wasn't everyone already here? She put her hand on Brett's arm. "I'll be right back."

Walking away from the light into the darkness, she took out a match and struck it. There had to be flashlights in this place somewhere. The person had disappeared into the darkness of the lobby area. Where did he go?

At the front desk, she shook out the match and lit another. Wait! It had to be Ernie. He was the only one who wasn't around. And he couldn't possibly be out fishing in a hail storm. She went behind the counter and knocked on the door to his living area. "Ernie? Are you in there? It's Robin. I'd like to talk to you."

Nobody answered and she pressed her ear to the door. Silence. It didn't sound like anyone was moving around in the space. She shook out the second match and sat down on the rickety chair at the front desk. This was all way too creepy. Where was that guy?

A shadowy form approached the desk and Robin's heartbeat accelerated. She lit another match, revealing Alec's face in the dim light. He leaned over the desk toward her. "Why are you sitting over here in the dark?"

"I saw something…or someone…outside, and then someone came inside. I realized it might be Ernie, and I thought he might be here somewhere. But I don't think he is."

"He's probably around somewhere. You should eat your dinner before they take it away."

Robin shook out the match before it burned her fingertips. "You're right. This is absurd."

As they walked back to the dining room, Robin leaned over and whispered to him. "Would it be okay if I sit at your table? There's this woman talking about golf and I'm not sure I can face hearing any more about the different types of drivers."

He laughed. "Sure. I hate golf."

The dinner plates had already been removed, so Robin went to the kitchen, got some more food from one of the roadies, and sat down next to Alec.

A large woman at the table looked up as they sat down. Alec said, "Loretta, this is Robin." The woman was wearing a flowing top and had an array of plates surrounding her. Robin remembered that Loretta was Terri's much-maligned cubicle-mate. Loretta's word had been *level-headed*, but it appeared her equilibrium had left the building. She said in a shrill voice, "Robin. You're the person I'm supposed to talk to about the accommodations. Well, I'd like to complain about the lack of electricity. I can't see my food. What if it's *touching*?"

Robin paused for a moment, considering how best to respond. Terri had mentioned Loretta's food hang-ups. "I'm sorry about the weather. I assume the storm knocked out the electricity. I'm sure it will be back on soon." She gestured toward the plates. "You seem to have everything quite well subdivided."

Brett walked to the table and put his hand on Robin's shoulder. "May I join you?" Robin smiled up at him. Apparently he couldn't stand any more golf either. "Certainly."

Loretta said, "Do you know when we're getting electricity back?"

"No, I'm sorry. I assume the power company is..."

A loud cracking noise interrupted Brett, and Robin looked toward the windows. A huge tree branch was pressed up against the glass, its wispy twigs and leaves waving in the wind.

Loretta's eyes were wide. "This place is creepy!"

Brett laughed, "Oh, it's just a storm. Those old ghost stories don't mean anything."

Robin cringed inwardly as Loretta whined too loudly, "What ghost stories? Are you saying there's a *ghost* here? You mean this place is *haunted?*"

The room fell completely silent as everyone seemed to digest this new information. In the most calm and reassuring tone she could muster, Robin said, "No. It's just a silly story. Apparently all the locals know about it here in Alpine Grove. There's nothing to worry about."

Nigel said, "Tell us! I love ghost stories."

Robin glanced at Alec, who smiled at her. "Aww, come on."

With a sigh, Robin said, "All right. I have heard from a couple of people that a ghost named Julia Lambert supposedly inhabits the North Fork Lodge."

Terri said, "Lambert? You mean like our boss Darrell Lambert?"

"Yes, Julia is supposedly an ancestor of his. Darrell's uncle Ernie Lambert owns this place." Robin went on to explain the story of Julia's fiery demise. "Apparently, Ernie and his wife used to play up the whole ghost legend by running a haunted house at Halloween. Until his wife died, it was a popular local attraction."

Angela piped up. "So his wife is dead too? That means there could be *two* ghosts!"

Robin waved her hands in exasperation, "Oh please, everyone, there are not any ghosts here. Don't be silly."

Suddenly, the lights flickered and came back on. Everyone cheered and Chuck came out of the kitchen. He motioned to Robin and mouthed "Dessert?" She nodded emphatically. Brett excused himself and Robin watched as he strode through the lobby and out the door. She smiled as a roadie placed a delectable-looking piece of chocolate cake in front of her. Thank goodness. It was definitely time to administer chocolate.

Alec inclined his head toward her and said under his breath. "Good thing the lights came back on. Telling that ghost story might not have been the greatest idea."

"I know. But what could I do after Brett opened his big mouth?"

"Well, you did a great job of keeping your cool while everyone else was losing theirs."

She looked at him in surprise. "Thank you. That's very sweet of you to say."

He flashed a conspiratorial grin. "Don't worry, only a few more days and we're outta here."

"I know. I'm counting down the hours."

～

After dinner, Robin sat with Alec, Nigel, and Darlene, who was still poking at her now-stale piece of chocolate cake. Everyone else had left the dining room and Nigel and Alec were exchanging customer-service stories. Nigel related a complicated tale of a customer who couldn't find the discount code printed on the back of her catalog. "A question like 'what is the number in the yellow box?' shouldn't be so hard."

Alec had his own story about a woman who called asking about a particular skirt. It was the day after Thanksgiving and Alec was answering overflow calls. The customer said that it was a blue-flowered peasant skirt with purple ruffles along the bottom. Since he didn't answer calls regularly, Alec didn't remember the item, but he spent ages on the phone talking to the woman, doing searches, and faithfully flipping through every available catalog looking for a skirt like the one she described.

At last he'd given up and said, "I'm sorry, I can't find any skirt that looks anything like what you're describing. It doesn't sound like any item I've ever seen in stock at Eagle River. Maybe it was another catalog?"

The caller had said, "No, I know you have it. You must carry it because I dreamed about buying it."

Everyone at the table laughed at Alec's reply, which had been, "Interesting. I dreamed you changed your mind and bought the skirt on page 42 instead because it's on sale." In the end, the customer had bought the skirt in the catalog, after all.

As the conversation wound down, Nigel stood up and said goodnight. Darlene thanked Alec for something and followed Nigel out of the building, leaving Alec and Robin in the dining room alone. Robin put her elbows on the table and leaned forward to rest her head on her arms. She peeked up at Alec. "I'm so tired I can barely move."

They both jumped at the sound of the lodge's front door opening. Robin sat up straight in her chair and her jaw dropped in surprise as Ernie walked over to the front desk. He stopped and looked at them. "Why are you two sitting there? You've got every light on in this whole building, wasting my electricity."

Robin scuttled over to the light switch and turned off the dining room lights before heading to the lobby area. Alec followed her to the front desk. Robin spread her arms and raised her palms to the ceiling. "Ernie, where have you *been*? I was getting worried about you."

"I've been around."

Robin looked at Ernie more closely. Although his face was only illuminated by the feeble light from the old lamp on the desk, something about him had changed. Somehow he seemed even more ragged than he had the last time she'd seen him. He was wearing old blue jeans with a faded red-and-black flannel shirt and suspenders stretched over his bony shoulders. His gray razor stubble had evolved into a scraggly thin beard and his unruly hair had frizzed out. Maybe it was the humidity from the rain, but his hair was practically standing on end, as if he'd stuck his finger in a light socket.

He thumped his cane on the floor. "Don't you people sleep? Go to bed."

Robin said, "I need to talk to you."

As he walked around to the other side of the desk, he mumbled something unintelligible, and with a groan, he sat down in the chair and leaned his cane against the wall. "So talk."

Robin glanced at Alec helplessly. She'd wanted to talk to Ernie about so many things, and now her mind was a blank. She cleared her throat. "Well, during the storm we heard some gunshots outside. And some strange noises. The guests were a bit frightened."

Ernie moved his shoulders slightly. "I didn't hear anything. I'll ask Myrtle."

Alec said, "So I've been curious. Could you tell us about Myrtle?"

Robin noticed that Alec had managed to phrase the question without implying Myrtle was dead. "Yes, I'd like to hear about her too."

The hard expression on Ernie's face softened. "No one can talk about Myrtle without mentioning her sense of humor. That woman—well, what can I say? Sometimes you meet someone and you know it's right. That's the way it was for me. When we met, it was like she could see into me. All the good stuff and the bad stuff too. But it was always okay, you know?" He shook his finger at Alec. "If you ever meet a woman like that…someone who totally understands you and who you can laugh with, don't you ever let her get away. I'm telling ya, there's not enough laughter in this world."

Alec nodded, but didn't say anything. Robin asked, "How did you meet?"

Ernie took a photograph out of the pocket of his flannel shirt. "Blind date." He handed the black-and-white snapshot to Robin. The edges were rough and the paper was criss-crossed with white creases. A woman wearing a classic sixties pillbox hat and a tailored suit was standing on a pier, obviously laughing at the person taking the picture. Robin smiled and handed it back to him. "That's a lovely photograph."

Ernie tucked the photo back into his pocket and looked away toward the windows. "Yeah. It was a great trip."

"Was it around here?"

Ernie looked startled. "No. I gotta lock up. You guys are staying out in the cabins, right?" He stood up and grabbed his cane. Walking around the desk, he escorted them to the door and practically shoved them outside.

Alec put out his arm. "It appears that the evening's activities are concluded. May I walk you to your cabin, my lady?"

Robin giggled as she linked her arm with his and they walked down the stairs. "Sure. Just keep an eye out for scary ghosts and monsters, okay?"

As they strolled along the path down to the Pine Cone cabin, tendrils of mist swirled in the moonlight. Robin reached up and swiped the cold mist from her cheek. The moist air seemed to muffle sounds and the earthy scent of sodden grass rose from the ground. In the murky muted quiet, the violent thunderstorm, hail, wind, and lightning seemed like a long time ago.

The moon emerged from behind a cloud, lighting up Alec's face. His expression was contemplative. Maybe he was thinking about what Ernie had said. It was obvious that Ernie had loved his wife and it was interesting to see that Alec had been sensitive to the fact that he might not want to talk about her in the past tense. Since Leroy had become their shared secret, being around Alec had been much more enjoyable. It was a relief to have at least one friend during this strange experience.

He glanced down at her, catching her looking at him. With a smile, he said, "Everything okay?"

She squeezed his arm. "Yes. Thanks for walking me home."

They stopped in front of the Pine Cone cabin and Alec released her arm. "See you tomorrow."

As he strolled down the path toward his side of the duplex, Leroy woofed excitedly from within, obviously delighted to see Alec. Robin smiled at the realization that tomorrow she'd be glad to see Alec again too.

~

At the sound of a dog barking, Robin opened her eyes. For a moment, she didn't know where she was. Then it all came back. The ceiling was knotty pine and the dog wasn't Emma. Her dog was off at a kennel and she was in her cabin. What time was it?

As she rolled over, another gleeful yipping came from Leroy, who was obviously excited about something over there on Alec's side of the Pine Cone cabin. With a glance at the old plastic clock on the dresser, she sat up. It was time to bravely face the arctic shower again.

Later, after getting some breakfast, Robin was walking back to the Pine Cone when Leroy ran up to her. She bent to ruffle his ears and marveled at how soft he was now that he was clean.

Alec walked up and grinned at her. "You're doing a whole lot of cooing."

"Cooing?"

In a high-pitched voice, he stroked Leroy's head and said, "Oh look at how pretty you are. What a sweet doggie." Leroy wagged and wiggled his long body, enjoying the attention.

Robin straightened. "I don't sound like that. And he *is* a sweet dog. Besides, I miss Emma." She gestured toward the forest. "So are you ready to go out into the trees for the scavenger hunt?"

"I'm exempted from this morning's activities. Leroy is going to help me prepare for the training I have to do this afternoon." He patted the dog's head. "Right, Leroy?"

"You did a great job yesterday."

He stopped and looked into her eyes. "You thought so?"

"Of course. Everyone was whining and you turned it around. I was stunned."

"Thanks. I've never done this before."

"Well, you said that back when you started at Eagle River, you figured out how to do a lot of stuff. It seems now you've figured out training too."

He laughed. "Yeah, we'll see. I've still got a few more days to have a spectacular screw-up."

Robin looked at the sky. "I should get back and change my clothes. It's starting to look like it might rain again."

"See you later. Happy hunting."

After outfitting herself in her raincoat and boots, Robin walked back to the theater building. She wasn't the only one who had geared up for the occasion. After the storm last night, everyone seemed to take the clouds more seriously and had prepared themselves for bad weather.

Robin took off her coat, sat down in her seat, and looked up at Brett as he walked by and handed her a sheet of paper. He had a stern expression on his face, which was unusual. Up until now, he'd seemed like an easygoing person, but this morning the muscles around his jaw and neck were tense and his lips were pressed together. Something was obviously bothering him.

He moved around the room passing out papers, then stood in front of the square of tables with his arms crossed across his chest. Once everyone was settled, he gestured toward the forest. "As you know, today we are doing a scavenger hunt. This exercise is designed to help you learn to work together to meet a common goal."

"I have divided you up into three teams. Robin will lead one, I'll head up another, and Terri will be in charge of the third. You'll find your name on the paper, and below the team listings are the items you need to find. He paused and looked around the room. "Here are the rules. If anyone on your team breaks the rules, your team is automatically disqualified. First, the items you find can be on your person, in your room, or on the grounds somewhere. Under no circumstances are you allowed to break into cars or premises that are not yours without the owner's permission. If a member of your team knows he or she has an item, for example, you can gain permission that way. Beyond that, you're on your own. We will meet back here at eleven thirty. The team who has collected the most items at the end of the hunt wins."

Robin looked at Terri, who had a determined look on her face. Some people thrived on competition, but Robin wasn't one of them. For the most part, contests were stressful for her because she worried too much about winning and upsetting those people who didn't win. Or not winning and letting down the people on her team. Either way, she hated it. Why had Brett made her a team leader?

The people on her team started gathering around, rustling their papers. Robin tried not to let anyone see her dismay at the fact that "expert Emily" and "ambitious Angela" were on her team. During training the day before, Emily had been a pain in everyone's backside. Although Alec had dealt with her patiently, Emily was such a know-it-all that by the end of the class, Robin wanted to throttle her. And of course, Angela was so critical that if they lost, the woman would probably file a lawsuit against Robin.

Looking up from the piece of paper, Robin smiled brightly. "All right everyone, please review the list. If you own any of these items, please mark them and we can compare notes."

Emily shook her head so vigorously that her short straight hair whapped her ears. "Why would I bring a seashell to a retreat?"

Robin laughed as she grabbed her handbag. "You may not have a shell, but I think I do. There might be one in my purse. I picked it up on a trip to the Washington coast last year. I bet it's still sitting there at the bottom."

Angela said, "Some of this is trash. A Pepsi can? Is this stupid scavenger hunt some type of trick to clean up garbage around here?"

Robin made an effort to suppress her exasperation. What a whiner. "Even if it does involve picking up litter, that's not such a bad thing, is it?" She looked at the group. "Does anyone drink Pepsi?"

Darlene said, "My church discourages the consumption of soft drinks."

Emily said, "Too much high-fructose corn syrup is bad for your health."

Robin pulled out her wallet. "Fine. Let's skip that one. Everyone, please look at your change. We need a 1979 penny and a 1994 dime." She scattered coins on the table and examined the dates. "Nope. I don't have them. Anyone else?"

The other women began rummaging through their purses. Darlene held up a plastic fork that was still hermetically sealed in its clear cellophane wrapper. "Look, here's something—it's on the list!"

Robin smiled. "Way to go, Darlene! Once we're done here, we can go outside and look for the plant-related items like the pine cones and leaves. There might be some stuff we can find in the kitchen too."

Everyone nodded as they continued to keep digging around for things to add to the pile. It was remarkable what people carried around. Even if Robin's team lost, at least their purses would be a lot lighter.

Robin dumped the change back into her wallet and rounded up the team to go outside. The other two teams had already disappeared. Maybe they had smaller purses. There were 60 items on the list and so far, her team had found about eight or nine things. Why Angela was carrying such a large nail around in her purse was unclear and Robin was pretty sure she didn't want to know.

They all trooped outside and stood on the porch looking out at the rain, which was now coming down in sheets. Emily said, "We should go over there toward those trees. There should be leaves and pine cones there."

"We need a heck of a lot more than pine cones," Angela said, looking down at her sheet of paper. "Some of these are impossible. A purple wild flower? Nothing is blooming right now. How are we supposed to find that?"

Robin said evenly, "I don't think we're supposed to find everything. Just as many as we can. If we can't find something, probably no one else can either."

"Well, Nigel might have an orange baseball cap. Too bad he's not on our team." Darlene said.

Angela snorted. "I don't think so. He's way too snappy of a dresser to wear something like that."

"Let's go down toward my cabin." Robin pointed across the lawn. "I think I might have a spool of thread in a sewing kit. It's been sitting in a side pocket of my suitcase for ages.

And maybe a paper clip too. I brought a bunch of office supplies. Look on the ground as we walk along. Maybe we'll see something."

The group slowly moved down the path toward the cabin. Darlene picked up a rock and held it out to Robin. "Do you think this counts as a pink stone?"

"Maybe. Under the mud there could be some pink. You can wash it off at my cabin."

Looking pleased, Darlene tucked the rock into her pocket.

Robin noticed that Brett's team had dispersed in the forested area behind the lodge. People were bent over poking around at things on the ground. Off to one side, Brett was standing facing toward the lake with his arms crossed. The hat he was wearing had a huge brim and rain was pouring off the sides onto his shoulders. Even from a distance, his body language indicated that something was wrong.

Robin unlocked the door to her cabin and invited everyone in. Having seven people in one tiny cabin was crowded, but the women were glad to be out of the rain. Angela said, "How come you get to stay in a cabin and we have to stay in the lodge? You have this cute little living area. All I got was a bed."

Robin rummaged through the papers and office supplies on the coffee table. "I had to bring a lot of materials for Alec and Brett, so I needed more space. Darrell set it up, remember?"

Angela shook the rain off her coat and paused at the sound of a thumping noise from the other side. "What's that?"

Robin said, "This is a duplex. Alec is staying on the other side."

Emily said, "What is he, an elephant?"

Robin stood up and held out a paper clip. There was no way she going to mention Leroy. "Please add this to our collection."

After dredging up a tiny spool of thread, Robin said, "Okay, do any of you have anything on the list in your rooms?"

Darlene said, "I think my comb is blue."

"Great, let's go."

∼

As she was locking up her cabin, Robin had an idea. She called out to the women. "I'll meet you up there. I know where I can get a binder!" Emily acknowledged her with a dispirited wave as the women trudged up the path toward the lodge.

Robin went over to the other side of the Pine Cone cabin and knocked. Leroy barked and Alec opened the door a crack. He peered out at her with a toothbrush hanging out of the side of his mouth. Through a mouthful of toothpaste, he mumbled. "What are you doing here?"

"Everyone else on my team is heading up to the lodge. But I need a binder and I know you have one."

He opened the door and waved her in. Leroy bounded over to her with an expectant look. As she bent to pet the dog, Robin glanced at Alec as he wandered back into the bathroom. He wasn't wearing a shirt, and her cheeks warmed in embarrassment. *Sweet blue blazes,* why wasn't he dressed? She shoved Leroy over so she could surreptitiously peer around the corner of the bathroom doorway to catch another glimpse of Alec's muscular back as he finished brushing his teeth. Her toe bumped into a heavy red metal box and Robin covered her mouth, so he wouldn't hear her yelp of pain.

This was ludicrous. What was she? Thirteen? It wasn't like she'd never seen a half-naked man before. What was wrong with her? Alec wasn't startlingly good-looking like Brett was with the whole dashing tall, dark, and handsome thing going for him. But it wasn't like Alec was unattractive either. Obviously, given his athletic build, he got out and did some form of exercise. He had broad shoulders tapering to a nice- fitting pair of faded Levis. *Heavens to Murgatroyd*, those were some impressive biceps too.

Alec walked out of the bathroom, grabbed an old Portland Trail Blazers' t-shirt off a chair, and yanked it over his head. "Why do you need a binder?"

"*Leaping lizards*, you have a *red* t-shirt. I need that too. This is wonderful. My team could actually win!"

"Did you just say *leaping lizards*? Who are you, Little Orphan Annie?" He looked down at his shirt. "Wait a minute. You want my *shirt* too?"

"Yes! It's for the scavenger hunt. This is great. I bet no one else has a red t-shirt." She paused. "Well, except maybe Nigel. But all the women are far too well-dressed to consider bringing a t-shirt, right?"

"I have no idea."

"Please take it off. I have to get back to the group." She paused. "Oh, wait a minute—do you wear boxers?"

He raised his eyebrows. "Why do you need to know *that*?"

"I need a pair of shorts. Boxers are close enough, don't you think?"

"You want to steal my underwear too?"

"Yes. And I need the three-ring binder. I know you have one."

"I'm not participating in the scavenger hunt. Isn't this cheating?"

"No! I would *never* cheat! I'm following the rules Brett gave us. He said we're not allowed to break into anyone's room without permission, but you let me in, so it's okay."

"Fine. Whatever you say. I've got to review more training material before the class and as I told you, I'm not exactly a speed reader." He pulled the t-shirt over his head and handed it to her. "But I want my stuff back, okay?"

Robin grinned involuntarily at another opportunity to see his bare chest. Nice. "Yes, that's fine. I promise I'll return everything."

"You're not getting sick or something are you?" He turned to the dresser, pulled out some boxers, and handed them to her along with an empty binder. "You look sort of flushed."

"I'm fine. I'll see you later. Thank you!" Robin looked down in an effort to mask her mortification as she moved toward the door. She really needed to get out more.

Leroy rushed out after her and ran past her toward the lake. Alec shouted the dog's name, followed by an extremely descriptive string of graphic expletives. She said primly. "You really are kind of a potty mouth aren't you? My momma would skin you alive if she heard you say that."

With an icy glare, he moved around her and ran out the door after the dog. Robin wasn't sure what to do. On the one hand, she needed to get back to her team, but she wanted to help Alec round up Leroy. But if she did that, her team members might come out looking for her and find Leroy. She stomped her foot on the old planks of the porch. Today she *had* to remember to find out if there was an animal shelter around here. After the scavenger hunt, she could call during the lunch break. She'd do it then. This time, for sure.

She looked down toward the lake. Alec had corralled Leroy and was leading the dog up the path back to the cabin using an old rope Leroy had in his mouth. The dog seemed inordinately pleased with himself and was marching along proudly behind Alec, obviously enjoying the impromptu game of tug-o-war.

By the time they reached Robin, both man and dog were completely drenched. Alec's brown hair was splayed in stringy, soggy clumps across his forehead. Leroy stopped in front of Robin, let go of the rope, and shook himself vigorously, spraying a plume of water across the two humans. Good thing she was wearing a raincoat. Alec wasn't so lucky.

As the dog strolled into the cabin, Robin looked at Alec and held out her hand. "Could I have that rope too? It's on the list."

He was shivering and had one arm wrapped around his bare stomach. Thrusting the rope into her hand, he growled, "Shouldn't you go find your team? Please leave before I get hypothermia and die."

"Thank you! Say thanks to Leroy too. I can't believe he found a rope. No one else will have that!"

Alec glared at her through the strands of his dripping hair, but said nothing. He went inside the cabin and slammed the door behind him.

Robin pulled the hood of her raincoat up over her head and practically skipped up the path to the lodge building. Now her team had a whole bunch of the hard-to-find items. Maybe the other members of her team had gotten some of the outdoor things too. They might actually win this silly scavenger hunt.

Even though the people on the other teams might be disappointed, maybe she'd finally have a couple of allies in her corner for a change. Being disliked by practically everyone she'd met here because of things that were out of her control, was getting depressing. And now Alec didn't seem too pleased with her either.

Robin walked into the lobby area where her teammates were relaxing on the willow furniture facing the fireplace. How irritating! While Robin had been off busy collecting things, no one else on the team had done anything. She stood in front of the coffee table. "How is it going? Did you find any more items on the list?"

There were a few negative mumbles and Darlene volunteered, "I have my blue comb. But I didn't bring a pair of shorts here. At my church, we prefer to wear less revealing clothing."

Robin pulled Alec's boxers out of her tote bag and held them up. "That's okay. I got a pair. And I got a red t-shirt and a binder. Oh, and then the dog...um...I mean, the *doggonedest* thing happened and I found a piece of rope too."

Darlene looked appalled at the wanton display of men's undergarments, but Emily sat up in her chair. "Hey, those are some of the tough ones!"

"I know! Isn't it great?" Robin said. "Let's go outside and get the easy stuff like the branch and the pine cone and then go to the theater building. We still have enough time to gather a few more items before the deadline."

With renewed enthusiasm, the women put on their foul-weather gear and went back out into the rain toward the woods. They collected various soggy pieces of flora from the ground and added them to their collection. Robin looked at her watch and called everyone. "We have to get back now!"

They all returned to the theater building, where Brett was standing at one end of the tables while the members of both of the other teams were busy counting up their items. Robin's group settled in and began crossing their items off the list. Out of sixty items, they had found fifty. Robin said, "Even if we don't win, I think we did really well and we should be proud of ourselves."

The women smiled and looked up at Brett in unison as he walked over to their group. He pointed at the pile of artifacts on the table. "That's quite a collection you have."

Robin smiled. "Yes, we found some difficult ones."

"How many do you have?"

"We count fifty."

He bent to look more closely. "Those aren't exactly shorts."

Robin said, "Yes, they are. They're boxer shorts. That's a type of shorts."

Brett crossed his arms. "I'm guessing they aren't yours. Where did you get them?"

The heat rose on her cheeks as she said, "Alec. It's his t-shirt too."

Curious about the discussion, members of the other teams started filtering over to their table. Terri pointed at Robin. "She cheated."

"I did not!" Robin stood up. She was uncomfortable having Brett towering over them, his dark eyes drilling into her. She stood up, although it wasn't really much of an improvement because he was so tall, but it helped her feel more like a grown-up instead of a recalcitrant seven-year old. "Brett said that we could go any place we had permission. Alec let me into his cabin and gave these things to me."

"Oh *reeeeally*?" Terri gave her a sidelong look. "Cheater."

"I did *not* cheat." Robin pointed at one of the piles on another table. "How many items did everyone else find?"

Brett said, "My team found forty-one."

Terri said, "Thirty-nine."

Robin gestured in the general direction of the Pine Cone cabin. "Even if you take out the things I got from Alec, we still won."

Terri mumbled, "cheater" again, turned on her heel, and went back to her seat on the other side of the room.

Brett said, "Congratulations to all of you. You all did well, but I'd like to recognize Robin's initiative and creativity. That is part of what this exercise is all about."

Robin sat down again heavily. Even though her team won, it didn't feel good. Competitions always ended this way. Like the old saying went, every time somebody wins, somebody loses.

Darlene said quietly, "I don't think you cheated. But I did pray for your eternal soul, just in case."

Robin turned to her. "Thanks Darlene. I appreciate that."

Chapter 8

Slamming

After Brett said a few final words about the importance of teamwork, he let everyone go. Robin ran over to the lodge building to see if she could get to the phone before Moira. Half the time she looked at the desk in the lobby, that woman was on the phone with her kids. But Robin was determined to get Leroy back home. The owners of that poor dog had to be beside themselves with worry by now.

She sat in the rickety office chair, picked up the Cedar County phone book, and flapped the thin publication back and forth. This wouldn't take long. She riffled through the pages and didn't find anything animal-related except for one veterinarian in downtown Alpine Grove. Maybe Kat knew of some type of unofficial organization that helped homeless pets. There had to be someone she could call about Leroy. She dug Kat's number out of her purse. If nothing else, she could get an update on Emma.

The phone rang a few times and Kat's voice greeted her. Robin said, "Kat, hi, it's Robin."

"It's good to hear from you. Emma is right here. She's asleep actually. We took a long walk and she's busy drying off now."

Robin giggled. "Oh, that's sweet. I miss her so much! I'm actually calling with a question I hope you can answer.

I looked in the phone book and couldn't find anything. I want to ask you if there's an animal shelter around here." She glanced up to make sure no one was near the desk. "There's a stray dog we found here at the lodge and the owner is against having dogs on the premises. We need to find this dog's family."

"There's not an animal shelter like you'd find in a city. Not exactly. There are some holding cages at the police station, where they keep strays that are picked up. But you don't want to take a dog there."

"Why not?"

"You don't want to know. Let's just say it's not what you'd call an adoption facility."

"Well, if someone lost a dog, who would they call?"

"Most people call Dr. Cassidy's office. She's the vet in town and their office tends to be in the know. A friend of mine just adopted a kitten that they saved from...well, ah... never mind. It's a long story."

"What should I do? This is such a sweet dog. Someone *must* be looking for him."

After a protracted silence, Kat said, "Well, I didn't know this until I moved here, but when it comes to animals, things are kind of different in rural areas. You met Joel, right?"

"Yes, he carried Emma across the creek."

"Joel has a dog named Lady that he found when she was about eight months old. From what he told me, it's not unusual for people to dump dogs out in the country. Five or six years later, he's still got Lady. No one has claimed her yet."

"You've got to be kidding."

"I wish I were."

"That's horrible. Who would do that? I don't want anything to happen to this dog. He's such a sweetheart."

"Well, if it were me, I'd call Dr. Cassidy's office. It's the Alpine Grove Vet Clinic. I can give you the number."

"That's okay. I found it in the phone book."

"If they don't know anything about the dog there, call the police station. Maybe someone called them to report a missing dog. There's not any animal control here exactly. One guy—the low man on the totem pole I guess—sometimes drives around town. He's supposed to pick up strays, but mostly he just sits in his car. But like I said, please don't take the dog to the police station."

"Okay. I won't."

"Sorry I don't have more advice."

"No, you've been very helpful and I appreciate it. How is your driveway doing? Would it be possible to pick up Emma again?"

"Not at the moment. Joel is out in the creek now, digging out the old culvert."

"In the rain?"

"Yes. He said he wanted to spend some time using the pick axe."

Robin glanced out the window. "It's such a cold rain today. He must be freezing."

"Well, he's not in a good mood, and I think he wanted to get out of the house for a while. A friend is going to pick up a new culvert for us, so with any luck, we won't be marooned for much longer."

"Oh, I'm sorry. Emma had so much fun here at the North Fork. She and Leroy are best buddies. It's so much fun to watch them play together."

"Leroy?"

"That's the stray dog who isn't supposed to be here."

"You named him?"

"Well, I didn't. Alec did. We had to call the dog *something*."

Kat laughed. "It's a good thing you like dogs. I think you're going to have two now."

"No, not me. Absolutely not! Leroy loves Alec anyway. I think they've bonded."

"I see."

"Well, thank you for your help. I need to make some calls now. I'll try to check in with you tomorrow and see how the road project is going."

Robin hung up the phone and looked up the number for the vet clinic. She gave a description of Leroy to a nice woman who unfortunately had no information about a large white dog that lived in the area. There was only one Great Pyrenees they had treated and he was an older dog with arthritis. Given his enthusiastic bounding around the beach, Leroy did not seem to be having joint pain. The only other white dog they knew about was a female Samoyed. Obviously that wasn't Leroy either.

Robin didn't want to call the police station, but she knew she had to. When she talked to the officer on duty, she reported a "sighting" rather than telling the man where Leroy was staying. In the end it didn't matter, since they had no reports of a missing white dog either. Robin stared down at her hands. She was out of ideas.

She looked up as Moira walked up to the desk. The woman looked anxious and Robin stood up. "Don't worry. I'm done."

The woman's brows pulled together in concern. "Oh, that's a relief. This soccer tournament is turning into a nightmare. I need to give Mrs. Johnson a call."

Robin waved toward the phone. "The phone is all yours. I hope everything is okay."

She went to the dining room and quickly made herself a sandwich from the lunch buffet. There was still enough time to go back to the Pine Cone, talk to Alec, and return his things.

As she slowly chewed the sandwich and walked down the path to her cabin, Robin gazed out across the lake. Even though the weather was gray and stormy, something about being near water never failed to make her happy. Growing up in Spokane, she had loved the trips they took to the lakes across the border in Northern Idaho.

Living near the ocean or a lake was one of those things she dreamed about, but it was probably never going to happen unless she won the lottery. Waterfront property anywhere was out of her price range. And to get a job, she needed to live in a big city, anyway. At least Portland had the river. Darrell was lucky to have spent so much time here with his family. Even though it was worn and broken down now, the North Fork had probably been beautiful in its heyday.

She knocked on the door of Alec's side of the cabin and Leroy barked. Alec opened the door, and she was relieved to note he was fully clothed. He said, "I assume you're here to give me back my underwear."

Pulling the tote bag off her shoulder, she nodded. "Yes. We won!"

He stepped aside so she could come inside. "That's good, I guess."

Robin sat in the desk chair, pulled out the rope, and handed it to Leroy, who was thrilled to have his prize returned to him. He sauntered over to Alec, proudly displaying it. Alec grinned at the dog and sat down on the end of the bed. The dog shoved the rope into Alec's lap. "That's great Leroy, but watch it with that nose, okay?"

Robin put the binder and clothes on the desk behind her and faced Alec. "I have some bad news about Leroy. After making some calls, no one seems to know about him. Kat says sometimes people just drop dogs in the country when they don't want them anymore."

He looked up from ruffling Leroy's ears. "There's no animal shelter?"

"No. Apparently, sometimes some officer of the law picks up strays, but then they throw the dog into a little cage."

"That's it? Then what?"

"I don't know, but Kat said not to take Leroy there. What she didn't say is more worrisome. With such a small facility, I don't think they keep dogs long."

Alec raised his eyebrows, obviously understanding what Robin meant. "That's definitely not an option then."

"I don't know what to do."

He returned to playing with Leroy's floppy ears. "Neither do I. I can't take a dog back to Portland with me. My apartment isn't a great place for a dog, and I work incredibly long hours."

Robin brightened. "Why not? Lots of people who have dogs also have jobs and your apartment is probably bigger than this cabin. And Leroy has done great here, right? I have a dog walker who comes in and walks Emma. It's expensive, but Emma has been adapting since we moved. I'll give you the card for the company." She clasped her hands together in her lap. "Please keep him, Alec. Leroy needs a home and he loves you."

"He *had* a home. I have to teach in a few minutes, but tomorrow morning while everyone's off team-building, I'll drive around and look for lost dog signs. I can make some flyers of my own too. And maybe knock on some doors around here. There's probably a local paper. Maybe I can put an ad there. I just can't believe someone would let this guy go like you're saying."

"According to Kat, it wouldn't be the first time. I met her husband, or boyfriend, or roommate. Whoever he is, he lives there and his name is Joel. I guess that's how he ended up with his dog."

Alec looked down at Leroy, who was enjoying the affection. "So are you my dog now?" Leroy wagged his tail happily.

Robin smiled. "Unless someone speaks up, I think he is."

~

For Robin, the next two days were filled with more complaints, ghost stories, team-building activities, training, and small talk. By Thursday afternoon, everyone was winding down and even Terri had stopped voicing her dissatisfaction as loudly. They'd all managed to survive an activity called "Two Truths and a Lie." Each person had to tell three stories and then everyone else was supposed to guess which story was a lie. Robin had been incredibly irritated that everyone thought one of her truths was a lie. Now Terri was convinced she was a cheater *and* a liar. Was it so impossible to believe that Robin could have been on TV? It wasn't a lie! Okay, yes, it was a commercial for Cal's used cars when she was six years old, but it was still true.

The Trust Walk activity had been far worse though. Being blindfolded and led through the woods was not Robin's idea of a good time. Then Terri accused her of purposely causing her to run into a tree, which Robin definitely did *not* do.

In retaliation, Terri had directed Robin so she tripped on a log and almost killed herself. The bruise on her arm still hurt. Brett had not been particularly amused by the whole situation. A muscle in his neck was pulsing in a slightly scary way, and he obviously had been trying to restrain himself from saying something unkind. Robin was mildly worried that he might have a stroke. The only good thing was that he was unlikely to pair her up with Terri again. As the week wore on, he seemed increasingly unhappy. Should she ask him about it or was it better to just let him be?

Fortunately, the training classes in the afternoons had been less hazardous. Robin could tell Alec was getting tired, though. They talked about the products, services, policies, procedures, and every possible Eagle River guideline for every possible scenario people might encounter. He'd gone over communication and listening skills and talked about tone of voice, and why people buy.

True to his word, Alec had also driven throughout the area putting up posters and notifying everyone he could think of about Leroy. So far, no one had any information.

He'd even brought Leroy by the vet clinic, so they could take a look at the dog to be sure no one had seen him before. While he was at the clinic, he'd made an appointment for an official veterinary check-up, since it was looking more likely that Leroy would be going home with him on Saturday.

Robin sat and watched as Alec patiently went through a role-playing routine related to a complicated return with an angry customer. Some of the role-plays had been funny, particularly when Alec played the clueless husband trying to buy a birthday present from the catalog for his imaginary wife. Apparently, a male caller shopping for his wife or girlfriend was a common occurrence.

Although it had been a long week, it seemed that Darrell's goal of bringing people together might be working out, after all. The level of animosity had dropped considerably and worrying about the ghost of Julia Lambert seemed to have brought people together. After all the shared weirdness, people were actually talking with one another a bit more.

Alec concluded the class and started gathering up his materials. As everyone filed out, Robin went up to him. "Only one more day!"

"It's a good thing. I'm so tired of talking. And if somebody tells me one more strange or creepy thing that happened at night in their room I may cry like a little girl. After this is over, I think I'm going to need to take a vacation from humanity. I want to go sit on a beach somewhere by myself and listen to the waves."

"Well, the sun is out for the moment. You could sit by the lake. The waves aren't very big, but it's still beautiful."

He smiled. "You're right. It is, and that's a good idea. I'll collect Leroy and find a quiet spot down the beach a little ways."

"Any word about his family?"

"Nope. My phone number is plastered over half this town. I keep calling my answering machine and the obnoxious techno-voice tells me I have no new messages."

Robin looked toward the North Star cabin. Brett was heading up the path toward them, and he stopped and waved to Robin, indicating he wanted to talk to her. Alec continued on toward the Pine Cone cabin and Robin walked over to Brett. He greeted her and gestured toward the lake. "Shall we stroll and look at the water? I need to discuss something with you."

They walked down toward the beach and as they walked, Robin got the distinct impression that something was bothering Brett. His head was bowed and he seemed upset. They sat down at an old picnic table and Robin folded her hands in front of her. "Is everything okay?"

He looked across the table at her with his intense dark-brown eyes. "I want to apologize for letting you fall the other day during the Trust Walk. I have not been at my best this week and my behavioral choices led to that situation."

"That was Terri's fault, not yours. She's not my biggest fan. In fact, I'm pretty sure she despises me."

"Whether or not that is true, as the leader, I must be conscious of everything happening with all participants to help guide their actions."

Robin shrugged. "You can't be everywhere at once. We were all wandering around in the trees."

"I wasn't completely present for you and the others. My mind has been elsewhere and that has governed my behavior."

"Well, you have looked like something is bothering you. Is everything okay?"

He reached out his hand across the table. "You are such a perceptive person, Robin. I have not been one-hundred percent in the moment and my performance has suffered."

"What's wrong?"

"I'm afraid I can't honor my commitment to be here tomorrow. In the morning I need to set out for home. There is a legal entanglement that I can't avoid and it's vital that I be present."

"I can tell everyone tonight at dinner. They might enjoy having a morning free before we all have to head back."

He squeezed her hand. "Still always looking on the bright side."

"You look so sad. Is there anything I can do?"

"No. But if you can avoid it, don't get divorced. And if you do get divorced, please do it before you decide to have children."

Robin's eyes widened. "I'm so sorry. I had no idea. I hope everything works out."

He released her hand and stood up. "I should go pack. It has been a pleasure meeting you, Robin. I hope our paths cross again."

He seemed to want to be alone, so Robin stayed at the picnic bench and watched as he slowly walked back down the path toward his cabin. The thought of legal entanglements involving kids was heartbreaking. No wonder he was having trouble concentrating.

~

After dinner, Robin got everyone's attention and announced that the team-building exercise had been canceled for the next day. She thanked Brett and wished him well on his trip home. Terri was sitting next to Brett and took his hand to pull him away for a private conversation at another table in the corner of the room.

An older woman named Trudy who had flaming red hair said, "Since we're almost done with the retreat, I wanted to share something."

Robin sat down and said, "What's that?"

"Tequila!"

Robin said, "Where did you get that?"

Trudy, whose word was *tidy*, stood up and smoothed the front of the pink and purple floral blouse she was wearing. "I brought it. It's in my room. I think we should celebrate that tomorrow is the last day of the retreat and that we get the morning off! Who's up for slammers?"

A few women voiced enthusiasm for the idea with shouts of "Yeah!" and "Bring it on."

Trudy stopped by Robin's table on her way out. "Could you find us some shot glasses and 7-Up?"

Robin wasn't sure what a slammer was and she hated tequila, but she went to the kitchen and returned with a large heavy shot glass in one hand and a liter bottle in the other.

Trudy returned with a big gold bottle and placed it in the center of the table. "Everyone gather 'round!"

Darlene said, "There isn't a worm in that bottle is there? I heard tequila has worms."

Trudy said, "No, that's mescal."

Darlene looked disappointed. "Well, I don't drink anyway. My church discourages it."

Robin said, "What's a slammer?"

Trudy held up the bottle of tequila. "You mix tequila and 7-Up, then put your hand over the shot glass and slam it on the table. It fizzes up and you drink it."

Robin cringed. How revolting. "We only have one shot glass."

Nigel reached into his pocket. "We can play quarters." He put a quarter on the table and moved his empty water glass in front of it. "If you can bounce the quarter into the glass, you don't have to drink. If you miss, you have to suck down the slammer."

Emily reached over and picked up the quarter, "I played quarters in college. I'm extremely good at this game."

Trudy poured some tequila and 7-Up into the shot glass. "You'd better hope so."

Emily flipped the coin into the glass, which landed with a clang. "See!" She handed the quarter to Robin. "You're up."

Robin whapped the quarter onto the table and the coin leaped over the water glass and rolled off the other side of the table. "Oops."

While Emily looked under the table for the quarter, Trudy passed the shot glass to Robin. "Slam it, baby!"

Robin did as instructed, putting her palm over the glass. She smacked the shot glass on the table, and the drink fizzed onto her palm. She tilted her head back and downed the shot, which flowed through her like agonizing molten lava. She coughed and licked the fizz off her palm. "*Flaming heck*, that's absolutely disgusting."

Trudy giggled as Emily passed the quarter to Alec. He smiled and quickly flipped the quarter into the glass. "I've played this before too."

Linda tried and failed to get the quarter into the glass. "Oh dear. Do I really have to drink?"

Every said, "Yes!" in unison and Linda downed her fizzy shot.

As they went around the circle, Robin discovered she was extremely bad at quarters. There was a trick to this game, which some people like Emily knew and she definitely did not. By the third trip around, they'd lost one quarter that had rolled off into oblivion. Maybe Chuck would find it again someday. But Darlene rummaged around and found a quarter in her purse, so the game was still on. After missing the glass yet *again*, Robin handed her shot over to Alec. "This isn't fair. You haven't had anything!"

With a grin, he slammed the shot on the table and drank it with a gulp. "Happy now?"

Loretta was almost as bad at quarters as Robin was. After taking another drink, she said, "I have a confession to make. After I heard the weird noises, I was so scared I had a cigarette. Then another. I have a pack in my purse, and I know I shouldn't have put it there. My husband doesn't know. He's going to kill me."

Robin was pretty sure this was not going to be much of a revelation to Loretta's husband, since the woman wafted eau d'ashtray wherever she went. Unless her husband had no sense of smell whatsoever, it wouldn't be a major news bulletin. She waved her hand emphatically, "You have to quit! Smoking is bad for you. And you shouldn't smoke in your room. Yuck!"

Emily said, "Smoking causes more than eighty percent of lung cancers."

Loretta glared at Emily. "Don't you think I know that? My mother died of cancer. I was just so scared. But I know I need to quit."

Trudy put her arm around Loretta's shoulders, "Aww honey, I quit last year. It's hard. But there's a smoking cessation group near work. I'll give you the information when we get back."

After taking her shot, Moira said, "I have a confession too. I'm the one who put the half-eaten tuna sandwich into Claire's garbage can."

Claire glowered across the table at her. "That was you? What were you thinking? That was the most revolting thing anyone has ever done. That nasty thing sat in the can over the weekend and my desk smelled like a fishing trawler for a week! If you didn't want to smell that stink, what makes you think other people would?"

"I'm sorry. I was in a rush. I should have admitted what I did a long time ago."

With a small smile Claire said, "Well, you did find the feather for our team during the scavenger hunt, so maybe I can forgive you."

Nigel's quarter missed the glass and he took a shot. "Man, that was one rank fish smell. Legendary even. It stunk up the whole building. Even the memory grosses me out."

The quarter was passed her way, and Robin bounced it so it flipped across the table and clattered onto the floor again.

Nigel laughed. "I think you win the prize for distance, Robin." He tapped the table "The glass is right in front of you. You don't have to whack the quarter so hard. It's quarters, not hockey."

Robin gulped down her shot. "These are kind of yummy. I haven't had 7-Up in a long time."

Trudy held up the bottle. "Well, ladies and gentlemen, I think with that last shot, Robin has killed it."

Everyone slowly got up and began to stagger back to their bedrooms. Trudy walked over to Loretta and put her arm around her shoulders again, inclining her head to whisper something to her. Robin stayed where she was, since getting up seemed strangely difficult. She needed a few minutes to collect herself. Maybe that last shot wasn't such a good idea. She should have made Alec drink that one too. Leaning forward, she placed her forearms on the table and let her head rest on them, so that her forehead was touching the nice, cool wood. It was a relief to close her eyes.

At the touch of a warm hand on her shoulder, she raised her head and opened her eyes again. "What?"

Alec smiled at her. "I think you should go back to your cabin."

"I will." She put her head back down.

"Come on, Robin." He gently pulled at her arm and lifted her out of the chair.

She got up, put her tote bag over her shoulder, and suddenly was dizzy. "The room is spinning."

"I know. Let's go."

He put his arm around her and they walked outside. The fresh air and the support of Alec's arm improved matters. Robin smiled up at him. "I think I might really, really suck at quarters."

"I think you might be right."

At her door, she rummaged in her bag for her room key. She tried to put it in the lock but couldn't quite find it. Alec took the key from her and opened the door. "Are you going to be okay?"

"I'm fine." She staggered into the room and heard Leroy bark on the other side of the duplex. "Hi, Leroy!"

Alec followed her in and steered her toward the bed. "Why don't you lie down?"

Robin did as instructed and flopped down on her back. It was wonderful to be horizontal. She closed her eyes and felt Alec remove her shoes and pull the blanket over her. He whispered, "Have a good night," next to her ear and a few seconds later the door closed.

The last thing she heard before falling asleep was Leroy's happy barking. Soon she'd get to see Emma again. She missed her sweet little dog.

Chapter 9

Packing and Hints

The next morning Robin rolled over and opened her eyes, staring at the ceiling. She was still fully dressed, and she *badly* needed to brush her teeth. Yuck. What a strange evening. Did everyone in the world play quarters in college except her?

Although her stomach was queasy, it could have been a lot worse. Once, in college, she'd thrown up all over her roommate's sweater. That was an all-time low. Even though this wouldn't be the worst hangover she'd ever had, it would be unpleasant. Loretta had been looking pretty ragged last night too. It could be a slow morning for a lot of them.

After her arctic shower, Robin was more awake but still headachy and vaguely ill. She took a couple of aspirin and considered the day's activities. It was way too late to bring Emma out to the lodge, but she did need to call Kat and arrange a time to pick up Emma the next morning. Maybe Joel would have to carry the dog across the creek again. Kat hadn't sounded particularly optimistic about the state of their driveway the last time they had spoken.

Robin went back into the bathroom, pulled back her hair with a couple of combs, and tried to do something makeup-wise. It was a lost cause. Tequila certainly wasn't much of a beauty aid. Maybe no one would notice the dark circles under her eyes if she put on a little more mascara.

After giving up on looking anything close to pretty, she pulled on a sweater and walked up to the lodge to get some breakfast. Some toast might help. At the sound of a bark, Robin turned. Alec was coming up the path from the beach with Leroy. He waved and she stopped to wait for them.

Alec looked disgustingly hale and healthy. He grinned at her as he approached. "How are you feeling?"

"I've been better. I'm hoping food will help my stomach. Every once in a while, it does a little flip-flop to remind me that tequila is evil."

He laughed. "I doubt you're the first person to notice that fact."

She reached out to touch his forearm and met his gaze. "Thank you for taking me home. That was kind of you."

"No problem. I'm glad you're okay." He turned toward the Pine Cone cabin and called Leroy to follow him. "See you later."

In the dining room, Robin sat down at a table with some dry toast. Loretta sat down next to her and Robin noticed that her hands were shaking, but she didn't smell like cigarettes. Robin pointed at the plate in front of Loretta. "I think the toast is going to be a popular choice this morning."

Loretta picked up a slice and took a bite. "I feel a little sick. Since I feel terrible today anyway, and I'll be trapped in a van and an airplane tomorrow, I decided to quit cold-turkey."

"That's wonderful, Loretta. I know you can do it."

"Trudy and I talked last night. She is a lovely person and we have a lot in common. I feel better than I have in a long time...about a lot of things."

Robin put her hand on Loretta's to help still the trembling. "I'm so glad, Loretta."

They finished their toast and Robin returned to the Pine Cone to lie down for a while and let her stomach adjust to the presence of food. A thud that was undoubtedly Leroy bumbling around, and the low sound of Alec's voice came from the other side of the duplex. It was comforting somehow to know they were there. She closed her eyes and let sleep overtake her.

When she woke up, she looked at the old clock. It was almost lunchtime. She sat up and evaluated her condition. Her blouse was completely wrinkled, and it looked like she'd been run over. She needed to stop sleeping in her clothes. With a sigh, she got up and looked through her remaining wardrobe options.

The rest of the day was going to involve a lot of work packing up everything. She also needed to call Kat about Emma. At least after the nap she felt a bit better. She found another blouse in her closet that was somewhat more presentable and went over to the lodge. Kat said picking up Emma would not be a problem, since they had a rudimentary fix for the driveway.

After lunch, Robin attended the final training class, which was basically a question-and-answer session. When Terri asked a question about doing a product exchange, it occurred to Robin that the woman had not partaken of the evil tequila. Where had Terri been last night? After the drinking started, Robin had forgotten about her. Okay, after a week of animosity, maybe she *wanted* to forget about Terri. But Terri had not been a member of the slammer circle. Where had she disappeared to? Did she go off somewhere with Brett? Robin frowned slightly at the idea. Brett had enough problems without adding Terri to the equation. Poor guy.

The questions wound down and Alec dismissed the class early. As everyone filed out of the building, Robin stayed behind to help him pack. She walked around the table picking up papers and stacking them in her arms. She looked at him. "Do you want me to move my car closer, so we can throw all this into the back?"

He looked up from the easel he was disassembling. "That would be great."

They continued packing and Robin said, "I can't believe we're almost done with this retreat. This has been one heck of a bizarre week with you and Leroy scaring me, Ernie disappearing, and that awful storm. At least the complaining slowed down a little. I was about ready to smack Emily if she mentioned her dripping faucet again."

Alec grinned. "You're too nice to smack her."

"Maybe. But it doesn't mean I didn't want to. Even Terri shut up about that problem with her closet door. She hates me, so I figured she'd keep whining at me until I got in my car and left."

"I'm sure she doesn't hate you."

Robin put her hand on her hip. "She tried to kill me with a tree."

"I think you're exaggerating."

"Well Brett apologized, which I thought was really sweet of him. It wasn't his fault, but he said he should have been paying more attention."

Alec threw a pile of catalogs into a box with a forceful thump. "I suppose."

She stopped and looked at him. "Is something wrong?"

"No. Well, not really." He shrugged. "You'll think I'm an idiot, but I'm actually going to miss this place."

She smiled. "You do seem more relaxed. I'll miss it too. I know we had problems, but it's beautiful here and I loved walking all over the property every day—even when it was pouring rain! After ghosts and scavenger hunts, spending all day staring at inventory spreadsheets again is going to seem sort of tame by comparison."

He laughed. "No kidding."

~

Robin went back to her cabin and resumed packing. She was supposed to make an announcement at dinner about reviews. Darrell had told her that after they returned to Portland, everyone would fill out an evaluation of the retreat. Knowing that Terri would be spelling out her litany of complaints in excruciating detail was depressing. It would be a miracle if Robin didn't get fired, and the worst part was that none of the problems were her fault. After his one appearance after dinner, Ernie had been MIA again. Although she wasn't worried he was dead anymore, the fact that he was never around his own lodge was disconcerting.

At dinner, Robin ended up seated next to Nigel and Angela who were chatting happily about going home and seeing friends and family. Angela said, "My husband has had to deal with two teenage boys for a whole week all by himself. I think he'll have a new appreciation for all the things I do around there."

At a break in the conversation during dessert, Robin clinked her glass a few times and stood up. She cleared her throat and waited for the chatter to subside. Finally, Nigel uttered an incredibly loud, jarring whistle and everyone was silent.

Robin smiled at him. "Thanks. Everyone, I have to make a little announcement before you all get ready to go home. When you return to work next week, you'll receive an evaluation form, so you can review this retreat and your experience. Darrell has asked me to tell you that he would like you to fill it out completely and honestly. I'll probably see you tomorrow when you check out, but I hope you all have a safe trip back to Portland." Robin sat down and breathed a sigh of relief. At last, her final official duty was complete.

Emily said, "An evaluation? Does that mean we're going to have to do this *again*?"

Robin shook her head. "I have no idea."

Terri said, "We'd better not. I certainly never want a repeat of that stupid team-building stuff!"

"I have an idea!" Nigel waved his hand. "What if we all say it's great? Darrell will assume everything went off perfectly and he'll decide everything is fine, right? We're all a team and have had all the training we could possibly have. Everything is marvelous and we're done forever!"

Alec made a wry face. "Maybe. Or he'll think it's such a fantastic idea, he'll turn it into an annual event."

"He wouldn't do that. We're already trained! What more could we learn?" Nigel said. "If we say we didn't learn anything, we'll have to do more training."

"Ugh." Terri put her forehead on her palm. "I have *got* to find a new job."

Emily said, "I think Nigel is right. Let's all agree to say the retreat was fine. Good, even." She smiled at Alec. "With special kudos to Alec for fixing the sink in my room!"

"And the broken drawer in mine." Moira said, "Yes, three cheers for Alec!"

A few more people mentioned other things Alec had fixed and Robin smiled at the uncomfortable look on his face. He got up and said, "It was no big deal. And now I need to finish packing. Safe travels everyone. I'll see you back in Portland."

More people thanked him before he left the lodge. Robin nibbled around the edges of her cookie. How had he fixed all those things? And *when* had he? No wonder the complaints had died down.

She got up, wished everyone a good night, and walked out into the darkness. A bark broke the stillness and Robin recognized it as a happy Leroy woof. Alec must have taken the dog for an evening outing. She walked down the path toward her cabin and looked up across the lake. The Milky Way was shining brightly, a band of sparkles across the huge blue-black expanse of sky, which made her perpetual worries about losing her job seem insignificant. Just one minuscule event affecting one tiny being in an enormous galaxy. If she had to get a new job and move, she'd figure something else out. She always did.

Leroy bounded up to her with the rope in his mouth. Robin took the end of the rope. "Hi Leroy. You're into this tug-of-war thing, aren't you? If you let go, I can throw it for you."

Alec walked up. "If you say, 'drop it,' he will."

She looked down at the dog. "Leroy, *drop it*."

The dog released his lower jaw, and the rope plopped to the ground. Robin bent to pick it up and threw it down the path. Leroy bounded after it, snuffling along the ground in the area where the rope had landed.

Robin said, "I'm guessing Leroy is going home with you."

"Yes. No one has called. The vet gave him a clean bill of health today. He's all vaccinated and legal now. I just need to put his new rabies tag on his collar. She also recommended some food to help fatten him up a little."

"Make sure you get an ID tag, but get a permanent marker and write your phone number on his collar too." Leroy bumped her leg with his nose and Robin threw the rope again. "I didn't realize you were fixing half the lodge this week."

"It's kind of falling apart. But it didn't take much to repair the little annoying things people were complaining about." He picked up the rope Leroy had dropped at his feet and threw it. "I don't understand why Ernie doesn't fix it up."

"Where did you find tools?"

"I had them with me."

Robin gestured back toward the lodge as they walked. "Who brings tools to call-center training?"

"They were in the Jeep, which I borrowed from my dad because I had to haul so much junk down here. My car is too small."

"What does your father do?"

"For years he was an electrician, but now he manages part of the complex where I live."

Robin turned to throw the rope. "That's great! Dad can be your dog walker."

"I don't think so. I'll ask him, but his arthritis is getting worse and I bet he'll say no. That's why he sold the business. All those years crawling around under houses in the mud is hard on your joints."

"I suppose so. I bet he'll love Leroy though."

Alec grinned. "Yeah, and like you said, I can get a dog walker to come in and give Leroy some exercise during the day."

Robin stopped at the path that led to her side of the Pine Cone cabin and faced him. "Well, I guess I'll see you back at work, assuming I still am employed after Darrell sees the reviews."

"I think you will be. You did a good job. I'll vouch for you, if that's what you want." His gaze met hers and he stepped closer to her. Extremely close, so their legs were practically touching. "Is that what you want?"

Robin stood mutely, staring into his eyes, which were an intense teal blue in the dim light. Unable to think of anything, she mumbled, "Um," as he tilted his head to kiss her. The kiss was gentle at first, then increased in intensity as he pulled her closer. Electric thrills shot through her body and Robin threw her arms around his neck. It had been so long since she had been in a man's arms. She'd been lonely for what seemed like forever. The contact was warm and intoxicating. One of the combs in her hair fell out and landed on the ground, but she didn't care. It would be fine with her if he never let go.

With a low groan, Alec stepped back, away from her. "I'm sorry. I've wanted to do that for a long time, but I shouldn't have. It was extremely unprofessional."

"Unprofessional? What do you mean unprofessional?" Robin said breathlessly. More like amazing. Hadn't he noticed? It couldn't just be her imagination. Could it? She put her hand on her chest, trying to catch her breath. "And you're sorry? Are you frickin' *kidding* me?"

He picked up the comb and handed it to her. "We work together."

"Yes, I'm well aware of that. But I barely saw you before this week. You were a name on an email."

"I haven't looked at an org chart lately, but technically, you probably work for me."

Robin glanced down at Leroy, who was sitting next to them with a concerned look on his face. "It's okay, Leroy." She looked at Alec again. Now that her heart rate and hormones had settled down a bit, her mental faculties were returning, along with a serious case of frustration-induced anger. "I promise I won't sue you for harassment. Is that what you're getting at?"

"No. It's just that getting involved with people from work isn't a good idea."

"*Son of a motherless goat!* I don't believe this. You've got a whole lot of nerve." Robin jammed the comb back into her hair. "Fine. I can take a hint." The sad lack of male company since she'd moved meant it had been a while since she'd been rejected too. As it turned out, the experience was even less fun than she remembered.

Alec took her hand and gave it a squeeze. "I'm sorry. Drive safely, okay?"

Robin shook her hand out of his and nodded, too infuriated to look at his face. She bent to give Leroy a goodbye pat. "Be good and have fun in your new home."

~

Robin slept fitfully, having spent most of the night reliving the kiss with Alec in her mind. What had happened? Yes, she hadn't had a date since she'd moved to Portland, but she couldn't have forgotten everything, could she? It hadn't been *that* long. Finally, she gave up on sleep, figuring that for once, the cold shower in her cabin might be a good thing.

She went to the front desk and collected all the keys as everyone checked out. The key to Pine Cone 2 was already on its hook, which wasn't a surprise. She knew Alec and Leroy had left at the crack of dawn. She rolled the office chair across the floor. It was no longer rickety. Apparently, Alec had fixed the wobbly chair at some point too.

After throwing the last suitcases into her car and writing a note to Ernie, she stood and stared out at the lake. It was a glorious morning, as if the sun were making up for its frequent absences during the last week. The air was vibrant and pine-scented. Taking one last deep breath, she got into her car and drove north toward Alpine Grove and Kat's house.

She slowed the car at the turn to the driveway. The creek was flowing through a large, shiny metal pipe that was covered with a lot of large rocks. A makeshift bridge had been constructed out of a number of long pieces of wood that traversed the rocks. Robin carefully drove across the bridge and down the long, muddy driveway to the house.

As she parked her car, she glanced in her rearview mirror. Kat was walking down the front steps of the house with Emma. Robin rushed out of the car, crouched, and held out her hands. Kat dropped the leash and Emma ran into Robin's arms. After getting many doggie kisses from Emma, Robin stood and picked up the leash. "Are you ready to go home, Em?" The dog danced around her with delight.

Kat walked up to them and smiled. "I love a happy reunion."

Robin untangled herself from the leash. "Let me put her in the car." After loading the dog into the backseat, she turned back to Kat and handed her a check. "I have a little cash-flow problem. It would be great if you could wait a week to deposit this. I put the date on the check. That's when my next paycheck comes in. Otherwise this check might not clear. I'm getting reimbursed for my expenses on this trip, but I'm not sure how long that will take."

Kat looked down at the piece of paper. "All right."

"I'm so sorry. This is embarrassing. But moving to Portland cost a fortune. Sometimes I wish I'd never taken this job."

"Well, no job is forever. If you don't like it, you can always do something else."

"I know, although I'm not sure what I'd do. I'm afraid I still haven't figured out what I want to be when I grow up."

Kat grinned. "Join the club."

Robin gestured toward the forest. "But you seem so settled. And you're doing the whole dog-boarding business and everything."

"In between panic attacks, yes. Starting a business is expensive." She pointed at the house. "Fortunately, Joel and my friend Maria spend a lot of time talking me down from the ledge."

Robin laughed. "You're lucky. I think the thing I miss most is just hanging out with my friends. Talking on the phone isn't the same."

"I'm sure you'll make new friends. I'm amazed how many people I've met since I moved here."

"It's different in a small town, I think. I spend all day working and never meet anyone new. And most of the people I work with are women. At this rate, I may never go on a date again."

Kat grinned, "Don't feel bad. My friend Maria is having the same problem here. She refers to Alpine Grove as a dating wasteland."

Robin said, "It's a good thing I'm leaving then. I certainly have enough problems in that area as it is." Being so egregiously rejected by Alec hadn't exactly done much to build her confidence either.

They said goodbye and Robin set out for home. Emma curled up in the backseat and settled in for the long ride. Robin was glad to have some time to think. What she'd said to Kat was true. Here she was, more than thirty years old, and she had never figured out a real career. It was just plain sad. In college, she'd majored in business and that had led to various boring jobs that mostly didn't use her degree. It didn't matter though, since it wasn't like she was utterly enthralled with business or the classes she had taken. In high school, her friend Amanda had been a math whiz, so it was no surprise when she majored in math and went on to get her PhD. She had loved math and everything to do with numbers forever. Now she was teaching math and got to talk about what she loved every day.

No one specific thing had ever interested Robin so much that she wanted to spend all day every day doing it. She was interested in lots of different things. Even though Robin liked science okay in school, she couldn't imagine how scientists could stand talking about nothing except science all day. How could anyone stand it? Robin's lack of specialized expertise was like the old saying—she was a Jacqueline of all trades and master of none.

Everyone seemed to have a dream job in mind except her. What were you supposed to do if you didn't know what your dream job was? Maybe something was wrong with her. All the career guides talked about combining your skills with your passion. But she wasn't particularly passionate about anything. Robin was sort of good at a lot of things, but not *really* good at one specific thing.

It had always been that way. Being average was so boring. Every time she read her alumni magazine, she got depressed. It seemed like all of her classmates were busily climbing the career ladder while she was still flailing around trying to get off the bottom rung. She couldn't even pay for dog boarding. How pathetic was that?

Everyone always said that Robin was great at dealing with people. That was her only definable skill, and she'd demonstrated it again by not killing Terri or anyone else at the retreat. But "able to put up with other people's petty nonsense" wasn't exactly something you could put on a resume.

Robin's experience with putting numbers into spreadsheet software was quantifiable, and it seemed like that was all the drones in human resources departments cared about. Most of the jobs she'd had bored her silly, and Eagle River was turning out to be no exception. How did those people in the magazines end up being vice-presidents at twenty-five? What secret did they have? Were they really so different? Maybe it was that elusive passion for something. Or more experimentation with new experiences. Robin could be like Grandma Moses and finally discover her true gift when she was in her seventies. Oh boy, only forty years to go.

If nothing else, the retreat had been a good escape from her regular life. Even if it hadn't been a vacation, she'd done a lot of different things and had new experiences. She'd solved problems and made things happen. And for once, she hadn't been bored. Not even once. So that was definitely an improvement.

Emma sat up in the backseat and stared out the window at the countryside flying by. Robin glanced in her rearview mirror and smiled at the contemplative look on the dog's face. "Oh Em, I wish I didn't have to go back to work. Maybe I should try to find another job. *Again.* Ugh, what are we going to do?"

Emma wagged her tail enthusiastically, but didn't seem to have any answers.

Robin sighed. "Yeah, I have no clue either."

∿

Kat walked in the front door, took off her coat, and went into the kitchen. Joel was sitting at the dining room table eating a sandwich. He had a number of purplish bruises on his forearms from various mishaps with wayward rocks during the Great Culvert Replacement Project. Kat's body had been equally battered by the experience. It would be a relief once the load limits were removed from the roads. Then they could have a truck come out with a big load of rock that would fix the entrance to the driveway permanently, so they could get rid of the temporary bridge. Joel had suggested that they redo the entire driveway all the way up to the house at the same time. It was a reasonable, if expensive, suggestion, since dodging the sucking mud bogs and swampy craters had become virtually impossible.

He put the sandwich down on the plate. "Is Emma gone?"

"Yes. Emma and Robin were so happy to see each other—it was cute." Kat flipped the check onto the table. "I can't do anything with this yet though. Apparently Robin is having financial problems."

Joel sighed and rubbed his eyes with his fists. "Great."

"I know. I've got to be the world's worst businesswoman. You know how Robin has that sweet sugary voice? It kind of makes you want to just nod and agree with anything she says. I just stood there like an idiot when she was talking about the money."

He scratched his chin. "Have you talked to Maria?"

"Not lately. She called and left a message the other day while I was standing in the creek and dragging rocks around with you."

"Okay."

Kat sat down in the chair next to him. "Is this seriously bothering you?"

"Yes."

"I don't see why. I called the people in Clark County, Nevada. No one with my name got a license to marry Ned."

"I know."

"I don't understand why you think I need to talk to Ned. Because I'd rather not."

"You know what didn't happen. Don't you want to know what *did* happen?"

"Not really."

He looked at her. "I do. You don't just abandon a woman in a bathroom in the middle of the desert for no reason."

"Well of course, *you* wouldn't. But you're not a loser. Trying to understand the inner workings of a loser's mind… well, to be honest, I don't think you can do it."

Joel shook his head. "It seems so wrong. I mean, he had to have stolen something. Or done something. You don't run for no reason. If he wasn't out to marry you, why go to Vegas? It doesn't make any sense."

"Not everyone is as rational as you are. But Maria said she'd ask around and see if anyone knows where he is now. The guy was Sharon's friend. I didn't know her well, but Maria is still in touch." Kat stood up, walked behind his chair, and started rubbing his shoulders. "I don't see why you care."

Joel groaned and leaned his forehead on the table so Kat could reach more sore muscles. "I don't know. It's probably stupid, but it bugs me."

Kat bent to kiss his neck. She whispered in his ear. "This may come as a shock, but I have no interest in seeing or hearing anything about Ned ever again. I love *you*."

He sat up straight and put his arms around her, pulling her into his lap. "I know. And I love you back. I just hate unanswered questions."

"I wish I'd never told you about this, not only because it's completely humiliating, but because you can't seem to forget about it and let it go."

He arched an eyebrow. "It took you a while to get over the supermodel thing."

"Touché."

"I was wondering why you decided to tell me about this now."

"What do you mean? I said I'm sorry it took me so long to muster up the courage. I was scared of what you'd think."

"I understand. But why now?"

Kat rested her head on his chest. "Well, Maria and I were talking about the invitation I got to Beth and Drew's wedding, so the topic of marriage came up."

"Like whether you were or not?"

"Not exactly. We've already hashed over that question many, many times. I've been lectured to about Ned the Loser more times than I care to think about. But in this case, Maria wanted to know if you were for or against the institution."

"Me? You mean the institution of marriage?"

"Yes. I told her I didn't know because we've never talked about it."

"Oh."

"So would you care to share your thoughts on the matter? Are you for or against?"

Joel squirmed in the chair and looked into her eyes. "Well, *for* I guess, if I were marrying the right person."

"Okay. That's good to know."

He tickled her waist. "So what are *your* thoughts on the institution?"

"Cut that out!" She kissed his neck. "Definitely against if it's someone like Ned. But I agree that I'm for the idea if you're marrying the right person for the right reasons."

"What do you regard as the right reasons?"

She faced him again. "Well, the typical reasons. Loving the other person, for one. And wanting to spend the rest of your life with that person."

"Those are good reasons. Romantic reasons." He kissed her. "But marriage also has legal and social implications. Combining finances. And potentially owning property, doing taxes, and having children together."

Kat's eyes widened. "Well, uh, you and I talked about kids before. I'm definitely not ready for that yet. At this point, you're pretty much living with everything that's mine."

He grinned. "So what you're saying is that your dowry includes lots of dog and cat hair."

"Yes. Sorry about that."

"My dog has contributed to the dog hair."

"So we haven't combined finances, but we have combined dog hair."

"Something like that." Joel splayed his hands across her back and started kneading her muscles. Kat collapsed like an overcooked noodle across his chest and wrapped her arms around him so she could massage his back in exchange. She gasped as he found a particularly sore spot and pressed his knuckle into it. She pressed her fingertips into his back, "I never *ever* want to move that many rocks again. Every muscle in my entire body aches."

Joel moaned and leaned his head forward. "Yes. Right there."

"I still owe you for the culvert. I'll write you a check later."

"Consider it a gift. Just keep doing whatever it is you're doing. I think moving that last boulder did me in."

"And you say I'm a romantic. No one has ever given me a culvert before."

He kissed her and smiled. "Nothing says 'I love you' like shiny, new corrugated steel pipe."

~

Bright and early Monday morning, Robin settled into her cubicle. Everything looked exactly the same. The same gray fabric walls. The same irritating low hum of conversation. And some literal humming from a peculiar little man named Barney who hummed to himself all the time for no apparent reason. And with no apparent tune. A few cubicles down, the woman with the perpetual allergies snuffled and coughed loudly. Although her name was Alice, in her head Robin referred to her as The Sniffler. More than once, she'd considered buying a case of Kleenex and placing it in Alice's cubby as a little hint.

Flipping the power switch on her computer, Robin waited while it went through its whole aggravating start-up parade. She opened her email program and started the laborious process of sorting through her email. It appeared that she had been copied on a whole lot of email that didn't have anything to do with her. Somebody needed a few lessons in the right way to use the "cc" and "reply to all" features.

Robin rested her elbow on the desk and scanned the list. Inventory problems. A screwed-up shipment that was supposed to have gone to the distribution center in West Virginia. A new project led by a manager who was desperately trying to make it sound more interesting than it was. Purchase orders. There were even a few missives from the guy who invariably included the words MY RESPONSE in all caps in the subject line. No one actually knew why he felt compelled to proclaim this fact on every single email. What the heck? Everyone knew it was his response. Duh.

She sighed at the sight of an invitation to a meeting with Darrell and Alec later in the day. Maybe they were going to fire her. Great. Would unemployment be enough to cover her rent? Probably not.

With a click on the icon to open her spreadsheet software, she tried to jump-start her brain and get back into the swing of things. Maybe she needed more coffee. Yes. Coffee. That might help.

Consuming several cups of coffee made it possible for Robin to slog through the rest of her morning. She picked up a notebook and grabbed the business card for her dog-walker out of her Rolodex for Alec. Leroy probably was working on adjusting to his new life. Maybe he'd even met Alec's dad by now. Robin smiled at the idea of Alec's little surprise for his father. Who wouldn't love a big goofy white dog like Leroy?

She walked over to the executive building and peered through the glass wall at Alec and Darrell. Alec was facing the glass and Darrell's back was to her, so she couldn't see his face. Alec was wearing a suit and tie, although it looked like he'd yanked the knot of the tie down away from his neck. His head was bowed and his hands were fisted in his hair. It looked like he was literally tearing his hair out. Ouch. That had to hurt.

He raised his head and his eyes widened slightly as he noticed Robin. Darrell turned and waved, encouraging her to come into the room. She opened the door, placed her notebook on the table, and sat down. After seeing Alec in his beat-up old jeans and Trailblazers t-shirt at the retreat, it was odd to see him dressed this way. That suit probably cost more than her car. She'd have to check the label to be sure, but she guessed it was Armani. It had to be custom made because it fit him perfectly. Wow.

Darrell glared at Alec before saying, "Okay, new topic. Robin, what were your impressions of the retreat?"

She glanced quickly at Alec, who was tapping his fingers on the table. The expression on his face didn't reveal much beyond the fact that he wasn't happy about something. "Well, I think progress was made as far as bringing people together." She gestured toward Alec. "And the training was well received. I know I learned a lot."

At her comment, the corner of Alec's mouth twitched, although the scowl didn't leave his face. He turned to Darrell. "I'm telling you, I think there might be something wrong. You need to talk to your uncle. He was never there—I saw him maybe twice. And the place is falling apart."

Darrell waved off the comment. "I went over to the call-center building this morning, and the difference was shocking. A woman from High Country was laughing with someone who has worked here for ages. I can't remember her name, but she's a big woman. Double chin, shoulder-length straight brown hair?"

Robin said, "Oh, that's Loretta. She was probably talking to Trudy. I think they're friends now."

"That's incredible." Darrell said. "Robin, the evaluations will give me the whole story, but so far, it seems like you have done a great job in pulling this off in a short time frame. I don't know what you did, but it worked. Make sure you get your expenses into accounting."

The dismissive tone in Darrell's voice indicated that Robin's part of the meeting had concluded. She stood up and picked up her notebook. "I will. Thank you."

Glancing at Alec, she stopped. "Oops, I almost forgot." She pulled the business card out of the notebook and handed it to him. "This is my dog-walker's card. The company is great."

Alec flipped the card around in his fingertips. "Thanks."

She hurriedly left the room, but peeked over her shoulder. Whatever Darrell was telling Alec definitely was not going over well. At least life in her ugly gray cubicle wasn't particularly stressful, but it appeared the same was not true of Alec's work life. Although he might be dressed better than he was at the retreat, he looked much worse. By the end of the week in Alpine Grove, Robin had forgotten how twitchy and jittery he'd been when they first met.

Here at work, Alec behaved like a nervous animal in a cage. Maybe going home and spending time with Leroy would help. Taking Emma for walks definitely helped Robin deal with the tedious monotony of her job every day. Maybe having Leroy around would help Alec too. She hoped so.

Even though she was still annoyed at the way he'd rejected her after shooting her hormones into overdrive, he'd also been really sweet after she'd had all those tequila slammers. He wasn't a bad person and she missed their walks around the lodge with Leroy, just hanging out and talking. It was distressing to see him so obviously unhappy.

Chapter 10

Performance Art

A few days later, Robin was staring at a spreadsheet wondering what she had done to make the formula in cell F135 stop working. It looked like it *should* work. She didn't think she'd changed anything and nothing else looked different. But the number it had calculated was impossible unless she was planning to ship something to outer space.

Barney the humming dude made a little squeaky noise and stopped humming. Someone shuffled some papers, the Sniffler snuffled extra loudly, and another woman whispered something. Robin turned to look behind her and discovered Alec standing in her cubicle. He looked like he should be on the cover of *Hot Young Executive* magazine. No wonder there had been a stirring amid her fellow cubicle dwellers. She looked up at his face. "Are you lost?"

His hands were in his pockets and he rocked back and forth on the balls of his feet. "No. I need to talk to you. Could you come with me, please?"

Robin clicked the mouse a few times to save the dysfunctional spreadsheet. Maybe Darrell had read the reviews and sent Alec here to fire her. "Do we have another meeting? I didn't get an invitation. I hope my email isn't acting up again. I'm pretty sure the people in IT are sick of me."

He turned and started walking down the corridor. She scurried to catch up with him. "Hey, slow down. What's the big rush?"

Slowing his pace, he turned his head to glance at her. "Let's go outside."

Robin looked around her. "Why? What do you need to talk about?" Although she had a pretty good idea she knew, she wanted to hear him say it. Everyone had *agreed* to say the retreat was fine. She was going to be so angry if they all went back on their word.

He pressed open the glass door for her. "Look, natural light."

"Are you sure that's allowed at Eagle River? How can I possibly work without a fluorescent tube buzzing above my head?"

"I think you'll manage."

"Where are we going?"

"To my car."

He was walking fast again and Robin increased her pace. Who fired someone in a car? That was too weird. Maybe she wasn't losing her job, after all. "Are you kidnapping me from work? I'm not an expert in human resources, but I'm pretty sure company policy discourages playing hooky."

"Then I'm taking you to lunch."

As they walked across the parking lot, she waggled her fingertips at him. "Oooh, my first executive luncheon."

He stopped at a deep-blue two-door convertible Mercedes, unlocked it, and opened the door for her. "Hop in."

"*Holy snapping turtles! This* is your car?" Robin stroked the soft tan leather seat. "Mmmm." Alec must want to talk about something other than her job. No one could possibly get fired in a car this pretty.

He started the car and let it purr for a moment. "Is it okay if we leave the top down? It's nice out for a change."

Robin grinned. "Definitely."

"You might want to do something with your hair or it will get tangled."

"Good point." She rummaged around in her purse, found an elastic band, and put her hair in a ponytail. "Okay, I'm ready. Where are we going?"

"Away from here."

As they drove, Robin relaxed and enjoyed the ride, marveling at the flowers that were blooming everywhere. Everyone had told her that she would love Portland in the spring. It was true—every plant in the city seemed to have awakened and it was truly gorgeous with vibrant color exploding everywhere she looked. Almost everyone who lived here seemed to have a garden, and the plants were bursting with springtime joy. At some point, she wanted to go see the International Rose Test Garden. It was supposed to be spectacular.

Alec drove toward the northwest side of the city, navigating through a bunch of swanky neighborhoods filled with lots of adorable upscale restaurants and shops. It was so pretty over here in the hills. Everything was so tidy, leafy, and opulent.

Alec slowed the car to turn into a driveway and stopped in front of a tall wrought-iron gate. Robin said, "Did you take a wrong turn? Do we need to go the other way?"

Reaching from the driver's seat, Alec pressed some buttons on a panel in front of the gate. "No. I want to check on Leroy."

"Is he okay? Nothing is wrong with him, is there?"

"He's probably fine. I wanted to get out of the office, so I thought I'd take the opportunity to give him another walk." He looked at her. "Is that okay?"

Robin looked around. "Good gravy, I can't believe you live in Nob Hill. It must be nice to be close enough that you can zip home like this. I live way over on the other side of the city. If there's any traffic at all, it's kind of a pain to get to my place."

They got out of the car and Robin looked around at the green lushness that wound through the condo complex. The gardens were beautifully maintained and it was so peaceful, it was as if she'd left the city entirely. Having worked for Eagle River for so long, Alec probably had money. Given his car and the swanky neighborhood, maybe he had a whole *lot* of money. Why hadn't she ever thought about that before? She knew the company had gone public at some point. Maybe he was a stockholder? It was so far outside of Robin's realm of experience that she had no clue how any of that even worked. She lived in a crumbly old house that had been converted into four rental apartments. It was a cute space, but the neighborhood was often loud. People were always walking by on their way to the funky thrift stores and a popular Indian restaurant that was located nearby.

Alec opened the door and Leroy barked a greeting as he skittered to the door, the clatter of his claws on the shiny hardwood floors breaking the stillness of the cool room. Alec and Robin walked into a large foyer with a mirrored wall. The living room had a fireplace and huge windows that looked out onto a deck and hillside view beyond. Although the space was utterly gorgeous, with the exception of some tufts of white dog hair on the floor, it looked like no one lived here. The place was like a model home. Given what a slob Alec was, he must have one heck of a cleaning service. Robin bent to pet Leroy. "Hey, it's so good to see you! Emma says hi."

Alec grabbed a leash off a hook in the kitchen and clicked it onto Leroy's collar. "All right, let's go."

"Where are we going?"

"We can walk over to a cafe that has outside seating. I'm trying to give Leroy more experience in behaving himself around people. He tends to get a little overly excited."

Robin giggled. "That's easy to imagine."

As they walked, Alec seemed to relax again. The pinched, perpetually annoyed look he had at work left his face as they strolled along the crowded sidewalks. Leroy was extremely enthusiastic about the impromptu neighborhood excursion, so Alec was mostly focused on keeping the large dog under control.

They walked in companionable silence for a while. Finally, Robin was too curious not to ask. "So, you brought me all the way out here and now you're going to feed me lunch. What did you want to talk to me about so badly?"

He stopped at the edge of the sidewalk, next to a gray stone wall, and told Leroy to sit. Turning to face Robin, he said, "I was wrong."

She moved off to the side next to Alec to let people pass. "About what? Did I say something I shouldn't have in the meeting the other day? I tried to remain professional. Maybe

I should have waited to give you that business card until Darrell wasn't around, but I work in another building, so I never see you. I didn't want to forget, since I know you need a dog walker."

He looked into her eyes. "No. The meeting was fine. I thought it would be a problem to see you at work."

"I don't think you have to worry about seeing me. I hardly ever leave my cubicle."

"I know. I can't stand it." He reached out to take her hand. "I can't stop thinking about you."

She squeezed his hand. "What are you saying? I still work for you. Or somebody. I never looked at the stupid org chart."

Alec pulled her closer to him. "I don't care."

Her proximity to the warmth of Alec's body awakened the memory of the last time they had been standing close like this and Robin smiled, "Really?"

Inclining his head to kiss her, he whispered, "I missed you."

Although he probably only intended to give her a peck on the lips, Robin eagerly returned the kiss, throwing her arms around him and melding her body to his as she reveled in the sensations. His fist holding the leash pressed into her back as he pulled her closer.

Someone walking by bumped into them and grumbled a half-hearted "sorry." With a giggle, Robin looked down. Leroy's large furry body was creating a serious impediment to pedestrian traffic. She took Alec's hand again. "I missed you too. But maybe we should get out of the way and go have lunch."

He brought her hand to his lips and kissed it. "Let's go."

~

At the cafe, any residual awkwardness from work evaporated and Alec's sense of humor returned. Robin laughed at his stories about his drive back to Portland from Alpine Grove. He'd stayed with his brother in San Francisco and poor Leroy didn't know what to make of the crowds and noise from unfamiliar things like cable cars. Alec stroked the dog's head. "This guy has had a lot to deal with over the last couple weeks, but he's doing really well."

Robin smiled. "That's because he loves you. It's so sweet. Dogs are wonderful that way. No matter how awful your day is, when you come home, they are thrilled to see you."

Alec looked down at Leroy. "I think the only bad thing is that witnessing all that joy makes you realize you can't remember the last time you actually experienced that kind of joy yourself." He looked at Robin. "Even though doing the training was a pain, I liked Alpine Grove, and even the broken-down lodge. It was nice just fixing things, walking the dog, looking at the lake. I haven't felt that good in a long, long time."

"It sounds like you seriously need a vacation." Robin nibbled on a potato chip. "But I know what you mean. Driving home, I had a lot of time to think. Am I truly going to spend the rest of my life putting numbers into spreadsheets? Is that what my life is going to be about? Eight hours a day, five days a week? How pathetic is that? But at this point, it's the only thing anyone will hire me to do. It's sad to think that *this* is my so-called career."

Alec put his hand over hers on the table. "You could do something else if you wanted to. There are lots of other things you could do. You were amazing at the retreat. Even Darrell thought so. You found people to clean that place, which was a miracle in itself. And somehow you even managed to get me to pay for it. Then you kept everyone happy and fed without any help from the slightly strange absentee owner."

She grinned. "Thank your lucky stars Chuck and the roadies showed up, or we all would have starved to death. It's also a good thing you brought your dad's tools."

"I think you're underestimating what it takes to operate a lodge like that. It's difficult for most people to deal with that many people and details every day. You could run a hotel or a bed and breakfast."

"It's no big deal. I make a lot of lists. And it doesn't matter, because no one would hire me. All anyone looks at is my past experience and the software programs I know how to use."

He squeezed her hand. "Don't sell yourself short."

Robin shrugged. He probably had no idea what it was like out there in the cold, unforgiving world of employment-seeking. When was the last time Alec had even looked for a job? She was pretty sure things were different over there in the executive suite.

Alec glanced at his watch and waved for the check. "We need to get back. I have a meeting later."

On the way back to Alec's condo, they held hands as they navigated the crowds on the sidewalk. Leroy led the way as if he knew where he was going.

At the condo, Robin waited in the hallway while Alec settled Leroy in with a toy filled with peanut butter. Once the dog was contentedly chewing, Alec walked toward Robin. Her heart rate increased again as he approached. Placing his hands on either side of her neck, he bent to kiss her. Something about the way he moved his lips was crazily sensual. The kiss was overwhelming and exciting to the point that her knees went weak. Who knew that was a real thing? Falling down in a heap right there in front of the door might be embarrassing, but it would totally be worth it. By the time Alec released her, they both were breathing heavily. Robin gulped. "*Jiminy crickets*. My lunch breaks aren't usually this exciting."

He grinned. "I know. I'm going to be so late for this budget meeting. Ralph is going to have a coronary."

"Ralph Andrews, the CFO?"

"Yes. I'm not sure the man has ever laughed in his life. This is not going to be fun at all. I was supposed to review the numbers at lunch, but obviously I didn't. We need to go."

They walked back to the car and Alec opened the door for her. "Even though I'd like to, I can't ditch work like this every day. I've got back-to-back meetings the rest of the week. In addition to the budget meetings, one of the photographers quit and the person who was supposed to be managing the catalog photography while I was gone completely screwed it up. Sue is furious, but she's still dealing with the copy situation, so now the photo mess is my problem."

Robin made a face. "That sounds like almost as much fun as my broken spreadsheet."

"Believe me, it's not." He leaned over, cupped her cheek with his hand, and looked into her eyes. "But I want to spend more time with you. I told Darrell that for a change, I am not working this weekend, no matter how far behind I am. Are you free?"

She nodded. "Where do you want to go?"

"There's a street fair. You could bring Emma. Maybe we can go to a park too. I read in the paper, although people are fighting about it, that a few of the city parks are allowing dogs now."

"That sounds great. I think Emma misses Alpine Grove. The place she was staying had all these trails through the forest. I think she got a lot more exercise there."

"So did Leroy." He smiled. "I guess I did too. And it was more fun than going to the Eagle River gym, which half the time I can't get to anyway, because of meetings."

As they got closer to work, Alec became more subdued. Having a conversation in a convertible was challenging anyway, but Robin could sense his mood deteriorating. She didn't understand it. Why did he continue to work doing a job he so obviously didn't enjoy? Was it the money? She ran her fingertips across the soft leather interior of the Mercedes. How much money did one person need? The money from this car could pay her rent for two or three years. Maybe longer. Why didn't he just find a new job? Of course, she was one to talk. It wasn't like she was doing terribly well on the employment front herself, so what did she know?

What she did know was that she liked Alec and had definite difficulties keeping her hands off him. He might be depressed about work half the time, but the other half of the time he was totally sexy. Robin smiled happily at the cityscape racing by the window. The upcoming weekend could be a lot of fun.

～

The next couple of days passed at a glacial pace and Robin pondered updating her resume again. Somehow, getting away and doing something different had led her to question everything. After college, she'd coasted for years, mostly hanging out with her friends and not thinking much about work, the future, or what she was doing with her life. It just was.

Now that most of her friends were far away and she only talked to them on the phone, it was harder to escape the fact that their lives were moving forward, while hers was not. Most of the people she had known in high school and college had careers, were getting married and having kids or traveling to amazing far-away places.

Everyone else seemed to be creating interesting lives for themselves, while she was still cooped up in a cubicle entering numbers in spreadsheets. She had been so sure that moving to Portland would change everything. It was supposed to be such a cool, hip place to be. Certainly more interesting than Spokane, which was a utilitarian northwest city suffering from a serious inferiority complex. The reality of moving was that it hadn't suddenly made her cool, just broke. When had she turned into such a painfully boring person?

At least going to Alpine Grove and meeting Alec had been something different. After she returned from lunch with him, she'd been all keyed up, so she rearranged her cubicle to burn off some nervous energy and try to settle her raging hormones. Barney stopped by and asked her why she was making so much noise. She wanted to tell him that continual humming counted as noise too, but she managed to control herself and simply said she'd try to be quieter.

She went down to the sample room and talked the guy who worked there into giving her some posters to cover up the dreary faded cloth walls of her cubicle. Ads for pretty clothes were better than Steelcase gray. Shaking up her environment had actually helped a little. She even fixed the aggravating broken formula in her spreadsheet.

That Friday evening, Robin spent several hours talking to her high school friend Amanda about her life as a math professor. Amanda was expecting a baby, so they chatted about everything from calculus to diapers and day care. Robin didn't know much about math or kids so she probably wasn't particularly helpful, but she was happy for her friend. It had been a pleasant conversation, but after Robin hung up the phone, everything in her world seemed more empty and depressing.

Since rearranging her cubicle had improved her mood, maybe moving the furniture in her house would help shake things up even more. She looked down at Emma, who was curled up on the old rug in front of the TV, which was playing an ancient rerun of *Magnum, P.I.* Robin had the TV on more for background noise than anything else. Listening to Tom Selleck and Hawaiian tropical birds was better than overhearing the inane conversations of the people walking by on the street in front of her apartment.

She put her hands on her hips and gazed at the blank white wall. There were old cans of paint in the laundry room. Although she probably wasn't allowed to paint her apartment, what if she painted a design on a sheet and hung it on the wall? That could be interesting. It would be like a tapestry. Well, almost.

Robin grabbed an old pizza box off the TV and walked to the kitchen to throw it away. Emma jumped up, looking interested. "Sorry Em. It's not food. I'm redecorating. This place is a dump."

She moved the TV and its stand into the bedroom and shoved the old sofa around, trying to find a new spot for it in the room. Emma sat in the middle of the room, supervising the operation.

A few hours later, Robin had the furniture in new locations, which had revealed gigantic clumps of dog hair everywhere. It wasn't necessarily an improvement, but it was different. After sweeping up the fur, she went to the laundry room to investigate. Along with the paint, she was pleased to discover a huge piece of cardboard from an old refrigerator box leaning up against a wall.

Robin laid out the cardboard and the sheet on the grass in the tiny fenced-in yard behind her house. Now all she needed was a design. She sat on an old chaise longue and pondered her color options. "What do you think, Em?" Apparently, all the supervision time had tired out Emma, who didn't seem to have much input on the matter beyond wagging the tip of her tail a few times.

The phone in her apartment rang and Robin jumped up off the chair to run inside and answer it. With a gasp, she picked up the receiver. Alec said, "Robin? Is that you?"

"Yes. I was in the back yard trying to figure out a design."

"A design for what?"

"I'm making a tapestry. Well kind of. It's an idea. I'm not sure it's going to work."

"Oh, so I guess you're busy?"

"Well, not *that* busy. I thought you had to work late every night. You said the dog walker had to do double duty."

"Yeah, I'm still here. Mostly I wanted to let you know that I need to go into work in the morning to get some stuff done, so I need to meet you later than we planned."

"Really? Yuck. I'm sorry. Go home."

"I know. I'm almost done. Sometimes I feel like I live here."

"Did you have anything to eat?"

"No. I was going to grab some Chinese on my way home."

"How do you feel about art?"

"What?"

"If you bring me Chinese food, I'll let you help me paint."

"You'll *let* me? You've got to be kidding. This is like *Huckleberry Finn*, isn't it? You're going to get me to paint a fence or something, aren't you?"

"No, this is art! My walls are boring and creating art is relaxing and good for you. You'll feel better, I promise. Leroy and Emma can hang out too. He's probably lonely."

Alec laughed. "Okay, fine. I'll bring you food and a dog."

"Be sure to wear old clothes." Robin hung up, returned to the back yard and did a little dance with Emma around the sheet. "Leroy is coming over, Emma. I got you a date for the evening!" And one for herself too.

~

Robin peered over the wooden fence. Alec and Leroy were walking up the sidewalk toward the front door. She yelled over the fence, telling him to come around back. He opened the creaky wooden gate and Leroy and Emma greeted each other in a flurry of wagging.

The sheet now had a stripe of blue paint and a few blue paw prints on it. Quite a bit of the paint was also on Robin's clothes and in her hair. Alec looked at her and grinned. "What happened?"

"I'm calling it my blue phase. Emma and I are expressing our creativity."

He laughed. "If you say so. I hope that's latex paint."

Robin held up her brush. "Hey, I'm not stupid."

Alec placed the boxes of food on the rickety metal table and sat down on the chaise. Emma and Leroy pointed their noses upward, enjoying the fragrance of oriental food, while Alec pulled apart little wooden chopsticks. "So can the artist take a dinner break?"

Robin put down the brush and closed the paint can. "Sure. I'm starving."

"You've been suffering for your art."

She took a box and pointed a chopstick at him. "We artists are temperamental. It's worse when we're hungry."

"At the risk of showing my lack of artistic aesthetic, what exactly are you trying to do here?"

Robin waved a chopstick toward the house. "I can't paint the walls in my apartment, so I'm painting a sheet to put on the wall. Like a tapestry. It will be cool."

"Have you thought about buying a tapestry? Around here, there must be fifty head shops with those Indian tie-dye tapestries everyone had in college."

"That would be more expensive and less fun. I don't have much money and I was thinking I need more excitement in my life since my job is so painfully dull. I rearranged my cubicle and the furniture in my apartment too."

"You've been busy."

Robin gobbled down some food and put down the box. "I'm trying to shake up my life a little. It's too boring." She went over to the cans of paint and selected a reddish color. "On that note, it's time for a new color!"

"Were you trying to do a stripe?" He shrugged. "I guess I'm a little confused about the overall design here."

"It's abstract."

"That's for sure."

"Everyone's a critic." Robin shook the brush to emphasize her point, splattering red paint on Alec's face, his shirt, and the top of Leroy's head. She gasped, uttered an obscene expletive and slapped her palm over her mouth.

Alec looked momentarily shocked, then burst out laughing and pointed at her, "I'm gonna tell your momma on you! That one is absolutely on George Carlin's list of seven dirty words. And then you even graduated to a *compound* word. My impression of you is completely shattered."

Robin grabbed a rag and tried to rub the paint off Leroy's head, turning the paint splatters into a huge pink smear. Alec was still laughing. He leaned back on the chaise, holding his stomach, gasping for breath. Pointing at Leroy, he said, "Stop turning my dog into a flamingo!"

Robin looked down at the spot on Leroy's head. It seemed that white fur mixed with old red paint turned into a flamingo-like shade of pink. Leroy didn't seem upset, but it was a little disturbing. "Oh *flaming heck*, Leroy, I'm so sorry. I know there are quite a few people in this neighborhood with pink hair, but I don't think this look works for you."

Alec got himself under control enough to sit up. He swiped a fingertip across his cheek, removing a big blob of red paint, and reached over and wiped it onto Robin's chin. He widened his eyes and said with mock sincerity. "I think this color works with the blue of your eyes and the blue of your hair."

Robin wiped her chin and looked at the red paint on her hand. She grinned and swiped the paintbrush across her hand. "Oh, you'll be sorry you did that. Never mess with the artist when she's in the throes of creativity."

He scrambled out of the chair and fell on the grass. "Don't you even think about it."

She jumped on his back and smeared red paint on his face. "Oopsie. I spilled."

Rolling her over onto her back, he pinned her wrists down and looked into her eyes. He kissed her and grabbed the paintbrush out of her hand, crawling over near the sheet.

Robin stood up and pointed down at him. "Cheater! You distracted me."

Alec turned and jerked the paintbrush at her, flipping a line of paint splatter down her pant leg. "*Leaping lizards* Annie, I believe I may have spilled too."

"I'm going to get you for that!" She dove for him and caught the can of red paint with her foot, knocking it over onto the sheet. He scurried backward and swiped at her with the brush, using it like a sword. "Get away from me."

Robin pushed the brush aside and pulled his other arm out from under him so he landed on his back with a thud. Jumping on top of him, she kissed him like she *really* meant it. Two could play that game. He was momentarily still, then flipped her over on her back, kissing her like he meant a whole lot more. Flinging the brush into the grass, he found other things to do with his hands, shoving them under her paint-splattered shirt.

Emma poked her nose in Robin's face, interrupting the action. Robin glanced up at the light shining from the windows in the house. At this point, all of her neighbors in the four-plex were getting a free show, watching her make out with Alec in a puddle of paint. Even in Portland this was taking performance art a little bit too far. She sat up and pushed Alec away.

He flopped onto his side and Leroy leaned over and slurped his ear. Pushing the dog's nose away from him, he grumbled, "Ugh, yuck. Stop that, Leroy!"

Robin looked down at herself, then over at Alec, who had rolled over onto his back and was lying spread-eagled in the grass. They were both covered in red paint. It looked like there had been a war and they'd both lost. She grinned at him. "I think we need to get a room."

"With a shower." He stood up and held out his hand to help her up. "I think your art project is complete."

"The smattering of red paw prints add a touch of panache. Thanks, Em." Emma wagged her tail proudly and Robin turned to Alec. "We should wash their paws and take them for a walk before we go inside."

He looked down at his clothes. "I'm not sure I should be seen in public like this."

"You obviously haven't spent much time in my neighborhood."

He grinned. "I guess it's time to change that."

Robin filled up a bucket with water and scrubbed the dog's paws. Leroy didn't seem convinced that the paw-cleaning program was a great idea, but put up with having his feet handled after Robin gave him a few treats to improve his mood.

They leashed up the dogs and walked through the gate, out to the sidewalk. A tall lanky man with a rainbow mohawk walked by them, held up his fingers in a peace sign and said, "Rock on, man."

Alec glanced at Robin. "I think the paint is drying on my jeans. If it stiffens up much more, walking is going to be seriously unpleasant. There could be chafing in places I'd rather not discuss."

"You probably don't want to know what your hair looks like then."

He touched the back of his head. "Eww."

After a short tour of the neighborhood, they returned to Robin's house. At the front steps, she pointed at his shoes, "Take those off. I have wood floors and my landlord will kill me if you get paint on them."

"Me?"

Robin pulled off her shoes and socks so she was barefoot. She and Emma scampered up the steps onto the porch. Alec followed with Leroy. They went into the house and Robin started unbuttoning the old oxford cloth shirt she was wearing while she walked toward the bathroom.

Alec followed her. "I think I like where this is going."

Robin peered down at herself. "Well, *horse feathers*, there's paint on my bra. That's never going to come out. It was expensive too."

Alec pulled his t-shirt off over his head, dropped it on the tile, and reached out to run a fingertip along a dribble of paint that had traveled along most of the curves of her body. "The paint is not just on your underwear."

Robin looked up at his face as she turned on the shower. "I'm pretty sure I have paint in places I can't reach."

He grinned and said in his best Eagle River customer-service voice, "I'd be happy to help you with that."

~

After a lot of soapy scrubbing, kissing, and laughter in the shower, Robin suggested they give up and try soaking off the last of the paint. She filled the old porcelain tub, threw in some bubble bath, and they settled into the warm sudsy water. Robin leaned back on Alec's chest as he ran his hand down her arm, rubbing at some lingering dried paint spots with his thumb.

She sighed and closed her eyes. "This feels so good."

Alec kissed her temple. "I know I'm relaxed."

Robin turned to glance at him, "Since I've been having my little career crisis, I've been wondering something."

"What's on your mind?"

"Why do you work at Eagle River?"

"What do you mean why? Why does anyone work anywhere? To earn a living."

Robin took his hand and wrapped his arm around her. "True. But you don't seem to like what you do very much."

"You're one to talk."

"I know, but I just moved and I'm broke. In fact, looking back on it, I probably shouldn't have moved to Portland. That was probably a mistake, but I thought things would be different here." She splashed at a mound of bubbles. "But that's not the point. I'm asking about you. I've seen where you live and your car. You could do something else."

He stroked her hair back away from her ear. "I guess I could. It's been so long, I guess I've invested a lot into the company."

"But you seem so unhappy. Away from work, you're like a different person."

"Not really."

"Yes you are. The first meeting we had, I thought you were kind of mean. Then I realized you were just angry and unhappy. In Alpine Grove, I found out you're way more than that."

He poked at some bubbles so they made little squishy popping noises. "Yeah, a dyslexic with illegible handwriting. I can't believe I told you that. I don't even think Darrell knows. It's a good thing typewriters and computers exist, or I'd be in trouble."

She turned to look at him again. "That's not what I meant at all. I didn't think about that. I meant *you*—what you're like. Now that I know you better, I know you like dogs, you're smart and a great teacher, you can fix things, you've got a great sense of humor, and you're totally sexy."

Alec kissed her earlobe. "Thank you. I don't think I'll put that last one on my resume though."

"Well, I suppose that would depend on the job." Robin held her hand in front of her face and examined her thumb. "I'm turning into a prune."

"Maybe we can throw my clothes in here and let them soak. I think my jeans are toast. What am I going to wear home?"

Robin stood up and stepped out of the bathtub. "Right now, I don't think you need clothes. Maybe you can figure it out tomorrow morning."

"That sounds like an invitation."

"It is."

He got out of the tub, threw the pile of clothes in, and took her hand. "Lead the way."

The next morning, Robin rolled over toward the edge of the bed and encountered two sets of black canine nostrils in her face. "Hi guys. Did you have a nice snooze? I guess you want breakfast."

The dogs wagged and looked enthusiastic at the mention of food. Robin sat up and nudged Alec, who still had some red paint in his hair. Oh well.

He opened his eyes and smiled. "Good morning."

Leaning over, she gave him a kiss. "Your dog is hungry."

"What time is it?" Alec turned his head to look around the room. "Don't you have a clock?"

"I think it fell behind the dresser when I was moving stuff around."

He sat up and rubbed his face with his palms. "I need to get to the office. I have so much to do and I was planning to get in by six."

"I'm pretty sure that ship has sailed." Robin got out of bed and pulled on an old t-shirt and sweatpants. She tossed a faded blue terrycloth robe on the bed. "I'll go throw your clothes in the laundry. It's in the basement, but I have to go outside to access it. The dog food is in the pantry in the kitchen."

"Thanks." He leaned over and reached for her hand, pulling her back to the bed. "Even though getting covered in paint was not how I expected to spend the evening, I had a really good time last night."

Robin put her arms around his neck and kissed him. "Me too. I'll be right back."

When Robin returned from the basement, she found Alec standing in front of her open refrigerator resting his arm on the door. He looked at her. "You have no food."

"There's a loaf of bread and a jar of pickles right there."

"If I hadn't called last night, what were you going to have for dinner?"

"I told you I don't cook. Check the freezer if you want to know."

He opened the door. "I see."

"I suppose you're a gourmet cook?"

"I eat out a lot because I'm too tired to cook by the time I get home. But I used to cook all the time."

"That works out well for me, because I like to eat." Robin walked over to him and pushed her hands under the bathrobe so she could enjoy the warmth of his bare skin. "I hereby invite you to cook for me any time."

"I have liked your invitations so far."

"I'm really good at scooping out ice cream from the container, so you don't have to worry about dessert."

He kissed her. "I'll keep that in mind."

Later, Alec left to go home, change his clothes, and spend a few hours at the office. Robin agreed to let Leroy hang out at her place, since they had plans for the afternoon to go to Mt. Tabor Park. They'd missed out on the street fair, but it was a beautiful day and Robin was looking forward to checking out the hiking trails. Alec told her that the park was actually an extinct volcano. It sounded pretty and they allowed dogs. Plus, how often did you have the opportunity to stand on a volcano and live to tell the tale?

By the time Alec returned, Robin had mostly cleaned up the paint disaster in the backyard and hung up the somewhat weird painted sheet aka "tapestry" in her bedroom. Although it added some much-needed color to the space, the swash of red paint and paw prints were a little creepy. It looked like something had died on it and an animal had walked away from the scene of the crime.

Alec leaned in the doorway. "You sure you'll be able to sleep with that on the wall?"

"I kind of like it. I was thinking I could call it *Werewolf Surprise*."

"It doesn't look like it was a happy surprise."

"Maybe if I added another color it would help."

"Yeah, well…maybe."

Chapter 11

The Bottom Rung

They leashed up the dogs and loaded them into the Jeep for the trip out to the park. Robin put her hand on Alec's. "So how was work?"

"Same old stuff. You don't want to know."

"Actually I do. You never answered me when I asked why you work for Eagle River. I'm wondering what you do every day that you dislike so much."

He shrugged. "I think mostly what I don't like is the stress. Managing people and dealing with the fallout when people don't do what they say they'll do, which seems to happen on almost a daily basis."

"At least you make a lot of money doing it."

"True. I've gotten performance bonuses and I own stock. Being the third employee has a few advantages."

"No doubt. I've been thinking about that kind of thing lately."

"What do you mean?"

"What it means to be successful." She motioned her hand toward him. "You pretty much define success. I think I missed something. Maybe I wasn't paying attention. When everyone else was working on having a career, I was coasting along, doing my kind of crappy job. Upward mobility never happened. My career trajectory is not on an upward trend. More like it's flatlined."

"I don't know about that."

Robin shook her head. "The most confusing thing to me is that you don't even like what you do. Most of my friends who are successful in their careers are obsessed with something. Like my friend Amanda, who loves math. I figured the reason my career is in the toilet is because I'm not that interested in my job and I never have been. But you don't seem to like what you do, either."

Alec parked the Jeep and they unloaded the dogs. As they started down the trail, he stopped and turned to Robin, "You're right. I don't like what I do."

Robin waved in exasperation. "Then why are you so successful? We're about the same age. It's not fair that I'm eating macaroni and cheese from a box and you drive a Mercedes. What did I do wrong?"

"Probably nothing."

As she waited for Emma to complete an important sniffing maneuver, Robin looked up into the trees. Chickadees, swallows, and sparrows were having a birdie celebration, singing and chasing each other through the green leaves. The spring weather was energizing to everyone. "Okay, if I didn't do anything wrong, what did you do right?"

"Probably nothing. Well, other than not getting fired over the years. I did get close a few times though."

"You're not being helpful here. How did you end up at the top of the corporate ladder while I'm parked here on the bottom rung?"

"Luck."

"Luck? That's all you can tell me? I was hoping for some meaningful career insights here."

"It's the truth. I was in the right place at the right time. Darrell and Sue lived near my parents' house and I had just dropped out of college. They needed help and I had nothing better to do, so I helped them out. That turned into a job. So yes, it was basically luck."

At the crest of the trail, they stood in front of a bronze statue of a man named Harvey W. Scott, who had apparently been an editor of *The Oregonian* newspaper from 1865-1872 and from 1877 until his death in 1910. Robin looked at Alec. "A journalist rated a statue, huh?"

"It looks like his wife gave it to the city. Having lots of money is handy for that kind of thing."

"Yeah, I wouldn't know."

He touched her arm. "Robin, just because you don't make a whole lot of money right now, doesn't mean you have no talents or you'll never find a job you like. You've got your whole life ahead of you."

She hugged him and rested her cheek on his chest. "Thanks. I'm sorry I'm having a pity party. You are a really nice person, you know."

"Not always, but I'm glad you think so."

"I do."

After the hike, they went to the grocery store and then Alec's place. He'd been mildly appalled by Robin's kitchen. The meager collection of elderly cast-off pots and pans was a little embarrassing, but she'd never worried about it. All she needed was a microwave and a pot big enough to boil pasta. Everything else seemed like overkill.

He put the grocery bags on the expansive kitchen counter and Robin sat on one of the stools at the island. Emma and Leroy stationed themselves at key locations in the kitchen to closely monitor any food that might land on the floor.

Robin waved her hand toward the shiny appliances. "I think your kitchen is bigger than my living room."

"It also has knives that have been sharpened within the last decade. How can you live in Portland and not be into food? We have gourmet grocery stores, locally grown produce, restaurants—it's incredible."

"Well, I haven't lived here long and all those designer goodies are expensive." She grinned. "You are kind of a foodie, aren't you?"

He looked up from the refrigerator. "You said you like to eat. So do I."

Robin watched as he chopped up some tomatoes. "What are you making?"

"Fast food. I'm hungry and the focaccia bread looked great. A few roma tomatoes, onions, olive oil, and a little rosemary and it's an appetizer." He put the bread into the oven.

"Your definition of fast food is a little different than mine."

"No doubt." Reaching up to a cabinet, he pulled down multiple jars of spices.

Robin got up and looked at the shelves. "I've never seen that many spices. What the heck is kasoori methi?"

"Dried fenugreek leaves."

"Right."

"It's an Indian spice. I'm making a Makhani gravy."

"I have no idea what you're talking about."

"It will be good. I promise." He turned and pulled the focaccia bread out of the oven and slid it onto a cutting board. "Technically, with Indian food, we should have naan, but I'm starving, so we're mixing ethnic groups."

She sat down at the island again. "Is that some foodie faux pas?"

"Probably. But I prefer to think of it as fusion." He put a plate in front of her. "Try it."

Robin took a slice of the bread and tried not to swoon. "How can something made with only four ingredients be so yummy?"

"It's the magic of real food."

Robin watched as Alec prepared some rice and then started chopping up something white. "Eww, is that *tofu*?"

"Yes. I'm a vegetarian. Usually vegan actually, although sometimes it's hard to avoid cheese when you go out." He shrugged. "Pizza is my downfall."

"*Son of a nutcracker*! I never noticed before—you're a health nut."

"Not really. But I work long hours, and it's too easy to fall into bad eating habits. About ten years ago when I started having enough money to go out to eat, I gained a lot of weight. The worst part was that I felt terrible. So I tried a vegan diet, lost the weight, and felt better again. Around here it's easy to get health food."

"No wonder the Chinese food yesterday was full of veggies." She chewed the focaccia bread slowly. "No steak ever again? I can't imagine that."

He popped a piece of tofu into his mouth. "Don't knock it until you try it."

"You lost weight? How much is a lot?" She shook her hands in front of her. "Wait, is that too personal? I'm being nosy. Don't answer if you don't want to. But um, well, now that I've spent so much time naked with you, I'm curious."

"Twenty or thirty pounds, I think."

"That's difficult to imagine."

"Growing up, I was the short fat kid who couldn't read right, so I got beat up a lot." He waved a spatula in her direction. "You might not know this since everyone loves you, but kids can be incredibly mean."

"Yeah, I was the cute little blonde girl who got to go to all the coolest birthday parties. You are definitely not short now."

"The summer between my junior and senior year of high school, I grew like seven inches or something. It was kind of bizarre."

Robin walked over to the stove next to Alec and looked down at the food simmering in the pan. "That smells amazing. There's tofu in there?"

"Yes, but don't worry. It's well hidden."

The next day, they drove out to Multnomah Falls, which Robin had learned was the second-highest year-round waterfall in the United States. They walked up the Overlook Trail and enjoyed the views of the water cascading down the cliff. The lush, misty, gorgeously green trail reminded Robin of Alpine Grove a little. Except with a whole lot more people.

After the walk, they settled in for a picnic in one of the grassy areas near the visitor's center. Robin leaned back on the blanket and stroked the fur on Emma's back. "I need to rest now. I don't know what you did, but that was the best avocado sandwich I've ever had. I could get used to eating real food and hiking every day."

Alec sprawled out alongside her. "I know what you mean. But tomorrow is Monday."

"That's going to be awkward, isn't it?"

"Probably." He reached over and pushed a blonde curl off her cheek. "It might not be a great idea to advertise the fact we spent the whole weekend together."

"I suppose you're right." She rubbed a bit of the red paint in his hair between two fingertips. "Maybe no one will notice this."

He leaned to kiss her. "We can go back to my place and you could help me wash my hair again."

"Okay. That was fun. Your bathtub is way bigger than mine. And the jets were, um, invigorating."

"So were you."

~

On Monday, Robin left Alec's condo in the wee hours of the morning. He had to go into work early and she had to go home to settle Emma back into her normal weekday routine. She also need to leave a check for the dog walker, which could be complicated. The bean counters in accounting were supposed to cut her reimbursement check from the trip to Alpine Grove this week. Maybe she could convince the dog-walking company to wait a day or two to deposit the check.

She left an apologetic note with the check and went off to Eagle River. Back in her cubicle, the posters she'd put up on Friday were different, but Barney was still humming and the Sniffler was still snuffling. Some things didn't change. She looked through her email. Lurking amid the dull missives was a meeting invitation from Darrell. In ten minutes. *Son of a gun!* What was he thinking? Half the time she wasn't even here at 8:00 in the morning. Of course, he probably didn't know that. And she certainly wasn't going to be the one to tell him. She gathered up a notebook and hustled out of the building and over to the executive offices.

As she walked up to the conference room, Alec glanced at her through the glass. Although the expression on his face remained serious, he nodded almost imperceptibly and a corner of his mouth turned up. She grinned at him and knocked on the door. Darrell told her to come in and she sat down at the end of the table. It was like *deja vu*, except that she knew Alec a whole lot better than she had before. Her cheeks were hot, and she was probably blushing like a complete idiot.

She cleared her throat and said "good morning" overly brightly. This would have been better if she'd had the chance to grab some coffee first.

Darrell said, "You look like you got some sun this weekend."

"Yes, I went hiking with my dog. Wasn't the weather glorious?"

After a few pleasantries about the beauty of spring in Portland, Darrell got down to business. "I got the reviews from the retreat and Sue and I went over them."

Robin put her hands in her lap. Uh-oh. "I hope it was everything you expected." She glanced at Alec, who smiled slightly.

Darrel said, "It was better than I ever imagined. People loved it. And over the last week, the call center has been humming. We've done some call monitoring and it's incredible. Even some of our lowest performers are making sales. Lots of sales. This next catalog drop with the spring clearance is going to break records. I know it."

Robin nodded at Alec. "As I said, the training was excellent."

Darrell put both palms on the table. "And that's why I want you to go back!"

"Go back?" Robin stared at him blankly. "You mean go back to Alpine Grove?"

"Yes!" Darrell stood up. "The marketing team isn't in synch with their messaging. The High Country catalog copy doesn't mesh well with Eagle River campaigns. We can't get Brett for the team-building aspect this time, but that doesn't matter. The marketing folks don't seem to have the same issues with animosity that the call-center folks did. The problem in marketing is that they're not presenting a cohesive image. We need to fix that, because everyone needs to be on the same page. From what I read in the reviews, being off-site seems to make a huge difference. So you and Alec need to work together to set up marketing training on Eagle River branding, visuals, methodology—the whole nine yards. I talked to Ernie and set up the dates."

Robin leaned back in her chair. "Alec and I have to work together?"

Darrell opened the door to leave. "Yes. I've got to get to another meeting. You'll figure it out. This takes priority over any other work you have. Make it happen, Robin. I'm counting on you again."

After he closed the door, Robin turned to Alec. "Did you know about this?"

"Not until this morning." He gave her a pseudo-stern look. "I'm terribly sorry to tell you this, but there will be no spreadsheets for you for a while."

She giggled. "Oh darn."

He stood up. "I have go fight with Sue now. Could you set up a few times for us to meet this week? My schedule is packed, but see what you can do. I can reuse some information from the call-center training, which is a start. But there's a whole lot of other information on branding, imagery, and marketing strategy that needs to be pulled together for this. Gloria can handle getting everything reproduced, but we need to get everything compiled for her. As usual, Darrell isn't giving us much time, so we've got a whole lot to do."

"Okay." She stood up and held out her hand. "I'm looking forward to working with you Mr. Montgomery."

He shook her hand, caressing the top with his thumb in a ridiculously provocative way. "I am too, Ms. Sanders."

Over the next few days, Robin talked to what seemed like half of the residents of Alpine Grove. She recruited Ellie and the church ladies to clean and wash all the sheets, since it was highly unlikely Ernie had done anything since everyone left.

Although she met with Alec a few times, she spent a lot more time with his executive assistant Gloria. She was about ten or fifteen years older than Robin with short, curly red hair and a slim build that Robin envied. No matter what Gloria wore, the clothes fit perfectly and she looked like a consummate professional. It was impossible to imagine her in grungy old sweatpants or covered with paint. Next to her, Robin always felt like a slob.

Gloria also was one of the most efficient people Robin had ever met. Her list-making and organizational skills put

Robin's to shame. Gloria had been an executive assistant for years, and the woman had a level of confidence in her ability to get things done that was inspiring. Robin had tried to set up meetings with Alec, but finally gave up and asked Gloria for help. She rearranged his schedule so Robin actually would have a chance to speak with Alec before they went to Alpine Grove. How could one human being stand to go to so many meetings every day? No wonder he was so stressed about being behind in his work. He had no time left to actually *do* any work.

Robin was sitting at Gloria's desk helping to collate some documents when Alec walked up. Gloria said, "Why are you here? You have a lunch meeting in twenty minutes. We have everything under control. Get out."

He said, "I need to talk to Robin for a second."

Gloria waved her hand at Robin, who stood up and followed Alec into his office. He closed the door and watched Gloria through the glass. "Could you stop by my place tonight? I'd like to have more than ten minutes to talk to you about this trip. Bring Emma too. I think Leroy misses his friend."

Robin turned so her back was to the glass wall. She grinned at him. "That would be great. I've missed you."

His expression remained impassive as he said quietly. "I feel the same way. I can't wait to get out of here."

"See you later."   .

Alec opened the door for her and Robin returned to her seat next to Gloria, who handed him a printout. "Read this in the car before you talk to John."

He rubbed his eyes with his fingertips. "Okay, thanks."

~

Much later that evening, Robin stood in front of Alec's condo with Emma and knocked on the door. It was late and she was tired. If she'd been smart, she would have taken a nap after work. It was way past her bedtime.

Alec opened the door and Robin dropped Emma's leash so she could run inside and greet Leroy. As Alec closed the door behind them, he took Robin in his arms and kissed her in that molten way he had. Emma woofed at Leroy, who play-bowed and encouraged her to chase him around the dining room table.

Alec released his hold on Robin and she smiled. "I'm glad to see you too."

"Come in. Sorry it's so late. But I wanted to see you."

Robin collected Emma's leash, walked over to the sofa, and slumped down onto it, even though the squishy pillows were likely to be a bit too much of a sleep aid. "I don't think I'm as much of a night owl as you are."

"We've got to head out Friday. Do you think we can cram all the junk we need to take in the Jeep? Or do you want to take separate cars?"

"Is your dad okay with you taking his Jeep again?"

Alec smiled. "Dad doesn't tend to mind trading cars with me, but he's visiting my mom in Hawaii, so he's not using the Jeep anyway."

"That's good. I'd rather not take my car if we can avoid it. My tires are old and I need new ones. Tires are on the long list of things that I can't afford right now. But my reimbursement request will be a little odd with no gas receipts won't it?"

"True. Maybe you can forget to do your expense report entirely, since I'd be happy to pay for your food and lodging." He sat down next to her. "Unless you want separate rooms."

"That seems uncalled for." She pointed at the dogs, who had exhausted themselves and were now lying on the floor at their feet. "If your father is out of town, who is going to take care of Leroy?"

"Leroy is coming with me. Emma can ride in the back seat with him if you want."

"Aren't you worried we'll get in trouble?"

"No."

"This is going to be fun." She tried to sit up straighter, but the pillows wanted to suck her into their soporific vortex. "I didn't know your mom lived in Hawaii. Where?"

"Kauai. I bought her a condo."

"I won't tell my momma that. She'd be so jealous. Are your parents divorced?"

"Not exactly. They just seem to like each other better if they spend time apart." He shrugged. "It's kind of odd. My mom wanted to move someplace sunny after my father finally sold his business, and he didn't. They sold the house I grew up in and Mom went to Hawaii. Dad got the job here at the complex because he couldn't stand the idea of having nothing to do. He has a complicated arrangement with the other managers, so he can take time off when he feels like it. The whole thing is a pretty sweet deal."

"Well, whatever works for them."

"Yeah, they're happy. And he has a place to stay in Hawaii when he needs sun."

Robin was having trouble keeping her eyes open. She slumped over, resting her head on Alec's shoulder. "Sorry I'm so tired."

"It's okay. I've gotta get through some more of this training stuff. You know where everything is."

She kissed him and went to the bedroom. Emma and Leroy followed, their toenails clicking on the floors behind her.

The next morning before they left the apartment, Robin was sitting at the kitchen island eating a bowl of cereal and trying not to dwell on the beany taste of the soy milk. Alec came into the room and kissed her neck. "Hi."

Robin waved her spoon and swallowed. "I had an idea!"

"Does it involve paint or stealing my underwear?"

"No. I was thinking about what you said about reading. That it's harder when you're tired."

"Don't remind me. I'm already exhausted and I've got so much more to get through before Monday."

"What if I read the training stuff *to* you on the way to Alpine Grove? Since we're going to be in the Jeep for hours, I could read while you drive. Then if we trade, you can read yourself while I drive, assuming it doesn't make you carsick or anything."

He put his hand on her cheek. "Thanks for thinking about the disturbing amount of reading I have to do and why it's disturbing. That would help a lot."

"How late did you stay up last night?"

"Too late. I'm looking forward to being in Alpine Grove. Opportunities for sleep and except for the class, no meetings."

"I might invite you to a meeting."

"That's okay. I like your invitations."

The drive to Alpine Grove was as much fun as Robin expected. Along with reading more than she ever thought possible about Eagle River marketing to Alec, they talked for hours. The topics ranged from family and friends to a few dopey stories about various childhood escapades. Alec was extremely easy to talk to and they'd even delved into the delicate minefield of past relationships. All the laughter and conversation brought home how lonely Robin had been since she'd moved to Portland.

The pet-friendly hotel they stopped at was far nicer than the dump Robin had stayed in on her last trip to Alpine Grove. Even Emma seemed to be able to tell the difference. As they drove up the mountain toward the lodge, the dogs stood up in the backseat, vigorously inhaling the piney scents coming through the windows.

They turned into the North Fork Lodge, which looked exactly the same as it had when they left. Robin was relieved to note that none of the roofs had caved in yet and everything had dried out substantially. The sun was out and the lake was a stunning aquamarine blue with magical little sparkles dancing across the water. The only noises were from birds singing in the trees. No one seemed to be around. Ernie was probably fishing again. Robin looked at Alec. "Wow. It was pretty before, but with sun, it's absolutely breathtaking."

"I know. This is like a postcard. The color of the lake doesn't even look real."

They unloaded the dogs and walked down the path toward the lake. Robin bent to unhook Emma's leash and Alec released Leroy. The two dogs rushed along the lakeshore, chasing and cavorting with one another. They ran in dizzying circles, leaping and play-bowing with utter abandon.

Robin smiled at the demonstration of canine joy. "I think they're glad to be here."

Alec put his arm around her shoulders and took a deep breath. "So am I."

Chapter 12

Jeepers Creepers

After the dogs had tired themselves out, Robin loaded them back into the Jeep, in case Ernie showed up. "We'll be right back, guys. Take a nap for a couple minutes while we get the key."

Alec and Robin walked up the steps to the lodge. They entered the lobby area, which was dust-free. Robin pressed her hands together and grinned at Alec. "Look, Ellie and the ladies were here. It looks great. Or as great as it can, anyway." She went around the desk and grabbed the keys to the two sides of the Pine Cone cabin and looked at the door to Ernie's living area. Maybe he was inside. She knocked on the door and it opened a crack. Raising her eyebrows at Alec, he shrugged his shoulders.

Robin placed her hand on the door and pushed it open the rest of the way. It creaked and Robin stepped into a living room that had been lived in a lot. She put her hand over her mouth. Every possible surface was covered with some residue of past meals. Old half-eaten bread, bags of chips, dirty plates and cups were everywhere. Ernie was slumped on an old plaid sofa, snoring quietly. He was wearing headphones and the TV was tuned to a soap opera.

Alec came up behind her and put his hand on her shoulder. "That's a mighty bad smell you've discovered."

She turned her head and looked up into his face. "I guess he's asleep. Do you think Darrell knows about this?"

"I tried to tell Darrell that Ernie might have some memory problems, but he brushed it off. He said that Ernie just misses his wife."

"That's what he said to me too. Something more is wrong here. This is awful. What should we do?"

Alec shook his head. "I'm not sure. If he's been using headphones, he might have been holed away watching TV the whole time we were here before. We never would have heard the TV or been able to tell he was in here."

"We should let him know we're here." She took Alec's hand and squeezed it. "I'll wake him up, if you agree to talk to Darrell. He listens to you more than he does to me."

"Deal."

Robin tiptoed over the debris to the sofa and tapped Ernie's shoulder. The older man shot up off the couch as if he'd been electrocuted. With a glare, he shouted at Robin, "Who are you? Get out of my house!"

Robin stepped backward and pointed frantically toward the headphones. "Ernie, it's me, Robin. Take them off."

With a befuddled look, he pulled the black earpieces away from his head, pulled the headphones off, and looked down at them. "Myrtle says to wear them, so I don't disturb the guests."

"I'm sorry to wake you up. I just wanted to let you know we're here."

He pointed at her. "I know you. Why are you here with the twitchy guy again? I thought you left."

"We did. But we're here for another retreat. Remember, Darrell talked to you about it? The attendees arrive tomorrow.

There will be only eight people this time. Well, ten if you count me and Alec. I talked to Chuck about the food. He'll be here tomorrow."

Alec said, "Ernie, do you have anyone to help you here? Maybe we could clean up your apartment a little?"

Ernie ran a hand through his wild gray hair. "Myrtle will get around to it. She's been busy."

Robin said, "We're staying in the Pine Cone cabin. We'll go unpack and come back in a little while. Is that okay?"

Ernie nodded and pointed to the TV. "I'm missing my show! Now I'll never figure out what happened with Luke and Laura."

Robin put her hand on his forearm. "All right. We'll leave you alone now, but we'll come back in a little while, okay?"

They turned and closed the door behind them. Robin looked at Alec. "I kinda feel like crying."

"Yeah, I know what you mean. As soon as we unpack and get back up here to the lodge, I'll call Darrell."

They got in the Jeep and drove down to the Pine Cone cabin in silence. Alec let out the dogs, who did some post-nap stretching and yawning while the humans unloaded the Jeep. Even though the North Star where Brett had stayed last time was a larger cabin, they had agreed to stay in the Pine Cone, since it was a duplex. Alec pointed out that they might not want to advertise the fact they were together. No one else needed to know they actually were using only one side of the building.

The attendees were all staying in the lodge, since there were only eight people and Robin didn't want to hear complaints about lodging inequities this time.

Emma and Leroy seemed content to snooze in the cabin, so Robin and Alec left them to their napping and walked up the path to the lodge.

Robin glanced at Alec's face. "Now that you've been to my apartment, you've probably figured out that I'm not the greatest housekeeper. But Ernie's apartment grosses out even me. I'm kind of afraid of what I'm going to find in there."

"I'll help you after I talk to Darrell. I recommend starting with a big garbage bag."

"Yuck."

In the lodge, Robin knocked on the door and when Ernie didn't respond she tried the knob. It was locked. She turned to Alec. "He locked us out! Do you suppose he's still in there?"

Alec sat down in the chair. "I don't know. See if you can find a key while I try Darrell."

Robin rummaged around the office area, but mostly listened to Alec's side of the conversation with Darrell. He wasn't having much luck convincing Darrell that his uncle was anything other than old.

Alec glanced at Robin and raised his eyebrows. "You're not listening to me, Darrell. I think Ernie has some type of medical problem. No one lives like this, and now he's locked us out. I think he needs to see a doctor. He's your uncle and there's something really wrong with him. You need to do something."

Robin watched Alec's face as he was silent for a while, listening to whatever Darrell was saying. Alec appeared by turns frustrated, sad, and angry. Finally, he said, "Yes, I am saying you should drop everything. That's *exactly* what I'm saying, in fact. Get yourself down here. You have to deal with this, since you just finished telling me you're his closest relative."

Robin smiled and gave him a thumbs up sign. Alec responded with a shrug and *maybe, maybe-not* waggle of his hand. He said, "Gloria knows all the arrangements and she can set it up. Just get on the Lear, okay?" He rolled his eyes. "Fine, we'll see you tomorrow with everyone else. In the meantime, I'll see if I can get into the apartment." He hung up the phone and looked at Robin. "Well, that was fun. How do you feel about a little B and E?"

"What's B and E?"

"Breaking and entering. I suspect your momma wouldn't approve of it, but Darrell told me to break into Ernie's apartment."

"No she wouldn't. But I think this is an emergency."

"Let's try pounding on the door again first."

They both hammered on the door and got no response. Robin turned around just as Ernie walked up to the desk. He waved a slice of bread at her. "Why are you trying to beat down my door? I'm right here. You people are really strange."

Alec said, "We came back to help you clean up, remember?"

Ernie walked around the desk and pulled a key from his pocket. "No. Go away."

Robin put her hand on his arm. "We talked to Darrell and he is coming to see you tomorrow."

"Fine. Put him in the North Star cabin."

"Okay, I'll be sure to do that." Robin glanced at Alec, who made a wry face. She turned back to Ernie. "May we please come in and help you clean up?"

Ernie waved his bread at her again. "No. I'm missing my show. Don't you have anything else to do?"

Alec said, "Are you sure you're okay?"

Ernie opened the door and turned around. "I'm fine. Get lost." He slammed the door and the lock clicked.

Alec sat down in the chair heavily. "Well, we tried."

"I'm glad you convinced Darrell to come."

"Me too. You heard what I said. I tried to explain what's going on, but I'm not sure he believes me. He went through a long complicated thing about how Ernie is the last surviving member of this branch of the family. I got a little confused, but the gist of it was that if something happens to Ernie, Darrell is next in line to own this place."

"Darrell? I got the impression it's been a long time since he's been here. Does he know what the lodge is like now?"

"No, and I think he's in for a big surprise."

∼

Later, Robin suggested that Alec go to town and pick up a pizza for dinner. After he returned, he set the box on the desk. "I don't know how you convince me to do these things. You must have some serious manipulative powers."

Robin looked up in surprise from her perch at the end of the bed. "I'm not manipulative!"

"And yet, I went and fetched dinner—*again*."

"If I were manipulative, I would be using my persuasive abilities for evil. But I'm not. Acquiring food benefits you. So did asking you to provide a small temporary loan to pay the church ladies for cleaning. I just point out possibilities and make suggestions."

He grinned. "I guess you do it in such a sweet way, sometimes afterward I wonder what happened."

She stood up and gave him a hug. "Thank you. Here's another point to consider. You're much more cheerful after you have had something to eat."

After dinner, Robin decided the dogs had the right idea, and she curled up on the bed next to Alec for a little nap. The travel and worrying about Ernie had worn her out. Alec was reading more information for his upcoming class and the only sounds were the occasional flipping of a page or a dog-dream snorfle. It was quiet and soothing in the cozy cabin and all Robin's tense muscles began to relax.

Robin jerked awake. "What was that?"

Alec looked down at her. "It's that animal cry again. I thought it was gone."

"Well, *fudge berries*. I was having the best dream too."

Emma and Leroy were both standing up, looking concerned. The piercing shriek echoed again and Leroy put his hackles up. Emma walked over to the bed and thumped her muzzle on the bedspread in front of Robin's face. Robin reached out and stroked the smooth fur on the dog's head. "I'm sorry, Em. I don't like it either."

Robin rolled over and put her arms around Alec. "At least we know the dogs are safe. The last time this…whatever it is…made this noise, I was sure something awful had happened to Leroy."

He pushed a curl of hair back away from her eyes. "And yet here he is, being our brave hero dog."

She hugged him more tightly. "I didn't think I'd need to wear earplugs out here in the middle of a forest. What *is* that? Should we go check?"

"I wish I knew. I could go look, but if it's something like an animal with rabies, confronting it might not be a great idea. I don't have anything to ward it off, except office supplies. Let's try not to think about it until tomorrow morning when we can see what we're doing. Why don't you tell me about your dream instead?"

Robin could tell that her cheeks were turning red. "Well, ah, you were there."

"Was that a good thing or a bad thing?"

"Good. *Very* good." She stroked his arm. "We were here in Alpine Grove, actually."

"And I'm guessing there was no creepy howling, since it was a good dream and not a nightmare."

"No. But I said something to you and now I think maybe I should say it in real life too, but I don't know what you'll think. Maybe I'm more sure of myself in my dreams. Sometimes my subconscious knows things before the rest of me, I guess."

"What do you want to say?"

She scrambled up and sat up straight, so she could look into his eyes. "Now that we've spent all this time together, I've found out that the more time I spend with you, the more time I *want* to spend with you. And, well, I think I'm falling in love with you. I've never felt this way about anyone before."

A spark of emotion flickered in Alec's eyes, but Robin couldn't tell what he was thinking. He took her hand. "I'm not sure what to say."

"The best answer is to say you feel the same way. But not if it's not true."

He laced his fingers with hers and kissed the top of her hand. "I like you. And I agree that spending all this time together has been great. We have a lot of fun and you're easy to talk to." A corner of his mouth turned up. "And, we have this amazing chemistry, so half the time I'm with you, I want to rip your clothes off."

Robin took her hand away. "I thought you'd say something like that. It's okay. I know we haven't known each other long. You probably think I'm some clingy woman who is after your money like that horrid woman Anita you told me about. Now I'm worried that telling you this might have ruined everything."

Alec looked at the window as the shrieking animal cry surrounded them again. He turned back to Robin. "No. It's fine. I don't think you're clingy, the death grip you have on my arm notwithstanding."

"I wish that creepy sound would stop."

He pulled his forearm out of her grasp so he could wrap her in a hug. "I know. I do too."

The noises finally subsided and they took the dogs out on leashes for their final walk of the evening. Although Robin was glad that it was quiet, she found herself lying wide awake listening to Alec's even breathing as he fell asleep. She was such an idiot. Why did she have to go and tell him how she felt? Well, it was too late now. Fortunately, nothing seemed particularly awkward between them after she'd opened her big mouth.

She should just forget about the conversation, but a wounded little part of her heart wanted to rail and cry because Alec didn't feel the same way about her as she did about him. It was like some dreary old country song. She could practically hear the steel guitar. How pathetic and girly could she be?

The next morning, they took the dogs down to the beach for some playtime. The sun had just come up and the air was crisp and energizing. Robin stood with her hands in her coat pockets and Alec put his arm around her. They watched as the dogs romped through the sand, trouncing each other at every opportunity. By the time Emma and Leroy had worn themselves out, their tongues were hanging out to the side. Robin laughed, "Oh Em, you have sloppy tongue."

Alec smiled. "They sure do get along well with each other."

They walked up the path to the cabin and settled the dogs in for a nap. Robin gathered up notebooks from the table and handed them to Alec. "Here you go."

Alec took the flip chart and stand and they went to set up the training area before everyone arrived later in the day. Once everything was set, they went back down toward the lake. A small rowboat was sitting on the shore. Robin walked up to it. "Where did this come from?"

Pulling on the rope, Alec dragged the boat farther up on the sand. He bent to look at the interior. "Look at this— under those chains, there's a huge hole."

"What?"

He pointed. "This boat will sink like a stone if anyone takes it out. And who rows around with a pile of chains like this?"

"Maybe Ernie is catching some big fish."

"Chains like this aren't generally involved unless you're on a trawler. Not a rowboat."

Robin turned her head to look at the empty beach. No one else was around. "We should see if Ernie is here somewhere. I'm starting to worry again that he's at the bottom of the lake."

They walked up to the lodge and found the door to Ernie's apartment slightly ajar. Robin tapped on the wood and pushed the door all the way open. Ernie was sprawled out on the sofa snoring with his headphones on. Robin put her hand to her chest. "That's a relief."

Alec said, "He's going to be pissed off when he finds out what happened to his boat."

"What if he doesn't notice?" Robin quietly shut the door and faced Alec. "Maybe we should move it farther up onto the grass so he doesn't try to go out in it."

"You're probably right. He probably can't drag it far by himself."

Back at the beach, they considered the damage to the boat and potential new locations for it. Alec gazed around the area. "Maybe we can walk it up to the parking lot. It would be difficult to get it back to the lake from there."

Robin groaned. "Ugh. That's so far away. And uphill."

"Hey, this was *your* idea."

"Don't remind me."

~

After dragging the rowboat up the hill, Robin was grumpy and almost every one of her muscles hurt. This was not a promising beginning to the retreat. The attendees were supposed to arrive in a couple of hours and Robin was already in a foul mood. As she and Alec walked back to the Pine Cone cabin to retrieve the dogs for an outing, her mind was cluttered with less-than-angelic thoughts. Alec seemed equally subdued. What was he thinking about?

She stopped to look out at the lake and he paused alongside her. The view was absolutely stunning and Robin took a deep breath.

Alec said, "Is everything okay?"

"I'm tired, sore, and pissed-off." She took another breath. "But it's so beautiful here. Sometimes I have to stop and enjoy it."

"I know what you mean. It's strange. Even though I'm worried about who or what might have damaged that boat and about seeing eight surly marketing people who *really* don't want to attend training, part of me just feels happy and relieved to be here."

Robin put her arms around his neck. "Have I mentioned lately that you should consider taking a real vacation?"

"Not lately." He bent to kiss her. "But we do have some time before everyone shows up, so we should enjoy our last moments of freedom."

"Good point."

Later, the dogs indicated they were unwilling to wait any longer for their afternoon walk, so Robin and Alec leashed them up and started down the path. Robin started to unhook Emma's leash so she could run and looked up ahead on the trail as she released the clasp. What was that? Emma took off and Robin started to run after her. She stopped when she reached a large red puddle. Emma's paw prints continued down toward the lake and Robin yelled for Emma to come back.

Emma returned, proudly carrying something large in her jaws. Alec ran up to Robin and held Leroy's leash back as he crouched down next to the paw prints. He didn't say anything for a moment, then looked up at Robin. "Given your artistic background, you can probably tell that's not red paint. It looks like blood."

Robin put Emma's leash back on and took the bone from her mouth. "Yuck, Emma!" She crouched next to Alec. "*Mother plucker*, that's disgusting! Did something just die here?" She stood up. "Where is it? Do you think it's related to the animal cries? But wait—shouldn't there be a trail if it wandered off?"

"I have no idea."

Robin looked at the bone in her hand and flipped it into the grass, waving her hand in disgust. "Eww, that looks like… well, it's *not* an animal bone."

Alec leaned over to peer at it. "Maybe a femur?"

She wrapped her arms around her waist with a shudder. "Ugh! I'm completely freaked out now. We need to get the dogs out of here. I'm calling Kat to see if she can board them. It's too late today with everyone about to arrive, but one or the other of us needs to stay in the cabin with the dogs. I'll see if I can drop them off at the kennel in the morning."

"Maybe this was just a coyote having a squirrelly snack or something."

"That bone is huge. It was *not* from a squirrel. It's big enough to be a person's leg. If something happens to Emma and Leroy, I'll never forgive myself."

Alec nodded his head. "You're right. I have to be in training a lot of the day, so we can't really watch them. I'll pay whatever the boarding costs."

"Thank you. Maybe you can watch the dogs while I deal with the arrivals. They're going to be here soon."

He took the leashes from her. "Good luck. Give my best wishes to Clark, the world-class marketing analyst—in his own mind anyway. I'm sure he'll be leveraging his core competencies."

"I'm guessing from your tone that you're not best buddies."

"No."

Robin walked up the path toward the lodge. Alec hadn't told her much about the marketing people who would be arriving. All Robin knew was that they were people whose position on the org chart placed them far, far above her pay grade. Of course that wouldn't be hard.

As she walked into the lodge, it seemed extra silent for some reason. She went behind the desk and sat down in the rolling chair. The door to Ernie's apartment was closed, but he was probably in there. Robin wasn't up for trying to rouse him again, since he'd probably just yell at her. Her nerves were already a little frazzled. Although she didn't necessarily faint at the sight of blood, it was not exactly one of her favorite things either. Maybe there really was a ghost. Someone or something certainly was doing its best to make it unpleasant to be here. If Julia Lambert wanted the place to herself for all eternity, fine. She could have it after this week.

Robin picked up the receiver and dialed Kat's number. With any luck, the check she had given Kat had cleared by now. If not, the woman probably wouldn't be too excited about boarding Emma again. After Kat answered, Robin tried to muster up her most syrupy and convincing voice to commence begging. "I hate to ask you this, but I really need your help. Something is going on here at the lodge and I'd like to board my dog Emma. And Leroy too. I know it's last minute, but it's kind of an emergency."

After a long pause, Kat said, "Leroy? Do you mean you want to board *two* dogs this time?"

"Yes, I'm sorry. The other dog is named Leroy. He's the stray dog I asked you about. No one claimed him and now he's Alec's dog."

"Alec?"

"Yes, he's um, well, we work together. We're doing another retreat here at the lodge and he's doing the training, so he can't really watch Leroy. I'm worried about the dogs. Is it okay if they stay there with you? I'd like to drop them off tomorrow morning. Is your driveway fixed?"

"Yes, the driveway is significantly better since it finally stopped raining."

"I know! Isn't the weather amazing? Please, please say yes. Oh, and Alec said he will pay for it. He is a bit more… affluent …than I am."

"All right. But please don't come out here before eight."

"Okay. I'll see you at eight."

Robin hung up the phone and placed her elbows on the desk. Thank goodness. The last thing she needed was for something to happen to Emma. Even the thought made her heart do a little lurch in her chest.

At the sound of the door opening, Robin looked up. A dark-haired man with a scowl on his face walked up to the desk. He placed his hand on the counter. "Well, we finally made it here to this miserable hole. Where's my room?"

Robin smiled sweetly. "You must be Clark."

"Yes. Have we met before?"

"No. Just a lucky guess."

Chapter 13

More Bold

R obin dealt with introducing herself, handing out keys, and showing everyone to their rooms. At this retreat, six women and two men were scheduled to attend. After Clark announced their arrival, the other people trickled into the lodge building. Robin mentally reviewed which names went with which faces so she could remember them at dinner later.

Apparently, Alec wasn't the only one who wanted to give Clark a wide berth. The man seemed to have nothing good to say about anything. After spending hours in a van with him, the others probably needed to decompress. Robin said a small prayer to the North Fork Lodge plumbing gods that the guy's shower was functional. It was daunting to consider how unpleasant Clark was likely to be during the training. No wonder Alec had been so quiet. He was probably bracing himself.

Robin checked in the kitchen and Chuck had already arrived with the roadies. She walked over to the large metal stove. "It's good to see you in person again after all that time on the phone."

Chuck brandished a long wooden spoon and bowed flamboyantly. "You guys are paying for my kid's braces. As far as I'm concerned, you can do as many retreats as you want."

Robin laughed. "Do you need anything?"

"Nope, we've got it under control. See you at dinner."

Pleased that as usual, Chuck seemed to have the food program well in hand, Robin walked back down to the Pine Cone cabin. She opened the door and Emma and Leroy launched into a cacophony of barking. "Shhh, you guys. You're supposed to lay low."

Alec sat up and rubbed his eyes. "So everyone made it?"

"Yes. Everyone is here except Darrell. Do you know when he's showing up?"

"Not exactly. It's a private jet, so he can get here pretty much whenever he wants."

"Okay. I think we're off the hook until dinner then." Robin crawled onto the bed next to Alec. "Chuck's here and it's all looking good food-wise."

He put his arms around her. "You can help me watch the dogs sleep."

"It looked like you were watching with your eyes closed."

"Maybe. Reading too much marketing-speak has that effect on me."

Robin jerked awake at the pounding on the door. The dogs leaped up and started barking and Alec launched out of the bed, tripping over Leroy. "Quiet, Leroy!"

He pushed the dogs back and opened the door. Darrell strode in and stopped when he saw Robin. "What are you doing here?"

"I'm supposed to be here."

Alec pointed to the piles of papers littering the bed, "She's helping me learn all this material I'm supposed to teach."

Darrell looked unconvinced. "What happened to this place and where is Ernie?"

Robin got up off the bed and tried to smooth out her hair. "He's probably in his apartment watching TV."

"I knocked on the door and no one answered." He turned to Alec. "Do you know why there is a boat in the parking lot? And there's a weird tarp and garbage can in the lodge. What's with that?"

Alec said, "Remember when I told you that the lodge might not be quite the same as you remembered it? That's what I meant. I *told* you it needs some help."

"I can't get a cell-phone signal anywhere!" Darrell pulled a phone out of his pocket at shook it at them. "No one can reach me."

"They can leave a message and there's a phone in the lobby you can use," Robin said. She touched Alec's arm. "Why don't you go up to the lodge with Mr. Lambert, so he can talk to Ernie?"

Darrell turned to Alec. "I need to talk to you anyway."

Robin said, "Please don't tell Ernie about the dogs. They're going to the boarding kennel tomorrow morning."

Darrell shook his head. "All right. I don't care. Let's go."

Robin closed the door behind them and breathed a sigh of relief. She stroked Emma's head. "Maybe we could go for a little stroll while they're gone. You probably need an outing by now."

After the dogs had a short on-leash tour of the grassy areas near the cabin, she fed them dinner and they settled in for more relaxation. She hoped Alec would be back soon, since she needed to make sure everything was still on track in the kitchen.

A woman screamed outside and Robin jumped up off the bed. Grabbing her key off the dresser, she rammed it into her pocket. She bent down and held her palms under the two canine chins. "If strangers try to break in, you need to bite them. I mean it. Bite them *hard*."

The dogs looked like they'd be up for some ferocity if it was warranted, so Robin left and locked the cabin behind her. It was just for a minute. The sound of the woman screaming echoed through the trees again and Robin ran up the path to the lodge. Alec, Darrell, and Ernie were standing on the porch looking down at a tall woman that Robin knew was Paige, the Creative Director. She was pointing at the side of the building.

Robin ran up to Alec and Darrell, who had walked down the steps. Paige hiccupped and waggled her index finger. "I… what…I don't…what…yuck!"

Robin walked over to the woman and put her arm around her shoulders. "Are you okay, Paige?"

Paige shook her head and Robin looked at the wall, which had a strange symbol on it that looked like it had been painted with red paint. Uh-oh. She glanced at Alec, who moved closer to the wall. He shook his head slightly. It wasn't paint. This was getting scary.

Ernie stomped over to Darrell and Alec and put his hands on his hips. "What is going on? I didn't give anyone permission to paint. And they aren't even good at it either." He glared at Robin. "Did you hire painters too?"

Robin said, "No! Just people to clean. I told you about that. I have no idea what this is." Maybe that was a little fib. She did have some idea. Some horrible person was wandering around with blood and a paintbrush. It was like some late-night horror movie.

She looked at the symbol more closely. The paint slashes almost looked like letters, but not quite. TUO TIG? What if it were reversed? She covered her mouth with her hand. In that case, it would say "GIT OUT" except with horrendous penmanship. Or brushmanship? Whatever it was, it was messy and the spelling wasn't the greatest either. Did poltergeists always write backwards? Or was that just a movie thing? Who did you ask to find out answers to this type of question?

Darrell pointed at Alec and said, "You. Clean up the wall."

Paige hiccupped again loudly and Darrell pointed at her. "You. Go have a glass of water." With one last horrified glance at the wall, she ran up the steps and went inside.

Darrell turned to Ernie. "We're not done talking. Let's go down to my cabin."

Robin said, "It's right down that path."

He glared at her. "I *know* where it is. I was coming to this place when you were in diapers."

Robin could tell her cheeks were red and she studied her tennis shoes for a moment as Darrell and Ernie wandered off. Alec came up to her and whispered, "Okay, now *I'm* getting freaked out too."

She looked into his eyes. "I've got to go. I left the dogs alone. When you're done with this, come get me and I'll deal with dinner and bring you back some food."

"You always have a plan, don't you?"

"When you return, the second phase of my plan is to give you a big hug. By then maybe I will have stopped shaking."

"If not, the hug will help."

"I'm counting on it."

~

After Alec returned and Robin got her hug, she went to the lodge to ensure that dinner went as planned. She sat down next to a woman named Jill, a marketing manager who had come from the High Country catalog after the merger. The woman had a pixie haircut and was wearing a moss-colored dress that brought out the flecks of green in her pretty hazel eyes.

Robin put her napkin in her lap. "Hi Jill. Did you get settled in okay?"

"Yes, although there certainly are a lot of odd noises here."

Robin didn't want to hear Jill's answer, but it would have been impolite not to ask. "Oh dear, I'm sorry to hear that. What kind of noises?"

"Well there are random doors slamming and I kept hearing the sound of water running somewhere."

"It's an old building and people were probably washing up before dinner." Robin twisted her napkin. At least the horrifying crying noises hadn't started yet.

"Yes, I know." She smiled. "I guess I'm used to my house out in the quiet suburbs. We just bought a place out in Lake Oswego, and I love it there."

Darrell walked up and sat down heavily next to Robin. Jill sat up straighter and said, "Hello Darrell, what a pleasant surprise! I didn't know you would be here. Are you going be participating in the training? I would welcome the opportunity to share my ideas about enhancing brand awareness with you."

Darrell gave her an irritated glance. "No. Alec is doing the training. Talk to him. I have other things to deal with here, and then I've got to get back to Portland as soon as possible." Ignoring Jill's crestfallen look, he turned to Robin. "You and Alec were right. It's not good. I left him in the apartment with a piece of bread. That's all he eats and that can't be healthy. I'm taking him to the doctor tomorrow. Gloria is getting names for me."

Darrell undoubtedly didn't want to reveal much about his uncle in front of Jill, so Robin said simply, "I'm so sorry, Mr. Lambert."

Darrell shook his head. "I know you're being polite, but I think at this point you can call me Darrell." He grabbed a piece of bread from the basket and took a bite. "At least the food is good. You took my advice there."

Robin smiled. "Chuck is completely unflappable and a fantastic cook."

"I suppose he told you all the ghost stories?"

"Yes, Chuck likes to talk while he cooks. I've heard quite a bit about Julia Lambert at this point. At the last retreat, there was a big storm and the electricity went out. Everyone thought it was Julia."

Darrell shrugged. "Hey, don't underestimate her."

Clark placed a glass of water on the table and sat down next to Darrell. "I'm glad to see you here, Darrell. I need to talk to you."

Robin could practically feel Darrell's muscles tense as he said evenly, "What do you want, Clark?"

Clark widened his dark eyes, which sported thick black lashes. "Have you actually *seen* the latest ad copy? It's boring. No one's going to read that. We need more bold. More flash.

How can we sell anything with these dull-as-dirt ads? I know there are ways to increase wallet-share on a customer-by-customer basis and I want to have some face time with you about it."

Darrell waved his hand dismissively. "This isn't my problem. You need to talk to Alec about advertising."

Clark slapped his palm on the table. "I already did. That guy is useless and you know it. Did you see the headline for the *Better Homes and Gardens* ad? Someone changed it from what I wrote. Now it's a warm bowl of nothing. We need to leverage some wordsmithing best-practices to add wow factor."

"So fix it."

"But what about the campaign? It has to be consistent. Why do I always get pushback? I have to have the same conversation with every ad agency I work with. Those people always throw me under the bus. No one understands my vision."

"Talk to Alec and figure it out." Darrell stood up. "I need to make some calls now. Robin, I'll talk to you tomorrow. Thanks for your good work here."

Robin smiled at Darrell and then glanced at Clark, who was glaring at her. She said, "I hope everything is okay with your room."

He took a drink of water and then slammed the glass on the table, causing a few droplets to spill on the tablecloth. "Who *are* you, anyway?"

"I told you, my name is Robin. Normally, I work in merchandising, but I'm managing the retreat this week."

"So I don't suppose you know where Alec Montgomery is, do you? I haven't seen that show pony anywhere and I need to touch base with him. He *is* here, right?"

"Oh yes, I'm quite sure he's around somewhere."

The rest of dinner was long and awkward, filled with attempts at warding off animosity from Clark and making small talk with Jill and another woman named Inga, who was an art director with the thickest, most luxurious light-brown hair Robin had ever seen. Finally, when she could gracefully excuse herself, Robin went to the kitchen, got a care package from Chuck, and returned to the Pine Cone cabin.

Alec glanced at her face and said, "What happened to you?"

"I had to sit next to Clark. He's looking for you, by the way. And he's not happy."

"Clark is never happy." Alec sat down at the desk with the plate of food. "I suppose he told you that the ads are boring and need to be rearchitected. I'm guessing he wants to have a skull session with a deep dive into recontextualizing the language of penetration pricing."

Robin giggled. "Yes! How did you know?"

"Welcome to my world." He pointed his fork at her. "Now you know why I like it here so much. No one ever asks me for more bold type."

Robin walked over and kissed his neck. "I'm sorry, but your world is unpleasant."

"Tell me about it."

The next morning, Robin loaded Emma and Leroy into the Jeep for the ride out to the kennel. The scary noises had kept her awake again and it was clear something was going on. It would be much easier to get through the rest of the week without worrying about the dogs. Escaping for a little while also made it possible to avoid people at breakfast who'd undoubtedly heard the eerie noises too.

The driveway to the kennel was covered with new, bright-gray gravel, which was a stark contrast to the deep green of the trees. The roadway had been smoothed, so it was almost like driving on a regular asphalt street. What an astonishing difference. Not even one pothole graced the long winding path through the towering evergreens.

Robin arrived at the house at precisely eight o'clock. As she drove up, Kat was sitting on the bottom step reading something. She stood up and walked toward the Jeep.

Robin got out and was relieved to find that Kat appeared to be cleaner and more awake than the last time she'd been here with Emma. "Hi! Thank you again for letting Emma and Leroy stay. And your driveway is amazing. What did you do?"

Kat shrugged. "Moved a lot of rocks and spent enormous sums of money. I'm glad you noticed the difference. I'd hate to think I spent all that cash for nothing."

"No, it's great. Really!" She turned, opened the back door of the Jeep, leashed the dogs, and they both jumped to the ground. "You know Emma already. This is Leroy."

Leroy wagged his tail at the new human and Kat smiled as she bent to greet him. "Aww, you remind me of Linus. It must be a big-dog thing."

Robin handed the leashes to Kat. "Oh wait—one more thing." She turned back to the Jeep and dug around in her purse. She handed a check to Kat. "I asked Alec to write the check in advance. After last time, I mean, that was so rude of me. Post-dating a check? I was so embarrassed and it's not very businesslike. I'm so very sorry about that."

"It's okay. Once it cleared, you contributed to the new driveway rock."

Robin brightened. "Oh, that makes me feel better. I should get back now, but I'll be back on Saturday to pick them up."

"We'll be here."

~

Kat and Joel did the canine introduction routine with Leroy and the resident dogs and discovered that like Emma, Leroy was a mellow dog who just wanted to be friends with everybody. After determining canine compatibility, they set out on the trail for the dog walk through the forest. Joel walked Leroy, Kat walked Emma and Chelsey on leashes, and the other dogs cavorted around them. It was quite a crowd.

Joel gestured toward Leroy. "Did you notice that this dog has sort of weird fur? His back has a white-on-white stripe."

"Robin told me Leroy was a stray. Even though he's a big dog, he's incredibly skinny. Now he's probably getting healthier, and that might be his new improved fur growing in. He sure is a happy guy."

"True. I'm still surprised you were willing to take on two dogs, given all the stuff happening right now."

"I know. But all that stuff is expensive. We need all the money we can get. The fact that Robin said she was getting someone else to pay improved my mood. She implied that Leroy's dad is more financially solvent than she is, so I agreed. In fact, she paid in advance and apologized for the problem with the check last time. So that made me feel better too."

"She paid in advance? Wow, that's a novelty."

Later, Kat was sitting at her desk staring at her computer and hoping that she'd suddenly gain a flash of inspiration on her latest article. Her office chair was surrounded by dogs. Leroy was lying on the left side, Linus was behind her, and Tessa was sprawled out on the right. She looked down. "Listen here, I need to get up, so somebody needs to move."

Leroy raised his head and wagged his tail a few times. Kat bent to stroke the fur on the top of his head. "You're such a sweet boy. No wonder Robin was worried about you." Linus got up and walked around so he could shove his nose into her lap. "You are too Big Guy. Don't worry, I still love you."

The phone rang and Tessa leaped up and started barking. Kat shushed at the dog and smiled at her friend Maria's voice. "Hi, how are you?"

"Working hard here in the advertising coal mine, girlfriend. But I have news."

Kat pushed Linus's nose off of her thigh. "You mean you found out about Ned?"

"You know it. And baby, have I got stories to tell!"

Kat laughed. "Okay, this should be good. Do you want to try out our sleek new driveway? I'll give you wine and Joel can make you a meal that's created from actual food-based ingredients, instead of the chemical concoctions you tend to eat."

"I suppose I should dine on something healthy every once in a while to keep my fine body working at peak performance. See you later."

Kat spent most of the rest of the day fighting with software, trying to get more words written on her article, and walking dogs. Leroy and Emma were obviously best friends, but didn't seem concerned about sharing some quality nap time with the rest of the pack.

After feeding the dogs, she let them all go upstairs while she relaxed on the sofa with Joel and some much-needed escapist fiction. At the knock on the door, all of the dogs launched into a parade of frantic running and barking.

Kat tried to quiet the cacophony and let Maria in. "Hi. Sorry about the noise."

Maria looked around at the canine faces that surrounded her sniffing at her dress. "You seem to have added to the furry collection."

"That white one is Leroy and the little red and white one is Emma."

"Why are the big dogs always rude?" Maria pushed Leroy's muzzle away from her. "Listen buddy, not on the first date. I don't know you that well yet."

Kat shooed the dogs back out of the entryway toward the living room. "Everyone go lie down." She turned to Maria. "Do you want wine?"

"Yes I do! I've been working like a fiend all day and I'm ready to kick back and imbibe a bit." She waved at Joel. "What's up in geek land?"

He smiled. "You don't want to know."

Maria pointed at him and grinned. "You are so right!"

Joel got up and walked into the kitchen. "I'll open the wine for you."

Maria nudged Kat and whispered, "Hey, he's downright talkative today. What happened?"

"Oh, spare me." Kat rolled her eyes at Maria's typical wisecrack about Joel's quiet nature. "Sit down and start spilling your story."

Maria took the glass from Joel and took a sip. "Oooh, my favorite vintage—cheap."

Kat waved her hands in a get-on-with-it motion. "So, I guess Sharon finally dredged up Ned?"

"Yes, she did! And she got him to tell *all*. Even I was impressed with her interrogation skills."

"I'm guessing it involved getting him drunk."

Maria tilted her glass at Kat. "Got it in one, girlfriend. I guess he's been living in Vegas, but he was in LA for some reason and Sharon convinced him to meet up with 'the old gang' as if it were something fun. Barb was there too for moral support, and Sharon brought the weird guys from the mailroom, so it seemed like more of a gang. Having more people there made it easier to run away from the loser once she scored her intel."

"She brought Frank and Duncan? They never went to the bar with us back then. Good thing Ned has killed so many brain cells by now."

"I know. I'm sure he wasn't any the wiser."

Joel sat down at the table next to Kat. "So what happened on the ill-fated trip to Vegas?"

Maria raised her glass toward Joel. "Wow, curiosity makes you downright chatty."

Kat said, "Get on with the story. This is my youthful indiscretions we're talking about, and I'd like to get it over with. Why did Ned abandon me in some creepy Vegas wedding-chapel restroom?"

"He was there for a business venture."

Both Joel and Kat said, "What?"

Kat continued, "What kind of venture?"

"The story goes that Ned had a great business idea. He believed that just because people like him have no friends, it doesn't mean they shouldn't be able to drive in the HOV lane."

"You mean the carpool lane on the freeway?"

"Yes. You need two people in the car to be 'high occupancy' or you get a ticket. But if no one wants to ride with you, there's a significant problem."

Joel said, "I get the impression Ned was familiar with that issue."

"He was disgusting," Maria said.

Kat nodded sadly. "Loathsome. I'd like to state for the record that my taste in men has improved dramatically since then."

Joel put his hand on Kat's. "I'm flattered, although it sounds like you had nowhere to go but up."

"This is sadly true and a point I have made more than once," Maria said as she peered at the burgundy droplets at the bottom of her glass.

Kat waved her hands in exasperation. "Let's not dwell on that. Could you please get on with it? What does the HOV lane have to do with anything?"

"Ned's big business idea was…" Maria waved her empty glass with a flourish. "…blow-up dolls for commuters!"

Joel laughed as he poured wine into Maria's glass. "You've *got* to be kidding."

"Thank you and no way. I would not kid about something like this. He got a line that the Elvis guy in Vegas had a close-out on inflatable dolls."

"*That* was what was going to change everything?" Kat put her forehead in her palms. "I was abandoned 400 miles from home for blow-up dolls? I can't believe this. Well, I sort of can, since it's Ned, but ugh."

"It gets better." Maria took a sip from her glass. "Apparently there was a chase—just like in the movies. You shouldn't have passed out. You missed everything."

Kat shrugged. "All right, lay it on me. I'm not sure I could feel any more humiliated than I already do."

Maria took a sip and cleared her throat. "Okay, while you were indisposed in the ladies room, apparently a guy in a clown mask ran in and said, "Freeze!" Ned and George were standing there with Elvis, holding the boxes of blow-up dolls. They dropped them and tried to hide behind a plastic plant. Ned started to cry and then wet his pants. George started yelling at him and then Elvis told them both to shut up."

Kat sighed. "Crying? Yeah, okay, this sounds like Ned."

"So the guy in the clown mask comes and drags Ned out from behind the fake shrubbery and George makes a break for it. The clown guy runs after him, but he's not too speedy with those big floppy shoes and all. Meanwhile, Ned's standing there with Elvis, not knowing what to do. So they grab the boxes and run out of the building."

"Okay, so there was a lot of running away." Joel held up his palms. "Where did they go?"

Maria waved her glass at him. "Hey, Mr. Impatient, I'm getting there. The story is that Ned saw the clown gesturing wildly at George in an alley. They were obviously yelling at each other and about to really get into it. Then the clown uses one of those water-squirting flowers and totally drenches George. I guess it was one serious phony flower, not a lame one that does a wimpy stream."

"Because no self-respecting clown would be caught dead with a wimpy fake flower." Joel said as he began chuckling.

"So anyway, getting all soaked by a clown really made George mad and he hauls off and tackles the clown."

Kat started to giggle. "Clown fight! Clown fight!"

"Stop interrupting me!" Maria said. "Okay, so George and the clown start rolling around in the alley, which is full of old, nasty garbage because of an unfortunate Dumpster accident. Ned isn't exactly a hero, but it's George's car, so even Ned is smart enough to realize he's got a major transportation problem without George. So he takes his box of blow-up dolls and runs toward them, screaming. Then he throws the box at the clown, which knocks him over because, you know, those clown shoes are kind of tippy. The clown is slowed down enough that Ned and George have a chance to haul their stinky butts back to the car and bail out of Vegas."

Kat stopped laughing long enough to inquire. "So after all that, Ned didn't even get the blow-up dolls?"

"Nope. And he lost the money he'd paid for them too. Apparently, he's still angry. I guess he tried calling Elvis for a while, but he didn't get anywhere. And then he found out that the guy stole his idea."

Joel said, "So Elvis started selling blow-up dolls to commuters?"

"Yup. He got busted though, and had to serve time in the pokey."

"I feel better about being ditched now, since I was *this* close to living a life of crime." Kat held up her fingertips and turned to grin at Joel. "I'm also never going to be able to listen to the song *Jailhouse Rock* again without laughing."

Chapter 14

Big Bad Werewolf

After dropping off the dogs, Robin's day was filled with complaints almost from the moment she got out of the Jeep at the lodge. She'd been late for the training and had been trying to catch up ever since. Everyone had glared at her when she walked in, and it appeared that she had interrupted Alec, who was vehemently telling off Clark. The tension in the room had been extreme and Clark sat with his arms crossed, glaring at Alec and saying nothing.

Later, in the middle of a discussion on the history of the Eagle River brand, Darrell walked in and demanded to talk to Alec. After Alec left the room, Robin had tried to smooth things over, but probably only made matters worse. She got an earful about why each and every person did not need marketing training.

Jill, the woman who had spent most of dinner trying to suck up to Darrell, proclaimed that marketing was not the problem and that the company needed to "re-engage our core customers with compelling and differentiated campaigns."

Paige the frightened crier disagreed, saying that all they needed to do was "drop the green-field thinking and get our name out there to gain traction."

Inga of the fabulous hair said that "We have the lay of the land—what worked in the past will work now."

A marketing manager named Tom agreed. "What's the problem? I don't have the knowledge density to understand what the issues are here."

The copy manager Dawn claimed that all they had to do was "drop the prices to kick off a feeding frenzy."

Clark said that they needed to interface with design and "frontburner the copy to make it more impactful with fewer acronyms and more bold text."

Georgette announced that the brand didn't matter and they'd gone "into the weeds." Meanwhile Deb, a woman about four levels above Robin in merchandising, wanted to know why they needed a strategy anyway. They didn't have time for a strategy, so what was the net-net? Why were they even talking about it?

Robin had zero answers for any of these questions. She couldn't think of one acronym related to clothing, so what was Clark talking about? And the words net-net made her think about flounder, not catalog retail. What was that all about? Mentally throwing up her hands in disgust, she continued to nod as the group argued with one another until Alec finally returned. The marketing department was quite the little jargon-filled hornet's nest.

After the class, Alec disappeared to deal with whatever Darrell wanted, and Robin didn't see him for the rest of the afternoon. She found an old beat-up copy of a book in the cabin and spent most of the afternoon sitting out by the lake oddly absorbed in *Zen and the Art of Motorcycle Maintenance*. Years ago, a couple of her friends had mentioned the book, but she'd never read it. As the light started fading, she moved her reading inside and was curled up on the bed with the book when Alec walked in.

He sat down on the edge of the bed. "I hope your day was better than mine."

Robin smiled and moved over to give him a hug. "I'm pretty sure it was. Where were you? It's almost time for dinner."

"I know. I want to take a shower first and clear my head before I have to deal with people again."

"I'm people and I think you're fine. What happened?"

"True. You're one of my favorite people." He gave her a kiss. "It's not worth talking about."

She held up the book with the cover facing him. "Is this yours?"

"Yes."

"Really?"

"Don't look so shocked. I may read slowly, but I do read."

"I didn't mean it like that. It doesn't seem like the type of thing you'd be interested in. You seem more like the business-book type. The seven habits of super business moguls or something."

He stood up and began unbuttoning his shirt. "I grabbed it when I was packing. The last time I read it was when I dropped out of college and I had no idea what to do with myself. It talks about taking care of the things that are important to you and asking questions about your life."

"I know. I'm reading it. The author and his son are in Montana somewhere now."

He threw the shirt over a chair and grinned at her as he turned toward the bathroom. "Well see, you know what I mean then."

Robin looked down at the book. She did know what he meant, and reading it had brought home how little inquiry she had done into her own life. Ever. Maybe it was time she put a little more mental energy into what she was doing with herself and what she wanted her future to be like.

Alec seemed much more relaxed after his shower, but the animal cries had begun again, which was getting on Robin's last nerve. Her irritation level was rising precipitously. More than anything, she would like to stay here and *not* have to eat dinner with a bunch of angry, complaining people. But she had to. Throwing the book on the bed, she said, "So are you ready? It's time to go and be all polite and social now."

Alec raised his eyebrows. "What's with you?"

"I'm tired and I want that noise to go *away*. And I know everyone is going to yell at me again about all the weird noises in the lodge." She waved her arms in frustration. "I don't know what to do about it. I want it to please just *stop*."

"Yeah, I heard all about the noises in the lodge before the class. At the risk of making you even more angry, you don't believe in ghosts, do you?"

"Oh please. No, I don't."

Alec took both of her hands in his. "Good. I don't think we're being haunted by Julia Lambert either. But I do think someone is trying to scare us."

"Well, it's working."

Alec squeezed her hands. "I know we have to deal with dinner now, but think about this situation a little. Who would want us gone from here? And why?"

"Well, that woman Terri obviously wanted to get into your pants. Maybe she's got some other agenda."

Alec grinned. "I think she gave up on me and focused her agenda on Brett's pants. I would have thought he might be up to no good, but he seemed sort of distracted by the end of the last retreat."

"He was having child-custody issues. I think he had way too much on his mind, worrying about his kids."

"Okay. We should go. But please think about it, okay? You're really good at reading people."

Robin smiled. "Thanks. Can I have a hug for the road?"

"Absolutely."

∼

As Robin put a forkful of salad into her mouth, something outside the window caught her eye. What was that? She looked around the room and saw that all of the retreat attendees were present. Touching Alec's forearm briefly, she raised her eyebrows at him and excused herself from the table.

She hustled across the lobby area and went outside. The air was scented with acrid smoke. As she went down the steps she turned her head in an effort to isolate the smell. The animal cry arose, echoing through the forest, and Robin cringed involuntarily.

She turned to look behind her as Alec came down the stairs. "What is that smell?"

"Maybe a campfire?"

He pointed and took her hand, pulling her forward. "It seems like it's coming from over there."

"*Holy mother of pearl.* Is someone trying to burn this place down now?"

They stopped in front of a fire ring that had what looked like garbage burning in it. Alec looked at Robin. "Do you suppose it was just some kids having a party?"

"I don't know." Robin threw some sand on the flames and looked around for a container to put water in. "We have a whole lake here, so it should be easy to put it out."

They paused at the sound of the lodge door opening again. Darrell came down the steps and walked over to them. "What are you guys doing? Why are you making a campfire?"

Robin said, "We're not. We're putting it out."

"Do you two have some type of thing going on?" Darrel gestured at the smoldering remains. "Was this some romantic rendezvous?"

Alec said, "No. You just saw us eating dinner five minutes ago. Robin came out here and I followed her to make sure she was okay."

"I thought there was something out here." Robin said.

Darrell put his hand on his hip. "You couldn't see the fire from inside."

"No, that's not what I meant." Robin shook her head. "I thought I saw a *person* outside the window."

"Really?" Alec looked at Darrell. "Ernie isn't here, right?"

"No. I told you. The doctor had me take him over to that assisted-living place."

"Is he okay?" Robin said.

"They aren't sure. All they could tell me was that he hasn't been eating very much or very well. All I could get him to eat was a piece of bread." Darrell shook his head. "Poor guy. You wouldn't know it now, but he was the best uncle. He was hilarious and we did all kinds of fun stuff together when I was a kid."

"I'm sorry." Robin stomped the sand to put out the last tiny smoldering embers. "It is beautiful here and it would be so much fun for a kid."

"It was." Darrell put his hands in his pockets. "I gotta tell you, it kills me to see how run-down this place is now."

Alec said, "It's mostly cosmetic except for the lodge roof, I think. Some money and TLC would go a long way. I don't think Ernie has been up to it for a while."

"I know. I feel bad about that. Since my father died, I haven't paid attention to what was going on here. My mother nagged me about checking on Ernie. The last time I talked to him much he said he was refinancing this place. And then Mom started having health problems, and then the merger took up all my time. Then dealing with Sue." He ran his fingers through his hair and turned away from them toward the lodge. "I didn't get to finish my dinner. Could you make sure that's out? Having this place burn to the ground is the last thing I need."

Robin glanced at Alec, who stepped into the fire ring and stomped around some more. Something was up here, and she didn't know what it was. But she was willing to bet that Alec knew more than he was letting on.

He stepped back out of the fire ring and stood next to Robin. "I think it's okay now."

Robin faced him. "Do you want to tell me what's going on? What was the huge emergency and where were you all afternoon?"

Alec looked back at the lodge. No one was around, and he took Robin's hand. "I'm sorry. No one is supposed to know about this, but Darrell and Sue are probably getting divorced. As you might imagine, that has a considerable effect on the company, because they're the largest shareholders."

"What? That's impossible. The whole story of them starting the catalog in their living room is a retail legend."

"The reality was significantly less pleasant. Sue wants to get out of the business entirely. Obviously, that has a lot of implications for Eagle River." He squeezed her hand. "You absolutely can't tell anyone. I'm probably guilty of insider trading or something by telling you."

"Since I can't afford to buy even one share of Eagle River stock, I think you're safe. Do you think their divorce has something to do with whatever weird stuff is going on here?"

"The thought did cross my mind. But I'm not sure how it would be relevant."

"What happens if Ernie is too sick to run this place?"

"I think he already is. That's why Darrell wanted to talk to me. This afternoon we drove all over Alpine Grove. We talked to a lawyer in town. Darrell had to sign a power of attorney for Ernie because he was involuntarily committed. Then we got some of the financial and legal documents about this place."

"Poor Ernie. Are Darrell and Sue the only relatives he has?"

"Ernie and Myrtle never had kids, I guess." Alec shook his head. "I'm not sure Sue has ever been here."

Robin gestured toward the beach. "What's going to happen to the lodge if they get divorced?"

"I have no idea. Maybe it will be sold. I didn't get to see the documents, but I assume lakefront property like this would have to be worth a fortune."

"That's so sad. The North Fork has been in Darrell's family forever. Even the ghost is related to him."

"I know." He squeezed her hand again and let go. "We should get back. Darrell's certainly not going to believe we're not having some romantic rendezvous now."

She grinned. "It *is* kind of romantic out here."

"Except for the whole scary haunted-werewolf thing."

"Well, yeah, except for that."

As they slowly walked back to the lodge Alec said, "The other sort of awful thing about all this is that I'm going to probably have to work longer hours as Sue transitions out of the company."

Robin stopped and faced him. "How is that even possible?"

"I don't know. To be honest, it kind of makes me sick to think about it. I'm already kind of burned out."

"Kind of? *Kind of?*" Robin could tell the tone of her voice was shrill, but she didn't care. "You have got to be kidding me. I'll never see you. And apart from that, you're miserable. How long do you plan to wait until you actually decide to have fun or be happy again? Don't you ever want to have a *life?*"

Alec looked somewhat taken aback by her outburst. "I don't know. I guess I didn't think about it."

"Maybe you should." Robin thumped up the stairs away from him. She wasn't exactly a model for great life choices, but at least she wasn't miserable like he was. And seeing someone she loved so unhappy made her want to scream or cry. Or throw something at a wall.

Robin returned to her seat and, not surprisingly, found that her food was gone. And Clark was now sitting at the table. Perfect. As if she weren't already in a bad mood. Dessert had better include a whole lot of chocolate or there was going be *h-e-double-hockey-sticks* to pay. She grabbed a roll out of the basket, scowling as she chewed, mentally daring Clark to say something snotty. He glanced at her and looked away, suddenly deeply interested in the coffee dregs at the bottom of his mug.

Alec sat down next to her, took the last roll out of the basket, and began chewing. They ate in silence and watched as people slowly filtered out of the dining room. After everyone had left, Robin went back to the kitchen and snagged some leftovers before Chuck and the roadies finished putting it all away.

She set a plate in front of Alec. "I'm sorry I lost my temper."

He looked into her eyes. "It's okay. You're right. I'm kind of angry at myself too. If I had a spine, I'd say 'no Darrell, I'm not going to do that,' but I didn't. I never do. Part of me thinks that if I lose this job, I'll never get another one."

Robin smirked. "Give me a break. I'm the unemployable drone, stuck in dead-end jobs until I die or spreadsheet software is replaced by robots. You, on the other hand, can easily find another job. Companies are probably clamoring for you. *Heck-fire*, you can do whatever you want."

"Sure, until they find out that I'm not qualified. People will find out I'm not talented at much of anything and I just lucked into this job."

"I can't imagine why you think that. You work so hard."

"There's so much stuff I don't know and so many things I do wrong."

Robin put her hand on his. "You are so hard on yourself. It's not like you have to be perfect. No one is. The thing that bothers me is that you don't like what you're doing and you're obviously not enjoying it. If I'd never seen what you're like when you're happy, it wouldn't be so apparent when you're not."

Alec chuckled. "You said I am like a different person here."

"You are. And the happy version of you is a lot more fun to be around."

He stroked her hair and smiled. "Since I'm happy here, let's go back to our little home-away-from-home. And thanks. I need to think about what you said."

"I do too. Let's face it. It's not like I'm enjoying great career satisfaction either."

~

The next morning, Robin got ready to go to breakfast and the training class. While she brushed her hair, Alec was lying on the bed reading the gigantic marketing notebook again. She pointed the brush at him. "You have to be tired of that by now."

He grinned. "What clued you in?"

"The fact that you when you blink, your eyes stay closed too long."

"You never miss a detail. At least I'm well-rested." Putting the binder aside, he got off the bed. "Are you ready to deal with people who seem to dislike us more every single day?"

Robin raised a fist in a mock-enthusiastic cheerleading gesture. "Oh boy! Can't wait!"

He laughed and gave her a kiss. "Let's go."

After breakfast and the class, Darrell dragged Alec off somewhere again. Since she wasn't terribly interested in marketing, during class Robin had been writing down names and doodling arrows, trying to figure out who would have an incentive to try to scare people. She came up with nothing except a well decorated list.

Maybe Alec would finally tell Darrell he wasn't going to become his work wife once Sue left. Or not. It seemed like Robin couldn't do anything right. Her life was a mess. This retreat was a mess. After the class, she couldn't face dealing with people anymore, so she ran into the kitchen, grabbed some food, and went down to the beach. She sat on a bench looking out on the lake. It was so peaceful here. Maybe if she sat here long enough, she'd figure out what to do.

After the marketing people did the reviews, she'd undoubtedly lose her job. Alec would finally wise up and get a new job. Their whole relationship was completely doomed anyway. He'd already said he didn't feel the same way about her as she did about him. What was the point?

Maybe it would be simpler to quit, get it over with, and go back to Spokane. At least she had friends there. But then she'd lose everything she'd worked for in Portland, which seemed like a waste too. And the idea of never seeing Alec again made her stomach do a miserable little back flip. It seemed that she was good at making decisions, except for when it came to her own life.

She sighed and laid her head on her arms. Everything was all wrong and she didn't know what to do. She turned her head to look down the beach. What was that? She sat up straight and stared at the spot on the beach where a person had disappeared into the trees. Who was that? It was definitely *not* someone from the retreat.

Robin reflected for a moment on what she'd seen. What should she do? The person had been a balding older man with glasses who was wearing black clothing. He had been walking toward her down the beach, but then turned into a forested area. It was definitely not Ernie. This guy was short and stout, whereas Ernie was tall, skinny, and residing elsewhere now. It also was not anyone from Eagle River who was staying at the lodge, or one of Chuck's roadies. She'd certainly seen all of those people enough to recognize them. A nearsighted rotund guy wearing a black turtleneck didn't seem like someone out fishing, either. What was he doing?

Robin got up and began slowly walking toward the copse of trees. It was probably a stupid thing to do, but what if this was the person who was trying to scare them? Why else would he be sneaking around like this?

She stopped at the edge of the forest and peered into the dark foliage. A narrow cleared area meandered through some shrubs into the trees. With a deep breath, she stepped forward onto the path. Even though the sun wasn't going to set for hours, it was shady among the evergreens and shadows fell across the way. Trying to step as quietly as possible, she moved forward until she came to a clearing. She stepped behind a huge tree and watched as the man sat down in a folding chair in front of a tent. He seemed to be messing around with something electronic. Robin put her hand in front of her mouth to stifle her gasp of surprise. It was a CD player! Maybe the horrible noises were from a gruesome audio recording. Who would record something like that?

She stepped backward and a branch snapped loudly, breaking the hush of the clearing. Stilling herself, she waited to see if the man had heard. He looked up, shook his head, and mumbled something.

There was no way she was going to confront an unknown man who probably was up to no good, but Robin wasn't sure she could leave without him noticing her exit. It was so quiet here in the forest, but eventually she'd have to move. If she could get back, she could return with other people. Like the police. If nothing else, this man was trespassing. She looked over her shoulder and tiptoed to a nearby tree. The man didn't look up. Repeating the process, she tiptoed from tree to tree until she was far enough away. Then she ran the rest of the way down the path and back to the beach and up to the bench again.

Panting, she sat down and looked up the hill at the lodge. Alec was standing on the front steps and he waved to her. She waved back and hoped he would come down to where she was because the idea of moving wasn't appealing after fleeing the forest. She put her elbows on her knees, closed her eyes, and rested her forehead on her palms, trying to catch her breath and allow her heart rate to return to normal. Maybe she should take up jogging.

Alec sat down next to her and she straightened and opened her eyes to look at him. He put his arm around her and pulled her close. "What happened? Are you okay?"

She turned her head to look up at the lodge. Darrell was standing on the steps looking down at them. Disentangling herself and moving away from Alec, she said. "I found someone in the woods and, well, basically, I ran away. But we should call the police."

"What do you mean? Like a transient?"

"No. A guy in black with an expensive tent and electronics. He had a CD player. I think he's playing those awful noises. And I'm willing to bet he's been sneaking around doing other stuff too. Maybe he set the fire. How horrible."

Alec leaned back and sighed. "So there really *is* someone behind all that?"

"Yes. We need to tell Darrell. It's his family's lodge." She turned and looked at him on the steps. "I hope he didn't see you."

"You're right, we should." He gave her a peck on the lips and grinned. "I don't care if he saw me because I already told him that we've been staying in the same cabin."

"I thought you didn't want anyone to know. Telling the CEO might not have been the brightest idea. Now I'm definitely going to get fired."

"You're not going to get fired."

"How do you know?"

"Darrell wants to send you to West Virginia."

"What? Why? Is this because I'm seeing you? I've never even been to West Virginia."

"No. Eagle River is opening a new distribution center there. He wants you to run it."

Robin put her hand to her chest. "Me? Is he insane?"

"No. He thinks you're amazing. Actually I do too, which is why I told him I thought you were qualified to do it when he asked me."

"Well, sending me across the country certainly makes breaking up easier." She wiped a tear off her cheek. "Earlier I was thinking it was inevitable, but still. I know this is a great opportunity, but the idea of not seeing you anymore truly breaks my heart."

"I don't want to do that." He took both of her hands in his. "In fact, being here with you, sharing the cabin, made me realize you are right. It's not just you. I want to be with you all the time too. I didn't say it before because I was too stupid, or surprised, or who knows what? You never know with me. But now I'm sure. I love you and if you want to take the job, I'll go with you to West Virginia."

Robin's eyes widened and she threw her arms around his neck and hugged him. "You'd do that?"

"Yes. But only if I can bring Leroy too."

"Absolutely. Emma would never forgive me if you didn't."

⁓

Alec cupped Robin's tear-stained cheek and rubbed it gently with his thumb. "So are you ready to meet Alpine Grove law enforcement?"

"Yes. We should go." She wiped her eyes hurriedly. "Do I look like a raccoon?"

"You're fine. Beautiful, in fact."

"Well then, all I can say is thank goodness for waterproof mascara."

He took her hand and they walked up to the lodge. Darrel waved in greeting when they reached the bottom of the steps. "So I guess you guys talked?"

Robin smiled. "Yes. Thank you for the opportunity, but we need to talk to you about something else that's going on here."

Darrell leaned against the porch railing and listened quietly as Robin explained what she had seen. He scratched his chin. "Yes, the person is trespassing. But I'm a little reluctant to call the police. Did the guy look dangerous?"

Robin shook her head. "No. He looked like an accountant. Or a fire hydrant."

Darrell chuckled. "That doesn't sound like Julia Lambert either."

"Not at all."

Darrell said, "The finances on this place are such a mess, I'm afraid I'm going to have to sell it. I can't stand the idea that it won't be in my family anymore, but Ernie has no kids and neither do I. Myrtle is going to roll over in her grave, but there's no way I can do anything with this lodge while I'm living in Portland. I've got enough problems dealing with Eagle River right now as it is. Maybe someone knows what's going on here and is trying to capitalize on that to get us to sell out cheap. I mean, this is Alpine Grove. Given the grapevine here, if the police come out, it could be the biggest news of the last twenty years. I'd rather not let the entire town in on Ernie's troubles."

Alec said, "What if we sort of casually go for a hike in the woods and have a chat with the guy?"

Robin looked at Alec. "What if he's got a gun? There was all that blood."

Darrell said, "Well, Ernie's got a hunting rifle. I'm not sure it actually works anymore, but I could whack someone with it."

After Darrell went inside, Alec took Robin's hand. "You could stay here if you want."

"No way. I want to find out who that guy is. I love this place and if Darrell is right and someone is trying to burn it down or drive out Ernie, that infuriates me. It's just wrong."

She walked down the steps. "There's a shovel and hoe leaning on the wall over here."

Alec picked up the shovel and examined it. "I'm not sure I've ever seen anything this rusty."

Robin picked up the hoe and the end fell off. "I guess it's lighter this way."

Darrell returned with the old gun and held it up. "Okay, I found it."

"What is that, a flintlock?" Alec said.

"I don't know, but it's so dusty in Ernie's apartment I feel like I need to take a bath now."

Robin pointed toward the lake. "The clearing is off to the left."

Darrell said, "I think I know where that is. We used to hang out there when I was a kid."

They walked down to the beach and turned toward the path. Robin put the stick over her shoulder. "We look like the seven dwarfs."

"Hi-ho, hi-ho," Alec said. "Sorry, but the dwarfs had better tools. Mining anything with this shovel isn't going to work."

Robin giggled and held the handle of the hoe up off her shoulder. "All I have is a stick."

They turned toward the path and Darrell said, "You two need to shut up."

Robin put her fingers to her lips and Alec smiled at her. They walked as quietly as they could toward the clearing. Robin lightly tapped Darrell's shoulder and pointed up the path. He nodded knowingly, and Robin could tell by the expression on his face that he'd been there before.

They hid behind the large tree Robin had used as camouflage and watched as the man sat in his folding chair, methodically picking at his teeth with a toothpick. His legs were crossed at the ankles and he looked relaxed, not threatening.

Darrell stepped into the clearing, startling the man, who waved his arms, flinging the toothpick away and tipping over the chair. He landed on the ground with a thud and Darrell pointed the gun at him. "Don't move. Who are you and why are you on my property?"

Robin and Alec stepped out from behind the tree to get a closer look at the man, who was trying to sit up, still waving his hands at Darrell. The poor guy looked like he might cry or vomit and he sputtered, "I'm just camping!"

Darrell said, "This is private property. What is your name?"

"Henry Wallace."

"Wallace?" Robin said. "Are you related to Moira Wallace?" Having spent hours doodling retreat attendee names, Robin was up on every person who had been in the vicinity lately.

Henry looked surprised, but said, "Yes. Moira is my wife."

Alec picked up the CD player. "What's this?"

"Just music. I like to fall asleep to classical."

Alec pressed the play button and the animal cry burst through the clearing, causing everyone to jump and Robin to drop her stick. Alec pressed the stop button, but the sound seemed to continue to echo off the trees.

Robin picked up the hoe handle again and waved it threateningly at Henry. "What are you doing, you horrid little man? Scaring people like that! We should call the police. Did you smear blood on the lodge building? How *could* you? What is wrong with you?"

Henry waved his hands back and forth in an effort to silence her tirade. "I didn't hurt anyone."

Darrell said, "You didn't answer me. Why are you here?"

The defiant expression on Henry's face devolved into despair. "Moira is going to kill me."

Darrell lowered the rifle. "Wait, *Moira?* Was her name Moira Laude before she got married?"

Henry nodded. "Yes. Her cousins had a place south of here and she went to the haunted house when she was a little kid."

Darrell said, "Myrtle laughed about the 'sticky kid' for years."

"The sticky kid?" Alec said.

"Yeah, Moira ate a caramel apple too fast and started crying when her fingers got sticky. She got to the point that she was completely hysterical and screaming—it was a serious temper tantrum with her lying on the floor and kicking her arms and legs. My aunt had to take her inside, clean her up, and calm her down because she was upsetting all the other kids."

Henry shrugged. "Moira is a little high-strung."

Darrell gestured toward the tent with the gun. "That doesn't explain what you're doing here."

"I thought Moira went home." Robin said. "Is she here somewhere too?"

Henry shook his head. "The idea of her spending time in a tent is preposterous."

Robin made a wry face. "Yeah, I can't quite imagine her camping."

Alec said, "You never answered Robin's question. Are you trying to scare people away?"

"It was Moira's idea." Henry sighed. "I just sold an apartment building we owned in Portland. After Moira got here, she wanted me to use the money to buy the lodge. The land is a gold mine and having those crummy old buildings on it is a waste. We want to tear it down and subdivide. She thinks condos here would sell like crazy. I'm not so sure. I think high-end homes would be more profitable."

Darrell said, "It's not for sale. Even if it were for sale, I'd never sell it to you."

Henry looked defiant again. "The place isn't yours to sell. Your uncle owns it. And I happen to know that he's mortgaged it to the hilt. The whole thing is about to go into bankruptcy auction."

"There are quite a few things you *don't* know," Darrell said. "But you can be sure that you are never going to own this property if I have anything to do with it, which I do."

Robin said, "So wait—Moira wasn't talking to her kids all that time, was she? She was talking to you. I bet you don't even have kids. No one would *really* name a child Mickey. You're bringing on a lifetime of mouse jokes."

"No, we don't have kids." Henry waved toward the lodge. "Did you know you can't get a cell signal anywhere in this stupid place? I had to walk up to the road and there's only one spot where you can sort of hear."

Darrell said, "Where's that?"

"On the road, up to the left near the mailboxes." Henry leaned back on his hands. "I'm exhausted from all that walking."

Alec said, "Darrell, do you want to press charges against this guy? Should we call the police? I don't know if you can bust someone for scaring people. But he is trespassing. And smearing blood all over the wall of the lodge is vandalism."

Robin said, "Where did you get the blood? And that huge bone? Did you kill something?"

Henry looked appalled. "No. I went to the grocery store. I told the butcher the bone was for my dog and I was making blood sausage."

"Gross." Robin turned to Darrell. "Let's call the police. You need to bust him for this!"

Darrell shook his head. "It's not worth it for this weasel." He brandished the gun at Henry again. "Get your car keys. You're leaving this stuff here. All of it. We are going to walk you to your car and Alec is going to follow you and make sure you leave town. If you ever, *ever* come back here, I'm calling everyone—the sheriff, police, and any other law enforcement I can find around here. I'll also call every developer I know in the western half of the United States to make sure you never buy another piece of property anywhere within 2000 miles of this lodge."

Henry nodded.

"And by the way, Moira is fired." Darrell smiled. "I'm pretty sure she's not going to get a good reference either."

Chapter 15

Inquiry

After escorting Henry off the North Fork property, Robin, Alec, and Darrell returned to the lodge and sat in the dining room waiting for dinner to be served. Darrell was flying back to Portland the next morning, and since no one else was around, he explained what Robin's new job would entail. Because so many Eagle River customers lived on the East Coast, they had determined it would be more cost-effective to ship from West Virginia instead of Oregon.

They planned to build a huge new warehouse in West Virginia that would employ hundreds of people. The old warehouse space in Portland would be converted into more call-center cubicles.

The people who worked in the warehouse were either going to have to move to West Virginia or get new jobs. They hadn't been told yet, and it was likely to be quite an unwelcome surprise. Robin had never been to West Virginia and had no idea what it was like.

Later, Robin was curled up with Alec in the Pine Cone cabin. He was reading marketing materials and she was sort of reading *Zen and the Art of Motorcycle Maintenance* again, in-between bouts of sleeping. When she opened her eyes again, the narrator was talking about climbing a mountain and adjusting the motorcycle's speed. It took a moment for her brain to reengage with the text, then a random and disturbing thought popped into her mind. What if the job in West Virginia turned out to be a more stressful version of what she was doing now at Eagle River? In many ways, what Darrell had described made it sound as if it would be. She sat up and nudged Alec's shoulder. "Hey."

He opened his eyes and picked up the binder that had slid off his lap. "What?"

"Have you ever been to West Virginia?"

"No. I've been to the East Coast, but not that area."

"After class tomorrow, do you want to go to the library and learn more about it? There must be a library somewhere nearby."

"Sure. That's a good idea."

The next morning, class went much more smoothly, probably because everyone had slept a lot better without the dying-animal noises. Alec and Darrell had collected all of Henry's stuff and gone through it. He'd used quite an elaborate collection of odds and ends to scare people. Everything from fishing line to fake spiders. The guy had certainly been creative.

After lunch, Alec and Robin went to the Alpine Grove library. It was an old two-story brick building with cast-concrete decorations around the arched doorways and windows. Two sets of concrete steps went up to the huge wooden doors. At the top of the steps, Robin pointed at a brick that had the year 1927 chiseled into it. "What a cool building for a library."

Alec smiled. "Alpine Grove takes its reading seriously, I guess."

They walked up to the front desk, where a woman with curly reddish-blonde hair was sitting surrounded by piles of books. She looked up and smiled. "May I help you?"

Robin said, "Yes. I need to learn more about West Virginia."

"What would you like to know?" The woman stood up and walked around the desk. "Are you doing a report? Research?"

"I might have to move there, but I've never been out East." Robin gestured toward the stacks of books. "Maybe there's something that explains what it's like."

Alec said, "All I know is that there are coal mines. Or there were."

The librarian said, "Yes. Fifteen percent of the nation's coal production comes from West Virginia, although tourism is now the major industry."

Robin raised her eyebrows. "*Holy schnitzel*, you sure know your state facts."

The woman smiled and gestured for them to follow her. "I'm Jan, by the way, and I'm one of the librarians here. I tend to remember trivia. It's an occupational hazard, I suppose." She pointed at a shelf. "This section has lots of state information. If there's something specific you need, I also can do some online searches for you."

Robin crouched down to look at the books. "Okay, thank you."

The librarian walked away and Alec crouched down next to Robin. He pulled out a book and stood up. "Hey, West Virginia was the first place to enact state taxes. Back in 1921."

"That's not a drawing card."

"Well, the first spa open to the public was located in Berkeley Springs in 1756."

"That's better."

"This is interesting. Approximately seventy-five percent of West Virginia is covered by forests. I bet it's nice in the fall when all the leaves turn."

Robin opened a book. "Famous West Virginians include author Pearl Buck and actor Don Knotts."

"That's Barney Fife from *The Andy Griffith Show*, right?"

"Yes. I'm not sure that's a drawing card, though."

They quietly flipped through pages for a while, whispering stats at each other. Finally, Robin closed her book. "I know many more facts about the great state of West Virginia now. But I can't tell if I would like living there or not. Particularly that part of West Virginia. It seems to be far away from everything."

"Except Ohio."

Robin shook her head. "I don't know. This whole thing feels so sudden. I can't decide if I'm anxious because I'm afraid I can't do the job or because I don't want to leave everything that's familiar. Or something else. I mean, this a huge opportunity. Why am I not more excited about it? Maybe I'm just a big fat chicken."

"We could fly out and visit." Alec wrapped his arm around her. "I know what you mean about it feeling kind of...funny, or wrong, somehow. Let's go back to the lodge and talk about it some more."

"I think I need to stare at the lake for a while. That seems to help."

Alec gave her a quick kiss. "Yes. It definitely does."

~

The next afternoon after class, Alec and Robin drove out to a hiking trail that the librarian had suggested. Robin said, "After all this time here, I'm finally going to get to enjoy some actual recreation."

"The waterfall sounds like it will be worth the hike."

"It's kind of cool that it was named after that pioneer lady, Lilly what's-her-name. That librarian, Jan, sure knows her local history. Even for a librarian, she's kind of scary smart."

Alec laughed. "I'm glad I wasn't the only one who thought so."

At the trailhead, Alec parked and they got out of the Jeep. He looked around the empty area. "It's a beautiful day. Where is everybody?"

"This is a little different than the Multnomah Falls trail. No people noises. Just birds and squirrels and whatever else is living in those trees."

"Lions, and tigers, and bears?"

"Oh my. I'll take them over rabid werewolves anyway. I've had enough fright nights to last me a lifetime."

They began walking up the sun-dappled path through the trees. Spring growth was bursting forth everywhere. Ferns, shrubs and countless other forest plants were producing lush new foliage, so it was as if they were viewing the entire trail through a green lens filter. The sweet earthy scent of leafy trees and pine needles surrounded them, and the only sounds were birds calling to one another occasionally.

They walked in silence for a while until they reached the overlook for the waterfall. Standing next to the railing, they gazed down into the stone canyon far below. Rushing water shot over a cliff into a deep blue pool. The roar of the water seemed to echo off the massive granite rocks.

Robin wiped some moisture from her cheek. "That is an impressive amount of water.

"Spring runoff, I guess." Alec took her hand. "Let's go over here. I can barely hear you."

They moved back, away from the overlook, to a mossy cleared area. Robin sat down and sighed as she leaned back against an enormous cedar tree. "This is amazing."

Alec sat next to her, leaned back, and closed his eyes. "I know. I wish I never had to leave here."

"What if we didn't?"

Alec opened his eyes and looked at her. "What?"

"Well, we've been talking about West Virginia and what it would be like. I'm sort of worried about what I'd have to do and your job would be pretty much exactly the same, except you'd have to spend more time on airplanes flying back to Portland."

"I know. I can't say I'm excited about that."

"What if we found jobs here? Or somewhere else we like. Just chuck Eagle River entirely. I don't have much to chuck and you have tons of money, so you could call it an extended vacation or a sabbatical or something."

He laughed. "You're really pushing that vacation idea pretty hard, aren't you?"

"Maybe. It's probably silly, but reading about traveling all over the country on a motorcycle makes me think about doing something different, I guess." She picked up a leaf and examined it. "When you talked to Darrell, did he say how Ernie is doing?"

"Yes, I guess he's improving. Part of his problem was a massive nutritional deficiency. Did you know that if you don't get enough vitamin B-1, it can affect your memory?"

"No. I've never heard of that."

"They aren't sure if he'll ever really completely recover, but I guess it's possible. Well, assuming he doesn't go back to eating junk again."

"Maybe that whole health-nut thing you have going isn't such a bad idea, after all."

He tickled her ribs. "My body is a temple."

"I know I like it." She grabbed his hand. "Do you think Ernie will ever be able to run the lodge again?"

"I don't know. I'm not sure anyone knows. It sounds like he's going to be in the assisted-living place for the foreseeable future. Darrell is distracted with the whole divorce mess, the new warehouse, and lingering merger issues you don't even want to know about." He slumped down against the tree. "I wish I didn't know. Returning to work is going to be a shock to my system."

"So are they just going to board up the North Fork? That's so sad. I can't bear the idea."

"I know." Alec sat up straight and looked into her eyes. "Unless I bought it."

"What? You want to buy a run-down lodge in Alpine Grove?"

"Why not? The location is beautiful. If we can successfully do retreats in a dilapidated haunted lodge, imagine if the place were actually fixed up!"

Robin grinned. "Are you serious? You might have to convince Julia Lambert to share it with you."

"Yes, I'm serious. As long you manage the place. We already know you're incredibly good at it, even under adverse circumstances."

"Adverse is a nice way to put it."

"You'd have to tell Darrell you aren't going to West Virginia though."

"That's fine with me! Do you think he'd really sell it to you?"

"I think he might. In addition to cash, I have an enormous amount of Eagle River stock I can negotiate with. If he were going to sell it to anyone, I think he'd sell it to me, since he's known me forever."

"*Jumpin' Jiminy*, with your advertising background, you'd be able to promote it. And unlike Ernie, you fix things. You'd be a fantastic owner!"

"There are a lot of details to work out, but I like the idea of doing something else with my life. Creating something that's actually mine, instead of making money for someone else, has a lot of appeal. No meetings and no one whining about stupid things like value propositions and bold type."

"This is so exciting!" Robin held out her hand. "Look, I'm shaking."

Alec wrapped her in a hug. "Let's go back and I'll call Darrell."

"I know he'll say yes. He *has* to!"

∽

On Saturday, after all the attendees had left the North Fork, Robin and Alec packed up the Jeep to get ready to go. Alec stood next to the open driver's side door with his forearm resting on the top. "Are you ready?"

Robin gazed out at the blue water. "Almost. I'm saying goodbye to the lake."

He walked over to her. "You'll be back here before you know it."

She whirled around and wrapped her arms around his neck and gave him a kiss. "I know. I can't wait!"

Alec hugged her. "I'm so glad I was able to convince Darrell to sell the lodge. Things were looking bad there for a moment."

"He did lose his mind a little about you quitting your job."

"I was going to do that no matter what he decided. I think he realized that if I'm here, he knows where to find me."

"Threatening to disappear to a remote island with me was a good strategy. But he should have known you'd never do that, because it would be too hard to bring Leroy and Emma with us."

Alec grinned. "True, although knowing you, you would have figured something out."

"But I don't have to! I'm so excited that the next time we see this place, we can let Leroy and Emma run and play to their heart's content at the new, improved dog-friendly North Fork Lodge."

"Let's go pick them up from Kat and give them the good news."

She gave him another kiss and waved at the lake. "See you soon!"

Chapter 16

Epilogue

They went north through the town of Alpine Grove and wound through the forested back roads toward Kat's place. Robin said, "That's it! Turn here."

"Wow, somebody redid the driveway. I bet that was expensive."

"It wasn't much of a driveway before."

As they drove up, Kat and another woman were sitting and chatting on the bottom step, holding Leroy and Emma on leashes. They all stood up and Kat made an obvious effort to restrain Leroy as the other woman pointed at Emma, who sat attentively.

Alec said, "Your dog is somewhat better behaved than mine."

"Leroy is still working on it."

They got out of the Jeep and the women let Leroy and Emma run up and say hello. Robin crouched down and hugged Emma. "Oh sweetie, I missed you so much!"

Kat walked up and waved at Alec. "Hi, I'm Kat Stevens. I'm guessing you're Leroy's dad. Thank you for the check."

Alec stopped petting Leroy and grinned. "Yes, hi. I'm Alec Montgomery. Leroy looks like he had a wonderful time."

Kat gestured toward the other woman, who had very large curly brown hair and a very small red dress. "This is my friend Maria."

Maria said, "It's nice to meet you. I like Emma. She's a polite dog, which I've learned is an unusual thing."

"She was a star at obedience classes," Robin said. "I'll work with Leroy more after we get back up here."

"When are you coming back?" Kat said.

"I'm buying the North Fork Lodge and it will probably close in the next couple of months. We're going to try to come back soon so we can start working on repairs," Alec said.

Kat said, "You're buying the lodge? I had no idea it was for sale."

"It was a private transaction, I guess you'd say. It needs quite a bit of work, but once it reopens, Robin's going to manage it," Alec said.

Maria put her hand on her hip. "So wait, am I the only person in this town who is dateless? Because I'm thinking you two are doing the deed. How does this keep happening?"

Alec raised his eyebrows. "What?"

Robin said, "Well, yes, Alec and I are together."

Maria stomped her foot. "This is starting to get to me. Why am I not meeting men who can afford real estate?" She waved her hand at Alec. "I mean, look at this guy. He's got all his teeth. And he's *hot*."

Alec glanced at Robin, then at Maria. "Thanks, I guess."

Kat's eyes widened and she turned to Alec. "Sorry. Maria feels there is a shortage of men with good dental hygiene here in Alpine Grove." She gestured at Maria in exasperation.

"Plenty of guys have teeth. You just moved here. Give it some time. Things will get better."

"Girlfriend, I'm telling you, it's time for you to start boarding cats. I *mean* it! This is becoming tragic." Maria crossed her arms in front of her.

Kat turned to Robin. "Will you need to board Emma and Leroy when you return? We might be in the middle of construction by then. They're pouring concrete for the new kennel building next week."

Robin smiled. "No. My first official management decision is that the lodge will allow guests to bring dogs as long as the dogs have had all their shots and are friendly."

"I know a few people who will like that." Kat said.

Alec said, "Robin has lots of ideas."

Robin nodded. "And once I have an idea, I can be quite persuasive."

Thanks for Reading

Thank you for dedicating some of your reading time to *Howl at the Loon*. I hope you enjoyed Robin and Alec's adventures. I'll be writing more books that will feature Kat, Joel and various other residents of Alpine Grove who bring dogs to the new boarding kennel. The seventh book, *The Good, the Bad, and the Pugly*, is available along with ten other books in the series.

If you would like to be notified by e-mail when I release a new book, you can sign up for my New Releases e-mail list at SusanDaffron.com.

I know that not everyone likes to write book reviews, but if you are willing write a sentence or two about what you thought of *Howl at the Loon*, I encourage you to post a review at your favorite book vendor site or share a message with your social networking friends.

If you would like to share your thoughts about the book with me privately, you can reach me through the contact page on the SusanDaffron.com web site.

I look forward to hearing from you!

~ Susan C. Daffron

Acknowledgements

Writing a novel is never easy and I'd like to thank my husband James Byrd for his support and encouragement throughout the writing and publishing process.

I'd also like to thank my alpha and beta readers for their eagle-eyed reading and great feedback:

- James Byrd
- Kate Turner
- Dian Chapman
- Clare Cinelli
- Adele Hudson

About the Author

Susan Daffron is the author of the Jennings & O'Shea series and the Alpine Grove romantic comedies, a series of novels that feature residents of the small town of Alpine Grove and their various quirky dogs and cats. She is also an award-winning author of many nonfiction books, including several about pets and animal rescue. She lives in a small town in northern Idaho and shares her life with her husband and three really cute dogs.